THE LONELY SOMMELIER

BOOK THREE IN THE CLEARWATER SERIES

JULIE MAYERSON BROWN

Cover and photography by Steve Blinder

For my girls…
All the women in my life who support, inspire, and encourage me every day

"Lots of people want to ride with you on the limo, but what you want is someone who will ride the bus with you when the limo breaks down."

Oprah Winfrey

1

*S*EPTEMBER

The last thing Tessa Mariano wanted on a Sunday morning was a visit from her nosy neighbor—or so she thought…

∾

The doorbell chimed at a few minutes after eight, and Buttercup, her massive St. Bernard, released a low bark.

Tessa set her coffee on the kitchen counter. "It's probably just Mrs. Nelson coming around to spread some gossip," she told the dog. "Come on, let's go see."

She tightened the sash on her blue robe and went to the front door with Buttercup close behind. Through the glass she saw that the person standing on her porch was not Mrs. Nelson.

It was Tessa's ex-husband.

She'd have preferred the nosy neighbor.

Tessa turned the knob and opened the door a crack. "What are you doing here?"

"Good morning to you, too." Victor stuffed his hands into his jeans pockets. "I know you're probably surprised to see me."

Surprised, annoyed—and curious. Tessa and her ex-husband did an admirable job of avoiding each other despite sharing custody of their thirteen-year-old son.

"It's not your weekend, and Marco's still asleep. "

"I came to see you."

She finger combed her disheveled hair. "Why?"

"Do you mind if I come in?" He took a step forward, making it impossible for her to close the door on him. His wry smile stirred something deep within her—something between butterflies and indigestion.

The dog nudged past Tessa and pushed her snout against Victor's stomach.

"Hello, girl," he said, patting the top of her head. "Long time, no see."

"All right, fine." Tessa opened the door wider. "You can come in, but you can't stay long. I have to get ready for work."

Victor entered as Buttercup sniffed him up and down.

He was a larger, older version of their son, and since the dog loved Marco, she naturally loved his father.

"So," he said. "Dog's getting bigger. What's she weigh, now?"

Small talk—Victor's way of leading up to something.

"A hundred and twenty-two pounds." She rested her hand on the banister of the staircase that led to her bedroom. "Is that why you're here? To talk about my dog?"

"No." He leaned past her and peered up the stairs, placing a foot on the bottom step. "I haven't been in the house since you finished the remodel. Can I go take a look?"

"You may not," Tessa said, still blindsided by his visit. In the seven years since the divorce, she had remained tolerant and accommodating. Friendly and welcoming—that was asking too much.

Victor removed his foot and turned toward the great room that opened into a large gourmet kitchen.

Tessa cut in front of him, blocking his view. "Are you trying to figure out how much money it took to turn our little bungalow into my dream home?"

"Come on Tessa, why do you have to be so snarky? I know you're rich now, and *Mariano's Cheese and Wine* is practically famous. I follow you on Instagram. I'm actually very proud of you."

"Oh, please." She closed her eyes to shut out his swarthy good looks. Why couldn't he have gotten bald and fat like other men over forty?

"It's true." Victor rubbed the dark stubble on his cheeks. "Listen, I'm here because I want to talk to you about something."

"Then talk."

"Will you at least offer me a cup of coffee? It is Sunday morning, you know. Remember how we used to sit out back at the rickety little table with the paper and—"

"Stop." Tessa held up her palms. "I'm going to get dressed. The kitchen's where it used to be, there's coffee in the French press and cream in the fridge. Mugs are in the cabinet over the toaster."

"Thank you."

"Whatever." She climbed the stairs with Buttercup trailing behind. But halfway up, the dog changed her mind and scampered after Victor.

Tessa entered her upstairs sanctuary—a master suite with a luxurious bathroom and walk-in closet. Her bed faced a set of French doors that opened onto a balcony with a view of Lake Clearwater. She threw on a white linen sundress, brushed her teeth, and ran a comb through her brown hair, a shoulder-length bob in desperate need of a trim. Before heading downstairs, she applied a quick swipe of pink lip gloss.

Victor sat on a stool at the end of the island, sipping coffee and flipping through the morning paper. He leaned on his elbows and a slow grin formed. "You look nice."

Tessa gave him a doubtful look while she made herself a cup of herbal tea.

"I mean it. You really do look good. Rested, in fact. I heard you took a little vacation."

Vacation? Not exactly. Six weeks earlier, stress and a debilitating migraine had brought about a severe case of exhaustion. Upon the advice of her doctor, she spent three weeks in the mountains at a wellness retreat—meditation, long walks in the woods, health food, no wine, and, to Tessa's dismay, therapy.

"Yes, I took some time off while Marco was at soccer camp. It was lovely."

"Where'd you go?"

She set her tea on the island. The porcelain mug clunked the granite. "Big Sur."

"Really? You go to one of those fancy resorts?"

"Something like that."

"Ah, massages all day and cocktails all night." He winked. "Bet you hated to leave."

Tessa pursed her lips. She'd wanted to flee the moment she arrived. The retreat director, a holistic psychologist, hovered over her as if he expected her to bolt into the forest, something she considered doing on more than one occasion.

After two weeks of deprivation and spiritual soul-searching, Tessa spent the third week in a reimmersion program learning how to balance her life.

"All good things come to an end, Victor. You know that." Her pointed sarcasm hit the mark. She sipped her tea, peering at him over the rim and enjoying his discomfort.

He adjusted his position on the stool. "Why are you drinking tea?"

"I already had coffee this morning. One of the things I discovered at the—the resort is that I consume too much caffeine. So, anyway, that's that." She steepled her fingers in front of her face and waited for him to share the reason for his visit.

Buttercup rested her head on Victor's lap, and he scratched her behind the ears. "Your dog likes me."

"She likes everyone," Tessa said. "She's unusually secure for a rescue."

"We should've had a dog, you know, back when Marco was little."

"Really?" She twisted the diamond stud in her left earlobe. "Do pets prevent men from sleeping with women who aren't their wives?"

Victor sat back. "Guess I deserved that. Still, it was good in the beginning."

A lump swelled in her throat. Good in the beginning—she'd forgotten how good it was because of how bad it got.

Victor stretched his neck to the side, and it made a popping sound. "We're coming up on the anniversary of our divorce in a few weeks."

"Divorceaversary," Tessa said. "It's a thing now. We make gift baskets for it at the shop."

"No kidding? You gonna send me one?"

"Doubtful." But if she did, she'd put in spoiled oysters, stale bread, and wine that tasted like vinegar.

Tessa recalled the day seven years ago when she stood in her lawyer's conference room and signed the papers that closed the door on her marriage. They'd started with a mediator, but when Victor hired a lawyer and claimed he had no money for child support, Tessa had no choice but to fight back. By the time the divorce was final, they both were broke.

"Is that what you want to talk about, Victor? Our divorce?"

"No." He drank down his coffee. "Actually, I have something to tell you."

"Must be serious if you couldn't just text it to me."

"Kinda is."

Tessa pulse quickened. "You're not sick, are you?" During the divorce, when Victor and his lawyer made everything as difficult as possible, she'd fantasized his demise every which way. But as she gained control over her life and success came her way, her ex-husband's existence on earth wasn't as annoying as it used to be.

"No." Victor's expression softened. "I'm not sick, but I appreciate the concern. At least you don't want me dead anymore."

"I never wanted you dead." Tessa looked out the window toward the lake. A few people strolled along the shore, and a boat floated out on gentle ripples. "Well, not really."

"Gee, thanks."

"So, if you're not dying, what is it?"

Victor cracked his knuckles. "I'm getting married."

Tessa drew back. "Married? To whom?"

"To Crystal. Who else?"

"Oh, right." She scratched the front of her throat. "I'd forgotten you were dating someone new."

"It's been almost nine months. I wouldn't call that new."

"I suppose not." Tessa sipped her tea. The liquid went down the wrong pipe, setting off a choking attack.

"Are you okay?"

Tessa nodded, held up a finger, and continued coughing. She took a cleansing breath, something she learned at the retreat, and mouthed one of her mantras—*calm as a morning breeze, morning breeze, morning breeze.*

She dabbed her eyes with a napkin, and her concern went

straight to their son who'd always wanted his parents to get back together. "Have you told Marco?"

"I did the other day." Victor rubbed the bridge of his nose. "He, um, he was a little surprised, but he's okay with it. He likes Crystal and Henry a lot."

"Henry?"

"Crystal's son."

Tessa's hackles went up. She'd never met either one of them, which suited her just fine. "Well, a ready-made family. That's just grand. So what can I do? Provide the wine for your wedding, give you the friends and family discount?"

Victor rubbed his palms on his jeans and got to his feet. "You know why our marriage failed?"

She released a bitter laugh. "Let me see if I can remember. Oh yes, you had an affair. Two, in fact. That was it."

"No. That's why we got divorced. Our marriage failed because you can't deal with your emotions. You pack them in a little box, put the lid on, and let them fester." Victor's jaw tensed. "No wonder you had a breakdown."

Tessa inhaled through her nose like a dragon about to exhale flames. She bit into her right cheek—physical pain was far more bearable than the emotional kind. "I didn't have a breakdown. I was just exhausted."

"That's not what I heard."

She stiffened. In the small town of Lake Clearwater, gossip was like a luscious dessert—impossible to pass up. And although everyone close to Tessa had promised to keep her *vacation* under wraps, news leaked out and spread outside of their insular community.

After all, she was one of the most well-regarded sommeliers in all of California and a celebrity in Sonoma wine circles.

Still, she wondered how her ex-husband, who no longer lived in Clearwater, heard about it. Marco didn't even know the details. Thankfully, he was already at camp when she'd left for Big Sur.

Tessa plucked Victor's unfinished coffee off the island. "I think it's time you left."

"Right." He snatched his car keys off the counter and headed out. She marched after him, furious he'd highjacked what should've been a lovely, relaxing day.

At the front door, he turned and faced her. "You know, I thought telling you in person was the nice thing to do. But I can see I shouldn't have bothered."

"We're divorced. What you do doesn't matter to me." Tessa leaned on the heavy foyer table for support. Of course it mattered. Anything that affected Marco mattered. "All I care about is our son."

"I care about him, too." Victor snapped back. "And I wasn't going to bring this up today, but I think now's as good a time as any."

Tessa fumed. "Of course it is. You've already psychoanalyzed me, so let's just keep going."

He opened his mouth, then closed it.

"For God's sake, just say it."

"Crystal and I might be moving to San Diego."

That news was more disturbing than the marriage announcement. Despite their many disagreements, Tessa was committed to Marco's relationship with his father. And to make it work, proximity was the key. Victor lived close enough for them to adjust the visitation schedule at a moment's notice and accommodate Marco's sports, activities, and friends.

"That's a problem, Victor, unless you're planning to live in two places."

He shifted his weight, and his jaw twitched. "If we do move, I think Marco should come with me."

Tessa stepped back. "You're not serious."

For seven years she'd had primary custody of their son. She

maintained strict control, and Marco did nothing without her knowledge. There wasn't a chance in hell she'd give that up.

"He's almost fourteen, Tessa, and a teenage boy needs his father."

"Then don't move to San Diego," she said, struggling to keep her voice even.

Her ex-husband looked away. "It's not that easy."

"It's never easy," Tessa said, expanding her chest. "Listen, you can live wherever you want—next door, down the street, across the country—I don't care. But this is Marco's home, and this is where he'll stay."

Victor's cheeks reddened. "Well, I can't say I'm surprised, but I have news for you. Marco's gonna leave sooner or later, and holding him back only postpones the inevitable."

Tessa wrapped her arms around her waist, well aware that her son would graduate from high school in exactly four years, nine months, and two weeks.

Victor opened the door, and sunlight poured in. His tall shadow stretched across the hardwood floor. "I know you control our son's life right now, but that won't last forever. And I hope you love your big fancy house, because someday you're going to be in it all by yourself."

2

$\mathcal{V}$ictor's warning had had its intended effect. He knew what buttons to push and where her weak spot was. And his parting words were a slap in the face.

But threats only strengthened Tessa's resolve. Nobody, least of all her philandering ex-husband, was going to throw her off-course. One visit to wellness-camp was enough to convince her of that.

She activated her Bluetooth and said to the mechanical voice: "Call Elaine Cooper."

Her lawyer's cell phone rang five times then went to voicemail.

"Elaine, it's Tessa. Call me back as soon as you can. It's a matter of..." The words caught in her throat. "It's urgent."

She pushed the button to end the call and blew right through a stop sign. Within seconds, flashing lights appeared in her rearview mirror.

"Shit." Tessa pulled to the side and lowered the driver's side window of her black Audi SUV. Hot air blew in as she shut off the motor.

The smug face of Glen Duffy greeted her. He had been a year

ahead of her in high school, not that Tessa had much memory of him or anyone else for that matter. Her teen years were best forgotten.

"Well, Tessa Mariano, how the hell are ya?" He rested an arm over the window and peered in.

"Hello, Glen."

"Been at least a month since you ran that stop sign." He grinned. His teeth looked like little kernels of corn. "And if I recall, I gave you a warning that time."

Tessa steadied her voice. "You did, and I appreciated it. You know, there's a petition going around to remove the sign. Even the town council wants it gone."

"Doesn't mean you can violate it."

"You're right." She mustered as much remorse as she could. "I've just had a bad morning."

"Not an excuse for running a stop sign."

"True." Tessa gave up. Talking her way out of a ticket, especially with Glen, was usually a piece of cake, but today she didn't have it in her to cajole. "If you're going to give me a ticket, just do it. I have to get to work."

Glen frowned as if disappointed she didn't want to play the game. "Fine, I will. Boy oh boy, you really haven't changed at all."

"What's that supposed to mean?" She'd already received Victor's assessment of her limitations. Why not hear more?

"Never could give anyone the time of day. Thought you were better than the rest of us." He started writing the citation.

Tessa said nothing. In high school, she'd been the smart girl who kept to herself. An aloof exterior could hide a myriad of faults and insecurities.

"And now that you're rich and famous," Glen continued, "you're that much more of—"

"Could you stop talking and just write the damn ticket?"

"Whoa, somebody woke up on the wrong side of the bed."

He finished the citation and presented it to her. "Sign it."

She scribbled her name and gave the slip back to him. "May I go now?"

"You may." Glen handed her the yellow copy. "But if you speed down Oak Tree Lane, I'll pull you over again."

"Got it."

He leaned closer to the window "I sure hope you're not the one teaching Marco to drive. Better let his father do it."

Tessa resisted the desire to wrap her hand around Glen Duffy's throat.

The air conditioning inside the gourmet shop circulated cool, soothing air. Tessa unfurled her yoga mat on the floor next to her most expensive wines. Expensive wine reminded her of her success, and her professional success helped her forget the shambles of her personal life.

She lowered herself onto the mat, crossed her legs, and reviewed the mantras she'd learned at the wellness center.

Calm as a morning breeze. No, already used that one today.
Gentle as a flowing stream. No, makes me want to pee.
I'm grateful for my...

"Shit." She stood, rolled up the mat, and threw it into the storeroom. How dare Victor accuse her of having a breakdown. It wasn't anything like that at all. Not really.

The callback from her attorney came at exactly the wrong time. A wealthy wine collector was sitting across from her asking questions about a rare French Bordeaux.

Tessa quickly texted: *Call you right back.*

"You know what?" She placed a hand on the man's arm. "I think we should do a little tasting. Do you have time?"

"Of course," the older gentleman said.

"Great. Give me a few minutes. I have something very special in mind." Tessa rose. "Have a look around, taste some cheese, and I'll be right back."

She exited through the swinging door into the storeroom and called Elaine. The efficient attorney picked up after one ring. "Hi."

"Hey, sorry to bother you on a Sunday."

"Sunday-shmunday, what's up?"

Just the sound of her friend's voice soothed Tessa's agitation. Almost seven years had passed since Elaine stood by her side, physically holding her up, as she signed the paperwork that ended her marriage.

Tessa made it quick. "Victor's getting remarried, possibly moving to San Diego, and says he wants Marco to go with him."

"Hmm," Elaine said. "You think he'll take you to court over it?"

"I don't know. I just have a bad feeling. I can afford to spend circles around him, but I don't want this fight. And I don't want Marco caught in the middle."

"Got it. Let me do a little snooping, and we'll discuss it over coffee this week. We're overdue for a date, anyway."

"Okay," Tessa said, blowing out a big breath of air. "Sounds good."

"I'll text you tomorrow. Chin up, sweetie. We got this."

"You're the best."

Two minutes on the phone with Elaine was better than an hour of therapy. Tessa returned to the shop with a Bordeaux from Pauillac, France, a wine that retailed for over six hundred dollars a bottle. She opened it without a second thought, certain it'd be worth it. Between his Cartier watch and Hermes belt, her client's wealth was on display. Plus, he knew all the right questions to ask.

An hour later, he ordered three cases.

At least something was going right today.

3

*T*essa merged across three lanes of traffic, cutting off several cars.

"Good heavens," said her grandmother. "Please slow down."

"Sorry." She glanced at her beloved Nonna sitting next to her. "I can't believe you didn't tell me how much your hip hurt."

"It wasn't so bad before you left," Nonna said, gripping the bar above the passenger door. "You've got to slow down. My appointment isn't until two."

Tessa lifted her foot off the gas. She pictured the forest in Big Sur, the location where she'd practiced meditation and chanted mantras. Despite the lack of massages and wine, she'd come home from the wellness retreat with a renewed sense of control. But in the last two days, ever since Victor dropped by with his big announcement, she felt as if she were walking sideways. Now, the startling news that her grandmother was seeing an orthopedic surgeon added to her distress.

"Who drove you to get the MRI?"

"For goodness sake, I drove myself. I'm eighty-five and perfectly capable of managing a simple appointment."

"I know you are." Tessa conceded and let the matter drop.

For a woman her age, Nonna was a dynamo. She shuttled her friends around town, delivered meals-on-wheels, baked cookies at church every other Friday, and participated in the senior-citizen walking club twice a week. Plus, she handed out sage advice to everyone at the salon where she had her silver-gray hair trimmed once a month.

A car cut in front of them, and Tessa hit the brake hard.

"Oh dear!" Nonna grabbed the armrest. "You're going to give me a heart attack. Why are you so agitated today?"

"I just don't want to be late for your appointment." Tessa wished she could talk to her grandmother about Victor, but it wasn't the right time. Her problems were of no importance when Nonna was in pain.

Traffic was beyond her control. As the therapist had drilled into her, she needed to let the little things go. If they were late, it wasn't the end of the world. Besides, doctors never ran on time.

"Your appointment was at two o'clock, Mrs. Mariano. It's ten after." The receptionist tapped her pen on the desk. "Dr. Barnes is with another patient, so you'll have to wait."

Tessa poked her head through the window separating the waiting room from the office area. "Excuse me. If we'd been here at two o'clock sharp, would we already be in with Dr. Barnes? Or did his next patient arrive early and take my grandmother's time slot? And oh, what about the gentleman waiting over there? What time is his appointment?"

"Tessa, please." Nonna pulled on her arm. "You're being rude."

"I'm just trying to understand why ten minutes makes such a difference."

"Let me see how the doctor's doing." The receptionist rolled her chair back and sprinted down the hall.

"Come with me." Nonna coaxed Tessa toward a couch on the

farthest wall. "Let's just relax. There's one of those fancy coffee machines. Do you want me to get you an espresso?"

The only thing that sounded better than espresso was red wine, but that wasn't an option. "I'll have a mint tea," Tessa said. She knew a jolt of caffeine would only hype her up more.

"Herbal tea, good choice. I hope it relaxes you a bit."

While her grandmother made two cups of tea with painstaking care, Tessa peered into the fish tank on the wall behind the sofa. The languid movement of the exotic creatures swimming through the water hypnotized her. It was probably why doctors put fish tanks in their waiting rooms—to distract patients from how long they had to wait.

Nonna handed Tessa a paper cup with a tea bag string hanging over the edge. She sat beside her granddaughter. "Now, let's catch up. I've hardly seen you since you returned. How did Patty do in the shop while you were away?"

"Fine," Tessa said. "Well, better than fine. She really stepped up for me."

Patty Sullivan, her new manager, had started working at Mariano's only four months earlier. In that time, she'd gone from fledgling trainee to confident manager, a transformation Tessa had nurtured. And just in time, too. Patty had kept the shop up and running throughout Tessa's three-week stay in wellness prison.

"I'm glad that worked out," Nonna said. "You're lucky she came around when she did."

"I really am." Tessa squeezed her grandmother's knee, grateful that Patty's presence now afforded her more time for Marco and Nonna.

"Now what else? How's my darling great-grandson?"

"He's, um…" Tessa faltered. She hadn't told Nonna about Victor's marriage and potential move to San Diego. "I actually wanted to tell you something that's—"

"Mrs. Mariano?" a nurse called from the doorway. "Right this way, please."

"See?" Nonna used the arms of the chair to get up. "That wasn't such a long wait."

The nurse escorted them down the hall to an exam room. "Dr. Barnes will be in shortly."

"How shortly?" Tessa asked. "It's almost—"

"Tessa, shush. I'm sure Dr. Barnes is doing his best."

"He is," the nurse said. "But I'll let him know you're in a hurry." She exited and closed the door softly behind her.

They seated themselves in two chairs against the wall .

"So, what were you going to tell me about Marco?" Nonna asked.

"Oh, yeah." Tessa decided it wasn't a good time to discuss her ex-husband's new life. "He, uh, he got an A on his last algebra test. Isn't that wonderful?"

"Good for him. He's a smart one." She wrapped an arm around Tessa's shoulders and squeezed tightly. "Just like his mama."

Dr. Barnes entered, and Tessa sat up straight. He had dark hair, flecked with a few strands of gray, and a closely trimmed beard covered a strong jaw. As handsome as he was, his lack of expression unnerved her, as if his mind were somewhere else and not completely focused on Nonna.

"Hello Rosa, how are you feeling?" the doctor asked, rubbing a bit of sanitizer into his hands.

"I'm fine, just anxious to know the results of my MRI," Nonna said. "Oh, this is my granddaughter."

Tessa extended her hand. "Nice to meet you."

"Likewise," he said, giving it a perfunctory squeeze. "So, Rosa, let me show you what your hip joint looks like."

Tessa sat on the edge of her chair, ready to learn everything about Nonna's condition.

The doctor flipped a switch, and the screen on the wall lit up with images of Nonna's hip. He swiped through them, droning on about arthritis, bone-on-bone grinding, osteoporosis, and how a hip replacement was the only option.

"Surgery?" Nonna's voice trembled. "I was hoping you could just give me a cortisone shot or something. My friend had one in her hip. She said it helped tremendously."

"Short-term fix," he said. "I don't recommend it."

His insensitivity to her grandmother's concern irritated Tessa, but she kept her mouth tightly closed.

"Hip replacements are easier than they used to be," he said.

Nonna fidgeted with the straps on her purse. "Oh, well, so you really think surgery is the best way to go?"

"That's what I said." His tone held a note of impatience. "And the sooner the better. Although, I do recommend you drop a little weight first."

"Excuse me?" Tessa leaned forward. "Did you just tell my grandmother to lose weight?"

"I did. It'll make her recovery easier."

Although Nonna could stand to lose a few pounds, his tactless comment astonished Tessa. She jumped out of her chair.

"I think we'll be getting a second opinion. I need a copy of the MRI report and access to the images immediately."

Dr. Barnes's face remained unchanged. "Not a problem. Would you like a referral to another orthopedist?"

"No." Tessa didn't bother to hide her indignation. "I'll find one myself."

"Very well."

"Sit down." Nonna tugged Tessa's arm. "I don't want a second opinion. Dr. Barnes is the best surgeon in the Bay Area. And this is my decision, young lady, not yours."

Tessa's cheeks burned. "I only want what's best for you, Nonna."

"A second opinion's always a good idea," Dr. Barnes said.

His agreement made Tessa less defensive. "Thank you."

"But there's not a surgeon in town who would advise differently. Your grandmother's case is textbook, and her recovery will be relatively easy. And the outcome, most likely, will be successful regardless of the surgeon." Dr. Barnes wheeled his stool to the sink. He stood and washed his hands. "Obviously, it's up to you."

"Obviously," Tessa said.

He extracted two paper towels from the holder and dried his hands. "My surgery schedule is busy, but you can check with the receptionist on your way out."

Nonna pushed herself out of her chair, favoring her sore hip. "I'll do that, Dr. Barnes. I'd like the surgery done quickly. I want it over with as soon as possible, however, I will not be losing weight. Not now, not later. Are we clear on that?"

Dr. Barnes's eyebrows rose, his first facial expression since Tessa laid eyes on him. His surprise lasted less than a second. The brows fell back into place, and his indifference returned.

"Okay." He opened the door and walked out.

Tessa and Nonna eyed each other, but her grandmother spoke first. "I'm going to use the restroom." She handed her sweater and purse to Tessa. "I'll meet you by the reception desk."

"Fine." Tessa said, feeling as if she'd been scolded.

As she followed her grandmother out, Dr. Barnes's framed degrees on the wall caught her attention—Washington University undergrad, Stanford Medical School and residency. Based upon his years of graduation, she guessed his age to be about fifty, maybe a bit younger. His level of education was impressive, to be sure, but it did nothing to assuage Tessa's concern. Besides, she couldn't stand him.

Tessa drove across the Golden Gate Bridge ignoring the sparkling bay below. "I don't like him, Nonna. He's rude, condescending, egotistical, and so full of—"

"Oh, stop, he's not that bad. I'll admit his bedside manner leaves something to be desired. But I don't care, I'll be asleep."

"You'll be asleep, and I'll be the one pacing the halls waiting for him to emerge with updates. And then when I ask questions, and you know I will, he'll have some flippant non-response." She couldn't understand why her grandmother was being so stubborn. "Nonna, I work with all kinds of men in my business, and I know what…"

"Tessa, please." Nonna put a hand on her granddaughter's thigh and squeezed gently. "You're worried about me, I understand. But it's going to be fine. Dr. Barnes can fit me in next week, and that makes the decision easy. I'll get a new hip and be back to my old self by Halloween."

An exasperated puff of air escaped Tessa's lips. "I still think a second opinion would be wise."

"Perhaps. But my mind is made up." Nonna returned her hand to her own lap and gazed straight ahead. "Someday you'll learn you can't control everything. At least I hope so. Trying to control situations that are not within your control is no way to live. Isn't that what you learned at the wellness center?"

Tessa tightened her grip on the steering wheel and clenched her jaw. Letting go, delegating, allowing others to be in charge— the therapist had drilled those lessons into her head. But she had resisted.

You want to prevent the storms from coming, Tessa, but it's not possible. Whether you're in control or not, the storms will come.

4

The day after the appointment with Dr. Barnes, Tessa immersed herself in work and forced the doctor's disagreeable manner, as well as his handsome face, out of her mind. Her worry over the surgery blended with her stress over Marco and San Diego, turning her stomach into an open invitation for an ulcer. No amount of meditation or creative mantras could calm her nerves.

The bells on the door jingled all day long as customers came and went. End-of-summer tourists flooded the shop, stocking up on wines and unique gifts to take home. Those in the know were practically star-struck to meet Tessa, and she tended to them with charm and equanimity, despite the turbulence churning inside her.

Finally, the rush subsided. Tessa dropped into a chair in the winetasting area, a mild ache pushing on the back of her head, and opened her laptop. The screen flickered to life, and a complicated spreadsheet appeared.

"Patty? Where are you?" she asked.

The petite redhead wearing a *Mariano's* apron over a short denim dress popped up from behind the counter. "Right here."

"What's holding up our shipment from that winery in Gilroy?" Tessa studied the spreadsheet on her screen. "I ordered it a month ago."

Patty leaned over her shoulder and scrolled to the left. "It'll be shipped next week. And look here, we have plenty in stock."

"Oh, you're right. Sorry."

Her manager pulled up a chair. She lived in the loft apartment above the shop with her younger sister, Liza. Tessa adored them and could hardly believe her luck that the Sullivan sisters both worked for her. Thanks to them, Mariano's Cheese and Wine thrived during Tessa's stint at the wellness retreat.

"Shouldn't you be taking it easy?" Patty asked. "I mean, aren't you still recovering from your, you know, episode?"

"Episode? Is that what we're calling it now?"

"You know what I mean." Patty's eyes were wide with concern.

"I do know." Tessa closed her laptop. "Please don't worry, I'm fine. Now, about tonight. How are the charcuterie platters coming along? Don't forget, I promised heavy hors d'oeuvres, so be sure to load them up."

That evening, twenty guests were attending a winetasting Tessa had donated to the animal shelter fundraiser.

Patty pointed at the trays on the bar. "They're so full I'm running out of room."

"Then use more trays." Tessa went to inspect them. "Very nice, but they could use a little more variety. And more cured meats."

"Are you sure we're not going overboard here? I mean, the wine and all this food—"

"Never skimp on a fundraiser, Patty, remember that. I always go above and beyond, especially when people have been so generous with their donations."

"It's you who's generous."

"I can afford to be. Besides, you never know who'll be in the crowd. Some of my best clients come out of these events."

"All right then," Patty said. "I'd better build up these trays."

"Build away." Tessa gave her an encouraging pat on the back. "And I'll select the wines."

She walked across the shop and climbed the ladder. Mariano's had expanded a year ago, which allowed Tessa to build an entire wall of floor-to-ceiling wine racks. Opposite the racks was a new refrigerated case packed with wheels and wedges of over a hundred different cheeses and other specialty foods.

The growth of her business had astounded everyone, everyone except for Tessa whose determination and belief in her vision never wavered

Tessa removed a bottle from the rack and came down the ladder. "By the way, I'm adding a Hawk and Winters Cabernet to the list for tonight."

"You are?" Beaming, Patty stopped slicing cheese. Her boyfriend owned the winery. "Adam's gonna be thrilled."

Tessa eyed her new manager. "You're quite smitten, aren't you? What's it been, a month?"

Patty grinned. "Almost six weeks."

It pleased Tessa to see her friend happy. Patty had been through her own tough time in recent months. Falling in love, or even just lust, was the perfect cure. Of course, she was young and starry-eyed, unsullied by the challenges of adult life like marriage, divorce, and custody arrangements.

Custody arrangements? "Oh, shoot. I need to go." She'd almost forgotten she was meeting Elaine Cooper at Nutmeg's.

Patty balked. "Wait. We have so much to do."

"I know, but this can't be helped. When's Liza coming?"

"Probably not 'til six," Patty said.

In addition to working for Tessa part-time, Liza had started a baking business that specialized in custom cakes.

"I'll call and see if she can get here earlier."

"Good idea." Tessa opened the door. "You can pull the rest of the wines for tonight. Wait, no, I'd better do it."

She knew where they were, how many she needed, and the setup she had in mind.

"I can do it," Patty said. "You sent me the spreadsheet, so I know exactly what you want."

"But I have a system."

"I know your system." Patty argued. "Geez, Tessa, I ran the shop for three weeks while you were away. I can do this."

Tessa hemmed. Delegating, even to Patty, made her nervous, but she needed to let her manager manage.

"All right. Stage everything, and I'll check it when I get back."

Tessa crossed Main Street into Town Square Park.

A gray-haired couple sat on a bench underneath a shady oak tree. Ducks swam around the small pond chasing bread crumbs tossed in by a little girl who watched from the bridge beside her mother. It reminded Tessa of how she used to bring Marco to the park when he was little.

A hot breeze blew, ruffling Tessa's skirt and the loose sleeves on her blouse. She couldn't wait for fall weather and a break in the heat. A woman clipping flowers in the community garden waved. Tessa waved back and picked up her pace.

In the back corner of Nutmeg's, Elaine Cooper sat at a round table texting feverishly.

Tessa tapped her shoulder.

"Oh!" Elaine jumped. "You startled me." She stood and folded Tessa into a firm hug. They hadn't seen each other in months.

"Sorry I kept you waiting. I meant to be here first."

Elaine, dressed in a royal blue pantsuit with matching pumps, brushed off the apology. "No worries. I had an appointment that finished early, so I came straight to Clearwater to enjoy this beautiful day. I even ate lunch in the park."

"Lunch in the park. I haven't done that in ages." Tessa wished she had time to picnic with Marco like they used to. Not that he'd want to picnic with his mother anymore.

"Next time we'll meet in the park." Elaine tucked a stray hair into the tidy bun at the nape of her neck. "Now, take a deep breath and tell me how you're feeling."

They sat across from one another, and Tessa forced a smile. "Fine. Better than fine. That wellness retreat did me a world of good. Migraines are better. And guess what? I meditate now. It's, like, well it's quite…"

"Oh, stop. I can see it in your eyes. You're a mess."

She wanted to object, but Elaine knew her well. "I'm not a mess exactly, but I am worried."

The barista, Trevor, set two cappuccinos and a pecan sticky bun on the table. "Hey, Tessa, welcome back. How was the, um, the vacation?"

The way he said *vacation* revealed he knew more.

"Thank you, Trevor," she said, glimpsing up at him. "My vacation was lovely."

"Cool." The twenty-something young man who'd been making coffee at Nutmeg's since he was a teenager topped off their water glasses. "Let me know if you need anything else."

"Will do." Tessa ground a sprinkle of chocolate over the foam on her drink. She inhaled the aroma of dark espresso and swallowed a sip. "Oh shit!"

"What? Did you burn your tongue?" Elaine asked.

"No. I forgot I've already had coffee today. I'm only allowed one."

Elaine's jaw dropped. "Nobody can live like that, and certainly not you. Coffee and wine, those are your two main food groups."

"Not anymore." Tessa sliced a tiny wedge off the sticky bun. "And I cut back on sugar, too. Healthy living just sucks."

"It sure does." Elaine slid Tessa's coffee over to her side of the table. "Let me order you a tea."

"No tea, I drink enough of that. Just tell me what you found out about Victor."

"Right." Elaine took a large bit of sticky bun and licked her fingers. "First of all, don't worry. Custody arrangements are rarely reviewed by the court unless there's a concern about a child's welfare. Even if Victor's lawyer files a motion, I doubt it would go anywhere."

Tessa exhaled, and the tension in her neck subsided. "You don't think so?"

"I don't. And he probably wouldn't spend the money anyway. Isn't he planning a big wedding?"

"I have no idea," Tessa said. "He didn't discuss that with me."

Elaine ate more of the sticky bun. "He told you about the baby though."

"What?" Tessa slapped the table with both hands.

"He didn't tell you? That weeny." Elaine did nothing to hide the fact that she didn't think much of Victor.

"His fiancé's pregnant?" Tessa couldn't believe it.

At one time they'd imagined a big family, but that was early on when they were young and in love. Tessa had wanted a sibling for Marco, but fatherhood failed to push Victor into adulthood. He continued behaving like a fraternity boy, and Tessa quickly realized that she needed to support their family.

The dream of a second baby vanished.

"How do you know?" she asked.

Elaine leaned in. "I had my assistant do a little, you know, poking around."

"Seriously? You had his fiancé investigated?"

"I wouldn't call it investigating as much as plain old snooping." The lawyer made it sound like child's play. "It's all about asking the right questions of the right people. Thanks to social media, we can track a common thread between people in minutes. We do it all the time."

"I'll bet she looks like Nicole Kidman." Tessa chopped a hunk off the sticky bun and ate it in one bite. "Victor always had a thing for her."

"I have no idea what she looks like," Elaine said. "So I can neither confirm nor deny."

"Doesn't matter." Tessa reached across the table and took her coffee back. "All I care about is Marco."

Elaine offered a reassuring smile. "As it should be. How old is Marco now anyway?"

"He'll be fourteen soon."

"That's good. At fourteen, a child can state his preference as to where he wants to live. Have you talked to him about it?"

"God no. He hasn't said a word about his father getting married, and I haven't asked either."

"These kinds of changes are so hard on kids," Elaine said. "He'll bring it up when he's ready. In the meantime, if it comes down to it, Marco will want to stay with you, right?"

"Of course he will. His whole life is here. School, friends, soccer team. He'd never want to leave Clearwater."

The lawyer narrowed one eye. She hadn't asked if Marco wanted to stay in Clearwater; she'd asked if he wanted to stay with *her*.

Tessa's shoulders slumped. "And he—he needs me. I'm his mother."

She didn't say what she really felt. *I need him. He's my son.*

*a*fter taking in all the reassurances Elaine could offer and promising to sit tight until something more transpired, Tessa bid her lawyer goodbye. She trudged back to the shop along the sidewalk in a daze, recalling the moment her lawyer had Victor up against the wall and tightened the screws on him.

They had slogged their way through the worst part of the divorce agreement when Victor's lawyer tried to force the sale of their house.

Elaine glared at Victor and leaned on the table, closing in on his personal space. "You want to kick your child out of the only home he's ever known?"

Victor's mouth opened, but no words came out.

"Ms. Cooper." The opposing lawyer intervened. "You're out of line."

Elaine turned on him. "That's the difference between you and me. I see it as my responsibility to advocate for a child's wellbeing. And you evidently don't."

"Fine. We withdraw the request."

The lawyer shrugged as if the concession were nothing more than a pebble in a pile of rocks...

A voice jolted Tessa from the memory.

"Tessa, hi!"

Her head snapped up.

Rebecca the dog walker, rescuer, and trainer, threw her arms around Tessa and squeezed the air out of her lungs.

"I just saw you yesterday, honey. We don't need to hug like this every time." She patted Rebecca's back and untangled herself from the young woman's embrace.

"I know, I get excited, though." Rebecca, wearing green overall shorts and hiking boots, had four dogs on leashes—the schnauzer boys, a basset hound, and a fuzzy brown mutt—along with a kitten in a baby carrier on her chest. "I was just at the shop looking for you. Wanted to know if you could help me out next week."

"What do you need?"

"A place to park a litter of puppies for a few days next week."

"A whole litter?" One puppy was a lot of work—a pack of pups was ridiculous.

"I know it's a big ask," Rebecca said, shoving her wild red curls out of her face. "But I'm desperate."

"It's not a good time. I have a—"

"Please, please, please. You're my favorite foster mom, and you have such a big yard, and I swear it'll only be for a few days, five at most."

"Five?"

"Okay, three."

The girl was clever, Tessa had to give her that. "I wish I could, but I've only been back a—"

"Oh, yeah, how was your, um, the trip vacation thingy?" Rebecca dragged the toe of one boot along the cement. "Sorry. I didn't mean to bring that up. I'm just glad you're feeling better."

"Well, thank you. And I am."

The kitten mewed. Rebecca scratched it between the ears.

She stepped off the curb, tugging the dogs along with her. "Okay, so I'll let you know when I'm bringing the puppies."

"Wait a sec, I didn't say I'd take them. How many are there anyway?"

Rebecca was halfway across the street. "Only nine. Thanks Tessa, you're a lifesaver!" She waved and jogged into the park with her rag-tag pack.

Tessa watched them disappear into a copse of trees, already thinking of everyone she knew who might want to puppy-sit.

A small door led directly into the quiet storeroom next to her shop. Tessa needed a few minutes to regroup and refocus.

She checked the thermostats on five temperature-controlled coolers. Fifty-five degrees—perfect. Next, she selected wine-glasses for the event and arranged them on the stainless steel counter in the order they'd be used for tasting.

A dull pain pushed on her forehead. Migraines were triggered by stress and anxiety, her constant companions these days. Tessa stopped and massaged her temples. She opened a bottle of water and gulped half of it.

The door between the storeroom and the shop swung open. "Oh good, you're back." Patty eyeballed her. "Are you okay?"

"I'm fine." Tessa rubbed the back of her neck. "How's the set-up going out there?"

"Great. I just need to get the clipboards, but I'm not sure where they are."

"I think I know." Tessa pinched an eyebrow. "I'll find them, you stay up front."

"Are you sure you're okay?" Patty asked. "Your face is a little pale."

"Don't worry," Tessa said, nudging her manager back into the shop. "Now off you go."

Patty's frown deepened, but she followed her boss's orders.

Tessa swallowed two Tylenols and went in search of the clipboards.

While the wine, food, and gift products were meticulously organized, her office was not.

A windowless alcove off the storeroom served as an office and supply closet. With an oversized desk and mismatched shelves, it was more a dumping ground for old electronics, folding chairs, and cleaning products

Tessa scanned the shelves for a box labeled "clipboards." It had been months since she'd used them. She climbed the step ladder and searched, frustrated by her lack of organization. "There you are," she said to a clear plastic storage container on the top shelf.

With her arms wrapped around the heavy box, she maneuvered herself off the ladder. Tessa dropped the box on the desk with a loud thud.

She lifted the lid and removed the clipboards. At the bottom of the box, underneath the boards, was a stack of construction paper folders. The top one was labeled: *second grade artwork.* She flipped through it. Picture after picture of their family, crayon drawings of her and Victor with Marco in the middle holding his parents' hands. Halfway through the stack, the arrangement of the stick figures changed. Victor had been drawn off to the side, smaller, with a downturned mouth.

The memory of that day came flooding back. Tessa had picked up her son from school, and he'd bounded into the car as usual. When they got home, she emptied the backpack and found his drawing squashed at the bottom.

"What's this, Marco?" She smoothed the paper, wiping off cracker crumbs.

"It's us." He pointed. "That's me and that's you. And Daddy's over there. When he comes home, I'll draw him next to me again."

Tessa caught her breath, and tears welled in her eyes. She allowed herself a moment to recall the guilt she'd felt at the time. Even though Victor was the one who'd had the affairs, she was the one who insisted they separate. The first affair she'd forgiven; the second one, no way.

Still, she bore some blame for their marriage's failure. Cheating was Victor's way of punishing her for being a workaholic and a micro-managing control freak. But she'd had no choice.

~

That night at the tasting, Tessa was renewed. Dressed in a black jumpsuit, her hair blown into loose waves and make-up done at the salon, she put her worries away and performed like the consummate professional she was.

Patty and Liza served the food, while Patty's boyfriend, Adam Hawk, assisted. The ruggedly handsome winemaker poured, making sure the guests had the right wine at the right time. Tessa loved having him at tastings. He could name and describe every grape grown in California as well as every winery in the region. His expertise and charm added an extra element to Tessa's events.

The guests, connoisseurs of food and wine themselves, made detailed notes on preprinted wine grids clipped to the clipboards as Tessa spoke.

When the tasting ended, they crowded around her with questions, compliments, and accolades.

Liza tapped Tessa's shoulder. "Sorry to interrupt, but I need you for a second."

Tessa excused herself from her audience. She followed Liza and her swishy blond ponytail.

"Someone wants to place an order and has some questions." Liza pointed to the wall of wine. "That tall, fancy lady over there."

An attractive woman wearing a gray pantsuit and carrying a

black Fendi shoulder bag waited with crossed arms. She had stick-straight dark hair cut to just above her chin.

"Hello." Tessa extended her hand. "Did you have a question?"

"I do." She gave Tessa's fingers a light squeeze. "I'm interested in a Syrah blend from Australia. I had it there last month, and it was just exquisite. Unfortunately I've forgotten the name.

"I carry a few. One of my favorites is an Australian Shiraz-Cabernet matured in Oak. Could that be the one?"

"Perhaps."

"Let me get one down." Tessa slid the ladder along the track, stopped midway across the wall, and stepped up a few rungs. She scanned the rack searching for the Shiraz blend. "Here we are."

She came off the ladder and handed the bottle to the woman. "Would you like to taste it?"

The woman smiled for the first time. Her teeth were large and very white. "Yes, please."

Tessa guided her to the tasting area and uncorked the wine. She inhaled the smoky, fruity aroma and poured a small amount into a glass. Tessa swirled the ruby-red liquid, tipped the glass, put her nose in, then tasted. It was excellent, but she said nothing.

"Let's see what you think." She poured the woman a generous taste.

"Thank you." The woman swirled, smelled, and sipped.

"Mmm, very good." She tasted it again. "Excellent, in fact. How much is it?"

"Ninety-five a bottle, but guests tonight receive ten percent off."

"And by the case?"

Tessa pinched her chin. Anything more than ten percent off was pushing it. "It depends on how many cases. Five or more, I can do a fifteen percent discount."

"Perfect. I'm hosting an art show next month with about three hundred guests." The woman pulled a business card from her purse. It was black with white lettering and said simply:

Angela Reid
Art Collector

No phone number, just an email address at the bottom.

"Let me know how much wine I should order. I'll need champagne as well, and a nice Chardonnay. Can you get back to me next week?"

Numbers buzzed through her brain like honey bees. "Absolutely. I'll run the numbers tomorrow and give you a call. Or an email if you prefer."

"Email is fine. I look forward to hearing from you," she said, securing the latch on her Fendi bag. "And I'll send you an invitation. I hope you'll be able to attend the event.

Tessa knew next to nothing about art, but any party serving that much wine purchased from Mariano's deserved her attendance. "Thank you. I'd love to come."

"Wonderful. May I purchase the bottle you just opened?"

Tessa went behind the counter. She sealed the bottle with a special cork to keep the oxygen out and placed it in a black wine sleeve.

"On the house," she said, handing it to her.

Angela exhibited no surprise. It was as if she'd expected the gift. But Tessa was accustomed to people who had an air of entitlement. And if they were going to spend thousands of dollars on her wine, she was more than happy to oblige.

"Thank you, Tessa. And just so you know, the event is black-tie." Angela seemed to be appraising her outfit, as if it weren't up to par.

"Well then," Tessa said with a hint of sarcasm. "I just might have to treat myself to a new dress."

6

A few days after the winetasting, which had been talked about all over town, Tessa visited one of her best clients.

In the kitchen of *Pierre's*, an exclusive restaurant in Napa, she sat across from the chef at a small table, dipping sourdough bread into spicy bouillabaisse infused with saffron and thyme.

"This might be the most delicious thing I've ever eaten in my life." Tessa wiped her fingers on a cloth napkin.

Pierre Fabron, a tall man with jet black hair and eyes to match, stroked the back of her hand. "I am pleased you enjoy."

"Yes, I enjoy very much." Tessa laughed, accustomed to his flirtation and adept at deflecting it. "And I'm pleased you like my design for the cellar. I'll have the architect finalize the blueprint for your contractor."

Pierre had sought her expertise on the layout of the new wine cellar he was building, a cellar that would hold two thousand bottles of wine.

"Ah, mon petit cher, you break my heart. It is all business for you, no? I beg you, come home with me. I will show you a pleasure more rapturous than you've ever known.

"I believe I've had all the delights I can handle in one night. Your bouillabaisse has sated my desires."

The chef leaned back in his chair, a smile on his lips. "Why do I pursue you?"

"Because you know I'll turn you down. It's the game we play. If I ever fell for your charm, you'd probably panic."

"I assure you, French men do not panic. At least not in bed." His affected accent faded. He'd lived in the United States for fifteen years and spoke English like a native. "So, my friend, how are you now?"

"How am I *now*?" Tessa cleared her throat.

The chef folded his arms. "Word is you had a..." he hesitated, "a disruption in your health."

Tessa flinched. Clients knowing about her trip to wellness camp was not good for business. "I'm absolutely fine, Pierre. I did take a vacation, though, a much-needed rest. I'll admit I was a bit exhausted. But I'm perfectly well. You have nothing to worry about."

"I am only worried for you."

"No need to be. Now, can I help you clean up?"

It was after midnight, but the offer was polite and a good way to escape the subject.

"I don't clean up." Pierre waved a hand, as if brushing away a fly. "I have people for that."

"As a famous chef should." She scooted her chair away from the table. "Oh, I almost forgot, you need to come by the shop soon. I've got a few new wines I'm carrying. You'll love them— delicious and well-priced."

"Two of my favorite adjectives." Pierre rose. "I will happily visit you, mon cher."

"Wonderful."

He walked her outside. A soft dry breeze carried the scent of honeysuckle.

Tessa opened her car door then turned and looked up at

Pierre. "You're a good friend, Pierre. Thank you for caring about me."

"Of course." He kissed both her cheeks. "I will see you soon. We have work to do. We must fill my new wine cellar before Christmas."

"Don't worry," she said. "We will."

Tessa headed home restless and annoyed. News of her *disruption in health* had spread all the way to Napa.

~

The next morning, bright sunlight penetrated her eyelids like a laser beam.

Tessa squinted at the clock on her nightstand. It was after nine. She never slept past seven, even on Saturdays, but after Pierre's bouillabaisse and the bottle of Sauvignon Blanc, no wonder she'd slept in.

Downstairs in the kitchen, Marco was standing in front of the stove frying bacon while Buttercup watched, drool dripping from her jowls.

She kissed her son's cheek.

He wiggled away. "Mom, stop."

"What? I'm your mother, and I don't care how old you are. I still get to kiss you."

Her little boy wasn't little anymore. His voice cracked, his upper lip hinted at a layer of dark fuzz, and his feet had grown two sizes in the past six months.

A mop of brown hair hung in his eyes. Tessa combed it back with her fingers. "What time's your dad picking you up?"

"I don't know. He said he'd text me."

Between school, sports, and friends, Marco's schedule had become chaotic, but Tessa was committed to the arrangements she and Victor had agreed to. He still had Marco every other weekend and took him to most of his soccer games. She handled everything else, managing her son's life like the captain of a ship. Somehow, it worked.

"You don't have to see him," Marco said. "I'll make sure I'm ready."

How could her son be so perceptive? "I don't mind seeing him."

His eyes flickered toward her then returned to the frying pan.

"I don't," she said, aware of her defensiveness. She poured coffee beans into the grinder and turned it on.

A week had passed since Victor delivered her the news of his engagement and the insane possibility of relocating to San Diego.

"So…" Tessa broached the subject with a vague question. "What's new with you?"

"Nothin'."

"Nothing at all?"

"Not really." He layered strips of bacon on a paper towel just the way Victor used to do it.

She proceeded with caution. "No news about your dad and Crystal?"

"Oh. You mean about them getting married." He said as if it were as insignificant as a trip to the grocery store.

She expelled a puff of air. "Well, that's news, isn't it?"

"I guess."

"Why didn't you tell me? I mean, it's a pretty big deal."

"I didn't want you to be upset." Marco concentrated on the bacon in the pan.

She took him by the shoulders and turned him. Marco was as tall as she was. Soon he'd be towering over her. But his face was still the face of her baby. "I'm not upset, honey."

Marco squirmed out of her grasp. "I just didn't want to talk about it. Still don't."

"I get that it makes you uncomfortable. I know you always wanted your dad and me to get back together."

"No, I didn't." He looked at her as if she were crazy.

Tessa recalled his second-grade drawings. "Yes, you did. When you were younger, anyway."

"Well, I don't remember." Marco wiped his hands on his boxer shorts. "Can you make me some eggs? I got to go pack my stuff."

"Of course, I will," Tessa said. "Cheesy scramble coming up."

"Actually, I like 'em fried."

"Fried?"

"Yeah. With hot sauce. That's how Crystal does it." Marco left the kitchen taking most of the bacon with him.

Tessa dropped a frying pan onto a burner with a clang. "*That's how Crystal does it*," she mimicked under her breath.

By the time Victor picked up Marco, Tessa was long gone.

$\mathcal{O}$n Monday morning, Tessa arrived at her grandmother's a few minutes before six. Nonna's cottage sat at the end of a country road lined with pepper trees.

It was the house of her childhood and held countless memories, both good and bad.

When Tessa was ten, her mother developed mysterious symptoms and eventually was diagnosed with kidney disease. Her father, a free spirited artist, couldn't manage the pressures of an ailing wife and precocious daughter. As he pulled away little by little, his mother-in-law took over. Rosa Mariano, a young widow at the time, moved her daughter and granddaughter into her home.

Shortly after Tessa's twelfth birthday, her mother died. Her father showed up for the funeral after being absent for months. A year later, he gave Rosa legal guardianship over his daughter. Tessa clung to her grandmother like a barnacle to a boat. She told her father she didn't care if she ever saw him again, and at eighteen she changed her last name to *Mariano*.

Tessa walked up the path toward the house. The tomato plants in the little vegetable garden were dry and spindly, the geraniums in the flower boxes almost dead. Tessa made a mental note to replant everything while her grandmother was recuperating.

She opened the door and stepped into the house. It smelled like vanilla and cinnamon. "Nonna, I'm here. Are you ready?"

"Of course I'm ready." Her grandmother held the handrail as she descended the stairs, her face pinched. "I can't wait to get this surgery over with."

"Me, too." Tessa hugged her tightly. She wanted her grandmother back to her old self as soon as possible. Hopefully Nonna's other hip wouldn't go anytime soon.

Once they were on the way to the city and making good time, Tessa relaxed. "How long do you have to stay in the hospital?"

"Dr. Barnes said a night or two. And then I'll go to a rehab hospital."

Tessa shook her head. "I've decided I don't want you to go to a rehab hospital. You'll come to my house." She couldn't stand the thought of her grandmother spending even one night in some depressing facility.

"I don't know. Let's just see what the doctor says." Rosa patted Tessa's knee. "Thank you, though. You're the best granddaughter. Now, let's talk about something else. You look very chic today. "

"Chic?" Tessa laughed. She'd been half asleep when she dressed, putting on jeans, a gray and white striped shirt, and red flats. "Yes, this is the latest in hospital waiting room attire—comfort clothing."

"Well, it's important to look nice. You never know who might pop up. There could be some eligible men wandering the hospital. Lots of handsome doctors."

Tessa gave Rosa a sidelong glance. "I have no interest in meeting anyone new. I'm quite content." She redirected the conversation with a sharp, sudden turn. "Have you spoken with Aunt Sophia? Does she know you're having surgery today?"

"She knows. I talked to her last night and told her you'd keep her apprised." Rosa inclined her head. "I'd prefer not to talk to her today. We all know how trying she can be."

Sophia, Nonna's younger daughter, had a way of exhausting everyone and twisting someone else's difficult situation into her own personal crisis. Lately however, she spent more time in Arizona with her daughter than she did in Clearwater, thank goodness.

"I'll be sure to keep her informed." Tessa added it to her mental list of things to do while she waited for her grandmother to get out of surgery.

When they reached the hospital, Tessa left her car with the valet and escorted Nonna to the surgical department.

The receptionist signed her in and directed them to a row of chairs in the waiting area.

Tessa crossed and uncrossed her legs. The reality of Nonna having to undergo anesthesia and a hip replacement struck.

"Are you okay?"

"I'm fine, Nonna. Just haven't had my coffee yet." She pressed her temples.

"Maybe you should go get one. I'm sure I'll be waiting here a while."

Tessa hesitated, but she needed to get a shot of caffeine into her system. "Okay, I'll be right back."

By the time she returned with a cup of lukewarm vending machine coffee, her grandmother and the receptionist were gone.

"Hello?" Tessa surveyed the area for a bell or something. "Anybody here?"

She waited, but when nobody came, Tessa marched through the "Staff Only" door and went in search of her grandmother.

At the end of a line of beds separated by blue curtains, she found Nonna propped against a pillow. Beside her, a young woman adjusted the incline of the bed.

"There you are." Tessa slipped in and closed the curtains.

The nurse, wearing a pink smock with puppies on it and white cotton pants, smiled. "Good morning! You must be Rosa's granddaughter."

"Good morning," Tessa said, unable to match the nurse's exuberance so early in the day.

"This is my nurse, Diane. She's such a dear."

"Nice to meet you." Tessa sipped the coffee and forced it down. She sat on the edge of the bed while Diane tucked the blankets around Nonna's legs.

"Okie-dokie. All comfy?" Diane had the voice of a children's television show host.

"I think she's cold," Tessa said with a shiver.

"I am a bit cold. Another blanket would be nice."

"Coming right up." She raised a finger in the air. "Now, Dr. Barnes is still in surgery with his first patient, so he's running a little late, but…"

"I thought my grandmother was his first case."

"Oh, no. His first case started at six-thirty. He has four hip replacements scheduled today." Diane's tone was almost reverential.

"Busy guy, isn't he?" Tessa said.

"Busy indeed! Now, you two sit tight. I'll be back in a jiffy."

When the cheery nurse slipped out, Tessa scooted closer to her grandmother. She drew the blanket up over Rosa's shoulders.

Nonna pulled an arm out and brushed a hand against Tessa's cheek. "My bambolina, we need to talk."

Tessa cringed. Any conversation that started with *we need to talk* would not be pleasant. Add that to *bambolina,* her grandmother's term of endearment for her from when Tessa was little, and she knew it would be serious.

"If something happens, you know, if anything goes—"

"Please Nonna, don't."

"Just listen. This is something I worry about, so keep quiet and let me talk. If I fall into a coma, take my tweezers from my cosmetics bag and pluck any chin hairs that pop up."

Tessa laughed. "You want me to make sure you don't sprout chin whiskers?"

"I know it's an odd request, but will you?"

"Yes. I will pluck your chin." She ran a finger along her grandmother's upper lip. "And anything else that needs it."

"Thank you. And one more thing."

"You want me to clip your toenails, too?"

"Be serious for a moment. I'm worried about you. I think all that good work you did at the wellness center has been forgotten. You're as stressed as ever."

"Please, Nonna, don't worry about me. I'm fine."

Nonna's eyes misted. "I know you better than anyone, my dear. And I know you're not fine."

It was impossible to deny it. Her grandmother had a sixth sense when it came to reading people, especially the people she loved.

Tessa kissed her cheek, inhaling the familiar scent of Ivory soap. "Let's get through today, and then we can talk about my stress, okay?"

The curtain opened, and Diane poked her head in. "Knock-knock. Got some warm blankets fresh from the oven."

"Perfect timing," Tessa said, grateful to have the conversation interrupted.

"They keep it freezing in here." Diane spread another blanket on top of Nonna then draped a second one around Tessa's shoulders. "How's that feel, honey?"

"So nice," Tessa said, enjoying the heat on the back of her neck. "Thank you."

"Doctor will be in shortly, but if you need anything in the meantime, just holler."

Tessa settled into a chair wrapped in the blanket and took a cleansing breath. She closed her eyes, but Nonna interrupted her moment of calm.

"You *are* stressed, you're not happy, and, to be perfectly honest, I think you're lonely."

"That's ridiculous," said Tessa. "I have you and Marco and lots of friends. Besides, you know how independent I am."

"Maybe too independent?"

Tessa squirmed as she recalled Victor's parting words the day he'd dropped his bombshell: *I hope you love your big fancy house, because someday you're gonna be in it all by yourself.*

"I don't want to talk about it, Nonna. You're about to have surgery, and we need to focus on that."

"Fine, I'll let it go for now." Nonna removed her watch, her wedding band, and a small diamond ring that had belonged to her mother. She pushed them into Tessa's hand. "Here, keep these safe for me. If I die, they're yours."

"Stop it!" Tessa wanted to crawl into bed and snuggle up to Nonna like she did when her mother passed away. She wiped her eyes with a corner of the warm blanket, leaving a spot of black mascara. "Now look what I—"

A large man in scrubs stepped into their cubicle. "Good morning, Rosa." He greeted her as if they were old friends. "I'm Dr. Kettleman, your anesthesiologist. How are you feeling?"

He had a mostly bald head with wispy gray sprouts and a soothing voice that put Tessa at ease.

"I feel fine," Nonna said. "A bit nervous though."

"Understandable. I can help with that." Dr. Kettleman smiled at Tessa. "And whom do we have with us today?"

"Oh, this is my granddaughter, Tessa Mariano."

Dr. Kettleman adjusted his stethoscope. "Tessa Mariano, the sommelier?"

"Yes!" Nonna said, overly excited.

Tessa raised her shoulders and smiled.

"I was in Clearwater last spring and attended an event," the doctor said. "It was a fundraiser, I think. And you were remarkable. You really know your wines." He turned back to his patient. "Do you know how skilled your granddaughter is?"

"I most certainly do." Nonna sounded like a proud parent at back-to-school night. "She's brilliant, successful, and single. Do you have a son, Dr. Kettleman?"

"Nonna!"

Dr. Kettleman chuckled. "I'm afraid I don't."

Tessa almost crawled under the bed. "I have some questions."

"Fire away."

"I, I'm…" she pushed the blanket off her shoulders. Tessa had spent hours researching hip replacement surgery and probably knew almost as much as he did, but she wanted to redirect the conversation. "I was just wondering how long you think she'll be in surgery."

"Probably two or three hours. And I'll be right by your grandma's side the entire time."

Nonna sighed. "You see, darling? I'm in good hands."

"You certainly are, Rosa. Dr. Barnes is the best orthopedic surgeon I've ever worked with. Not much personality, but a magician when it comes to fixing joints. So, let's get started." He wheeled the IV stand over and prepped the thin skin on Nonna's inner arm. "Look at me Rosa, just a teeny pinch, and…" he expertly poked the thick needle through her grandmother's skin into a vein, making Tessa wince.

"And we're done. Did it hurt?"

"Not at all, Doctor." Nonna's head sunk into the pillows.

Dr. Kettleman pushed a syringe of medication into the bag on the IV stand. "Just a little something to relax you. Kind of like drinking a glass of fine wine."

He winked at Tessa like an adoring father and gave her shoulder a reassuring squeeze.

8

*W*hile Nonna was in surgery Tessa texted Patty, reviewed some contracts, and thought about Dr. Kettleman and his patient, understanding demeanor. The polar opposite of his colleague, Dr. Barnes.

A long morning stretched before her, so she tried to relax and get a few things accomplished.

Tessa called Rebecca to let her know she'd found a spot where the nine puppies could stay until they were adopted, a farm owned by one of her old classmates.

"Really?" Rebecca shouted as if she'd just been told she had the winning lottery number. "That's totally amazing!"

"I'll text you the information," Tessa said in a low voice.

"Why are you whispering?" Rebecca asked, now whispering, too.

"I'm in the hospital waiting room. Nonna's having surgery today."

"Oh my God, I totally forgot!" Rebecca returned to shouting. "Please tell her how much I love her. She's my favorite grandma in all of Clearwater. I even love her more than I love my own. I don't really love my grandma. She's such a—"

"Rebecca." Tessa cut her off. "I've got to go."

"Right. Okay. Thank you. Goodbye."

Talking to the adorable but nutty animal rescuer was like running the fifty-yard dash. Tessa closed her eyes and mouthed one of the mantras and visualizations her meditation coach made up for her: *I am a boat upon the still water.* And while saying it, she pictured a wooden rowboat floating over gentle swells on Lake Clearwater.

She dozed, but awoke with a start.

It had been an hour since she'd watched two nurses roll her grandmother's gurney down the hall. Tessa left the waiting room and went in search of a status report.

At the nursing station, a young man in blue scrubs sat at the desk behind a computer screen.

"Excuse me, I'm just checking on my grandmother, Rosa Mariano. She's in surgery, a hip replacement. Her doctor is—"

"Yup, got it right here." His fingers flew across the keyboard. "Still in surgery."

"Can you check on her? I just want to know she's okay."

"Sure. Wait right here." He disappeared through the double doors at the end of the hall.

She paced back and forth, stopping to examine the prints on the wall, count tiles on the floor, and observe the busy nurses. Finally, the doors swung open.

Tessa hurried toward the young man in the blue scrubs.

"Everything's fine," he said.

"Are you sure?"

He returned to his desk. "Don't worry. If there's anything you need to know, they'll come tell you. She's got about another hour in surgery, and then she'll be in recovery. Why don't you go down to the cafeteria and get a snack?"

Tessa considered the suggestion. What she wouldn't give for a Nutmeg's cappuccino. "I really don't think I should leave the floor."

"It'll be fine. I'll call you if anything changes."

"Are you sure?" she asked again.

"I'm sure."

"You have my cell number?"

He pointed at his computer. "Got it all right here. With the information we collect, we could track you down anywhere."

"Right." Tessa tapped a nail on the smooth surface of the counter between them. She and Nonna had provided enough personal information to get a job at the CIA.

The crowded cafeteria smelled of cooking oil and toast. At the hot drink station, she studied the tea choices and selected one touting a calming blend of peppermint and chamomile.

At the register, she picked up a package of gourmet cookies. "Huh," she said, reading the description. They came from a bakery in Mendocino. "Are these any good?" she asked the cashier.

"No idea. But for what they cost, they should be."

"Stunning endorsement." Tessa put the box on her plastic tray alongside the paper cup of herbal tea.

She wound her way through the dining area toward an open table and sat in a hard plastic chair.

Nibbling on a piece of macadamia nut shortbread, she scrolled through her phone and responded to several texts. Then she snapped a photo of the cookie box and sent it to Patty telling her to order a couple of cases. The cookies would pair nicely with a crisp, citrusy Prosecco.

Moving on to voicemail, she discovered three messages from Sophia. The first one calm, the second one concerned, and the third one frantic.

"Damn." Tessa had forgotten to keep her aunt in the loop. She sent a quick text:

Everything fine. Will call later with update.

That ought to keep Sophia from flipping out for a while, or so she hoped.

Tessa broke off another bite of cookie but was distracted by the jarring buzz of her phone. An unfamiliar number appeared on the screen.

"Hello?"

"Tessa Mariano?" The connection was weak, and she could barely hear the caller's voice.

"Yes?"

"I'm calling from the nursing station on five."

Her stomach dropped. "What's wrong?"

"We need you to come—"

A high-pitched alarm sounded in the background.

"Are you there? Is my grandmother okay?" She yelled into the phone, but the caller was gone.

Tessa snatched her purse from the table, sprinted to the elevator, and jabbed the button repeatedly.

"Come on, come on," she said to the numbers on the wall. When the doors parted, she entered with a bunch of other people. Tessa gripped the handrail with clammy hands as they stopped on every floor. Her breaths came short and fast.

The doors finally opened on the fifth floor, and the alarm was still screeching. Tessa dashed toward the nursing station, but before she reached it a wave of dizziness struck. The noise faded, her vision blurred, and everything went black.

a cool hand held her wrist, and bright fluorescent lights blinded her. Lying on a gurney in the middle of a busy hallway, Tessa peered into the serene face of Dr. Kettleman.

She bolted upright. "Is she dead?"

"No, she's fine."

"You're sure?" She swung her legs over the side and tried to stand, but Dr. Kettleman stopped her.

"I'm sure. She's okay, and you need to stay put. You passed out."

The last thing Tessa remembered was stepping off the elevator. "When I heard the alarm, I freaked out."

"The alarm was for a different patient. Your grandmother is already in recovery." He pumped the bulb attached to the cuff on her arm. A concerned frown appeared between Dr. Kettleman's gray eyebrows.

"Do you typically have low blood pressure?"

"No. There's nothing wrong with me. Can I please—"

"Have you eaten today?" The doctor's frown deepened.

"I, um, I had a cookie in the cafeteria." She licked her dry lips. "A piece of one anyway."

"Hmm, you're probably a little dehydrated and low on blood sugar." Dr. Kettleman turned. "Can I get a juice over here?"

One of the nurses brought a juice box and poked the straw in for her.

"Thank you." Tessa breathed more easily. She swallowed the apple juice, and the fuzziness in her head dissipated.

"Oh look," said Dr. Kettleman, checking her pulse on the inside of her wrist. "Here's Dr. Barnes. He'll give you the update. You take care of yourself, dear. Drink more juice and don't forget to eat lunch."

"Okay, thanks," Tessa said, sad to see him go.

The two doctors switched places. It was like trading sweet for sour, light for dark. The surgeon's face revealed nothing.

"Everything went fine. Rosa will spend two nights in the hospital, and then I'll transfer her to rehab." He glanced at the clock behind the nurse's station. "Do you have any questions?"

"I do." Tessa got to her feet and brushed off her pants. "Are you always in such a hurry?"

"Generally, yes." His serious expression softened slightly. "I heard you passed out. Are you feeling better?"

She couldn't tell if his question was genuine concern or idle curiosity.

"I'm fine. Dr. Kettleman took care of me."

"I know. He's very caring."

Unlike you, Tessa thought. "Dr. Barnes, about rehab, I want my grandmother to come to my house. I'll take care of her. And I'll hire someone to be with her when I'm not there."

"No."

"No?" Tessa did not take kindly to be told *no.*

"I've already discussed it with Rosa, and we agreed she should stay in rehab for at least a week."

"But I—"

Dr. Barnes held his hand up. "I realize you're usually the boss, Ms. Mariano, but in this case, I am. The therapist will work with her several times a day. There's a state-of-the-art physical therapy gym, and at her age it's best she be at a facility where her vitals will be checked regularly and a hospitalist is on call at all times."

"Well," Tessa said, making herself taller. "That's quite a laundry list of reasons."

"I have more, but my next patient's waiting. Any other questions?"

Tessa seethed, but she tamped down the urge to argue. Besides, what he said did make sense. "Not at the moment. Can I see her now?"

Dr. Barnes gestured toward the nursing station. "One of them will escort you. I assume I'll see you at her follow-up appointment next week?"

She straightened her back. "You most certainly will."

A slight smile touched the corner of his mouth as if he were amused. And that made her dislike him even more.

~

Nonna dozed throughout the afternoon while Tessa sat beside the bed, staring at her grandmother's pale face and stroking her arm. At some point, she leaned back in the large chair and fell asleep.

A soft voice roused her. "Excuse me."

Tessa jumped, and the recliner bounced upright.

A nurse stood above her. "I'm so sorry, I didn't mean to startle you, but it's almost shift change. I'll be leaving soon."

Tessa rubbed her eyes, surprised to see a blanket spread over her lap. "Did you put this here?"

"I did."

"Thank you. I can't believe I nodded off."

"You and your grandma have been sleeping all day. Easiest patients on the floor." The young woman patted Tessa's shoulder.

"Anyway, the night nurse will be in shortly, and I'll be back in the morning. Have a good night."

The nurse left, and the room fell silent until Nonna stirred a few moments later. "Tessa?"

"I'm right here, Nonna."

"What time is it?" Her voice slurred.

Tessa caught a glimpse at the window, surprised to see the sky streaked with the colors of sunset. "Almost seven."

"Why are you still here?"

"Where else would I be?" Tessa asked. "Marco's with his dad tonight, so I'm staying with you. That chair over there converts into a bed." She eyed the chair-bed with its rock hard cushions.

Nonna reached for her with both hands. "Come, my girl."

Tessa took hold of the hands that had supported and soothed her for all of her forty-two years. The loose, wrinkled skin was lined with blue veins, fingers twisted from age and arthritis. Yet her touch was pure comfort.

She moved to the bed and rested her head on Nonna's chest. Her grandmother smoothed her hair like she did when Tessa was a little girl. Through every loss Tessa had suffered—her mother, her father, her husband—Nonna had been there for her.

A tear slipped down the side of her nose. "I'm so glad you're okay. If anything ever happened to you, I don't know what I'd do."

"Look at me, bambolina."

Tessa raised her head.

Nonna's sleepy eyes shimmered. "Nothing's going to happen to me, at least not yet. Goodness knows, I hope to get a few years out of this new hip. But you and I both know, my dear, I can't live forever."

"I—I know," Tessa said, her voice barely audible. She wiped a tear off her cheek with the back of her hand.

Her grandmother closed her eyes. Tessa thought she'd gone back to sleep, but then her eyes fluttered open. "We've been saving each other for many years, ever since your beautiful mother got sick. Because of you, my first *bambolina* is still with me."

They were tethered like two lifeboats on the ocean, weathering every ripple and storm together.

"And because of you, my mama is still with me." Tessa struggled to get the words out. The implication could not be ignored—when the time came for Nonna to go to heaven, Tessa would be alone. Of course she'd still have Marco, but he would grow up and live his own life.

"I don't want you to live your life alone."

There was no denying it—her grandmother could read her mind.

"Nonna, I—"

"Listen to me. I've been a widow for thirty-five years. That's a long time to live without love."

The words sunk in. Papa had died young, and then Nonna lost her daughter. Tessa couldn't imagine the pain of losing a child; the thought of anything happening to Marco halted her breathing.

"You always had me."

"And thank God I did." Nonna placed a gentle hand on her cheek. "But it's not the same."

"Are you saying I wasn't enough?" Had her grandmother made sacrifices beyond Tessa's comprehension? "Did you give something up because of me?"

"No, my love. I had your papa in my life for a long time."

Tessa tugged a tissue from the box on the bedside table and blew her nose. "Then what are you saying?"

Nonna's eyelids drooped again. "I'm saying that *you* have given up. You have closed off your heart to protect it."

Of course she had. Victor, the only man she'd ever fallen in love with, had betrayed her, leaving behind painful scars that would never heal.

Her grandmother tried to sit up, but she fell back against the pillow as if it were too great an effort. "I'm thirsty."

Tessa poured water into a cup and held the straw in front of Nonna's lips so she could drink.

"More?" Tessa asked.

Nonna shook her head. "Listen to me. A hard heart is a weak heart. I beg you, trov… l'am…"

She was mumbling in Italian, trailing off as she started to doze.

Tessa ran to the nursing station. "I think something's wrong with my grandmother, please, can you come check?"

The night nurse, a woman of about fifty with dark curly hair, followed Tessa into the room. She checked the bags on the IV stand and glanced at the monitor beside the bed.

"Her vitals are stable," she said, pressing a few buttons.

Nonna said something else unintelligible, as if agitated. The nurse leaned over her. "Rosa? How are you feeling?"

Nonna's eyes flew open. "What? Who are you?"

"I'm your nurse, honey. Just came to see how you're doing. Do you have pain?"

"A little." She made a noise, like a whimper.

Tessa moved closer. "Nonna, you're in pain?"

"Tessa?" she said, as if seeing her for the first time. "What are you doing here? Is it morning?"

"Why is she so confused?" Tessa asked the nurse. "We just had a conversation, and she was completely lucid."

"It's the anesthesia wearing off. And she's on pain medication, which I just increased slightly. Nothing to worry about." The nurse's voice was soft and calm. "Why don't you go home and get some sleep?"

"I can't leave her." Tessa shook her head. "She needs me here."

"Is it morning?" Nonna asked again.

"No, Rosa." The nurse stroked her arm. "It's nighttime. You

had your surgery this morning. And now you have an excellent new hip."

Nonna brightened. "New hip, that good."

The nurse was an angel, and Tessa had faith in her.

"Maybe I will go home—if you're sure."

"I'm sure," said the nurse. "She'll be much better in the morning, I promise."

"Okay." Tessa kissed her grandmother's forehead. "I'm going home, Nonna, see you tomorrow."

"Yes, darling, go. You need sleep." She closed her eyes, and the lines in her face relaxed.

"Don't worry about a thing," the nurse said. "I'll take good care of her."

"You'll call me if anything happens, right?"

"Absolutely."

"Thank you." Tessa gathered her things. She stopped in the doorway and turned for one more goodbye. Her grandmother looked small and helpless in the big hospital bed surrounded by pillows and machines.

"Bye, Nonna. I love you."

"Goodnight, dar..." Nonna coughed, her voice raspy. "Ti amo mia regazza."

10

Only two days after her surgery, Nonna was discharged by Dr. Barnes. Finally, Tessa could breathe again.

At rehab, Nonna had a private room, attentive nurses, and pretty good food served in a restaurant setting. On the night Tessa ate dinner with her, they enjoyed white fish, baked potatoes, and roasted brussel sprouts.

Tessa hadn't spoken to Victor since his unpleasant visit almost two weeks ago, so there'd been no more discussion about custody change. Perhaps he'd just floated the idea to test her reaction. Victor seemed to enjoy pushing her buttons every now and then. Besides, Elaine had reassured her that the likelihood of a judge even considering the idea was slim to none.

For the first time since she was released from wellness camp, Tessa looked forward instead of back.

~

Late Friday afternoon, the bells jingled on the shop door just as Tessa finished placing an order. Natalie Lurensky, owner of the ballet school just across the park, walked in. She had on black dance pants and a sleeveless leotard.

"Hello there." Natalie perched on the stool beside Tessa. "I'm exhausted."

"Long day?" Tessa asked.

"Long week. I'd love a glass of wine."

Tessa hopped up. "I have something new I want you to try." She selected a bottle from the rack. "It's a Merlot Cabernet blend. Spicy sweet, fruity finish, hint of dark chocolate."

"Hmm, sounds a little weird." The willowy brunette removed two stemmed glasses from the rack above her head and placed them on the counter.

"Unique, maybe. Calling wine *weird* is not permitted, even if you don't like it." Tessa uncorked the wine and poured it through an aerator into the glasses.

"Where's Patty?" Natalie asked.

"Out with Adam." Tessa removed the plastic wrap from the tray of samples and ate a few olives. "They're inseparable. It's sweet."

Natalie helped herself to a slice of brie. "Ah, yes—young love, new love, a beautiful thing."

"I detect a hint of cynicism," Tessa said.

"Probably." Her friend crossed her long legs. "That's what happens when you spend six years with a man who ends up breaking your heart."

A broken heart—enough to make anybody cynical. Tessa swirled her wine. "Yes, but you're too young to give up on love."

"Some might say you are, too." One of Natalie's eyebrows lifted. "

"Now you're starting to sound like Nonna. She thinks I'm lonely."

"Are you?" Her friend tucked a few stray hairs into the brown bun on top of her head. "I mean, you haven't been with a man since Victor."

"Thanks for the reminder." Tessa gazed into the wine, transfixed by the color, a deep dark red, the symbol of rage and love and longing. Abandoned by her father then betrayed by her husband—was it any wonder she didn't trust men?

"Just because Victor cheated," Natalie said, "it doesn't mean all men do."

"If you're trying to read my mind, you've succeeded." Tessa exhaled. "Can we move on, now?"

"Sure." Natalie raised her glass. "At least we have each other."

Tessa smiled at the sentiment. Platitude or not, it was true.

They clinked glasses and sipped.

The dancer held the wine in her mouth, closed her eyes, swallowed. "Mmm, good."

"I knew you'd like it," Tessa said.

"You know me better than I know myself."

"When it comes to wine, yes. It's my job."

Knowing what wine would please what person gave Tessa immense pleasure. It was like matchmaking. Except the wrong choice never ended in heartbreak.

"How's Nonna doing?" Natalie ate another piece of brie.

Tessa clicked a fingernail on her glass. "She's doing well in rehab, already taking laps around the hall. And of course the physical therapists love her."

"No surprise there. Everybody loves Nonna."

"And what about your mom? Any change?"

"She's slowly getting worse." Natalie's mother, a prima ballerina from Russia, had dementia. "The other night, she thought we were in Moscow performing *Don Quixote*. It was always her favorite ballet."

"Really?" Tessa pictured Natalie's mother twirling around the living room. "That's kind of sweet."

"It was. I put on the music for her, and she danced as beautifully as she did when I was a child. Then I went to the kitchen to check dinner and came back a minute later to find her pirouetting on the coffee table. Nearly gave me a heart attack."

Compared to Natalie, Tessa had nothing to complain about. She chastised herself for indulging in self-pity. "You need a little break. What are you doing tonight?"

"Nothing. My mom's caregiver is with her so I'm free. Want to do something?"

"I have to deliver some wine to a client. Come with me, and then we can grab a bite."

Natalie finished off her glass of wine. "It's a date."

∾

The kitchen in *Pierre's* bustled with servers passing through swinging doors, dishwashers spraying tubs of dirty dishes, and sous-chefs arranging plates into artistic creations.

As soon as Pierre saw Tessa, he broke into a smile. When he noticed her friend, he reacted just as she'd expected him to. Natalie had transformed her basic ballet uniform into a night-on-the-town outfit by throwing a leopard print pashmina around her shoulders and replacing her ballet flats with black sandals.

The chef practically tripped over his own feet.

Tessa introduced them.

"Miss Lurensky," he said, his French accent in overdrive. "The pleasure is mine. How can it be our friend has kept you hidden? Ah, your beauty is blinding like the sun."

Natalie, as tall as Pierre, shook his hand. "You are the charmer, aren't you?"

"Oui, oui, mademoiselle."

"I brought you some wine, Pierre." Tessa set the box on the far end of the stainless steel counter, steering clear of the food preparation and plating.

"Merci, I've been looking forward to—" A deafening crash drew his attention. "Dammit Tomas! You know what Chilean sea bass costs?"

"Sorry, boss." The young sous chef wiped his brow with his sleeve. "I'll eat it."

"Damn right you will. And next time I'll be deducting it from your pay."

"He's a tough one," Natalie said under her breath.

"Chefs can be difficult." Tessa patted the top of the box to get his attention. "Pierre, let me know what you think of these. Some are limited editions, so we'll want to place orders soon."

"You're not leaving, are you?"

"I'm afraid I am."

"But we must taste the wine together." He waved his arms. "And we must eat."

Tessa shook her head. "No, Pierre, really, we can't stay."

Another clatter stole his attention. "Just a minute," he said, holding up a finger. "Don't leave."

Natalie bumped her shoulder into Tessa's. "I'm starving, and it smells like heaven in here. And I haven't had a man buy me dinner in ages."

"I'll buy your dinner, Nat."

"Nice, but not the same. Besides, we're here, and I don't have much time. My mom's caregiver leaves at nine."

The scent of browned butter wafted in her direction, and Tessa's stomach growled. "Fine, you win."

When Pierre returned, Natalie stepped toward him. "I convinced Tessa we should stay," she said, her long lashes fluttering.

"Tres bon!" Pierre rested a hand on her lower back. "Right this way."

Tessa had become an after-thought as he led them through a narrow door into a tiny wine cellar with a carved wooden table and four chairs that looked like small thrones. Pierre snapped his fingers, and a waiter quickly set the table with white linens, china, and multiple wine glasses.

The chef slid out Natalie's chair, and she sat like the graceful ballerina she was.

Tessa stood with her arms crossed.

"I have not forgotten you, mia cara." Pierre seated her with a flourish. "Now, give me a moment in the kitchen, and dinner will be served."

As soon as he left the cellar, Tessa leaned toward Natalie. "What the hell was that? I've never seen you flirt so blatantly."

"Of course you have. Besides, you taught me how to flirt. That's why you were my favorite babysitter."

With an eight year age difference, Tessa had loved babysitting Natalie. "And I thought it was because I fed you fancy cheeses and grape juice."

"I liked that, too," Natalie said.

"Of course you did. But still, don't get ahead of yourself with Pierre. He's quite the womanizer."

"I can tell."

The waiter entered with a silver bowl of warm bread and salted butter. He opened a bottle of wine and poured it into a decanter.

Finally, Pierre returned. The three of them dined on filet mignon drizzled with Bordelaise, crispy pommes frittes, and steamed asparagus. The Cabernet Tessa brought paired perfectly. Throughout the meal, Pierre dashed back and forth into the kitchen, hardly sitting for more than a few minutes at a time.

"I could get used to this." Natalie swiped up the last drop of sauce with her finger. "And he is a cutie."

"Do I detect my cynical friend has had a change of heart?" Tessa asked.

"Just because I've given up on love, that doesn't mean I've given up on men."

Tessa mulled her friend's idea over. "Well now, there's something to think about."

11

One week after Rosa's surgery, Tessa drove her back to the city to see Dr. Barnes for the follow-up.

The receptionist behind the glass shuffled some papers. "I'm afraid he's not here."

"What do you mean?" Tessa's blood-pressure ticked up. "We have an appointment with him."

"He had an emergency, so—"

"I'm still here." Dr. Barnes appeared. His beard was thicker than it had been the day of the surgery, and instead of scrubs or his white coat he was dressed in khaki pants and a polo shirt.

Tessa stepped away from the glass, unnerved by a flash of attraction.

"How many patients are left on the schedule?" the doctor asked

"Just one," the receptionist said. "Mrs. Mariano is here."

Dr. Barnes lifted his gaze and acknowledged Tessa with a quick nod. "Hello, Ms. Mariano."

"Dr. Barnes." Tessa returned the polite nod.

"I'll be with you shortly." He said something to his receptionist before disappearing down the hallway.

"Tessa?" Nonna called from a chair across the waiting room. "Is everything okay?"

"Yes. Dr. Barnes will be right with us. I'm sure he just needs to check your incision so you can be cleared to go home. We'll be out of here in no time."

A minute later, the nurse summoned and guided them to a room. Tessa helped Nonna settle into a chair and rolled the walker out of the way.

Her cell phone chimed, and she glanced at the screen.

Call me when you have time to talk.

"Is it Marco?" Nonna asked.

"No." She sat next to her grandmother. "It's from Victor. He wants me to call him."

"Go outside and call, I'll be fine."

Tessa hesitated. "It can wait. I'll just let him know I'm busy."

With my grandmother at doctor. What's up?

Call me when done. Tell Nonna hello.

Just tell me what it's about.

Better if we talk.

Tessa rubbed her forehead, worried he wanted to bring up custody again. If she ignored the subject, it might go away. All she had to do was avoid it for a few years.

Her thoughts were interrupted when Dr. Barnes entered the room.

"Sorry about the confusion. I'm afraid I'm in a bit of a hurry today. Something came up." He lowered the examination bed and helped his patient onto it.

"I hope everything's okay," Nonna said, her voice tender. "An emergency can be very upsetting, so I understand."

The doctor tilted his head, and his eyebrows drew together. "Thank you, Rosa. I appreciate that."

His reaction gave Tessa a moment's pause. She didn't think he had a sensitive bone in his body. The cold doctor seemed to be warming up a bit.

"My grandmother has an uncanny ability to say the right thing at exactly the right moment," Tessa said.

Dr. Barnes turned his attention to her. "Yes. I'd have to agree."

"Oh, well," Nonna said, brushing away the compliment. "Most everything I say is just common sense."

"I am a fan of common sense," Dr. Barnes said with a firm nod. "We could use more of it in this world."

As the doctor examined his handiwork on Rosa's left thigh and asked about her exercises, Tessa reread the text exchange with Victor, jiggling her foot. If her ex-husband had any *common sense* at all, he'd never bring up the idea of Marco moving again.

"All right." Dr. Barnes helped Nonna off the table and positioned the walker in front of her legs. "Keep up the physical therapy. I'm pleased with your progress."

"It's not easy, but I'm determined."

"Good. I'll remove the staples Thursday or Friday. And you don't have to come back here. I'll do it at the rehab hospital."

"Oh, wait," Tessa said. "She won't be there. I'm taking her home today."

Dr. Barnes frowned. "I don't advise that. I'd like your grandmother to stay put until Friday. Is that all right with you, Rosa?"

"It is. I think it's a good idea."

"But Nonna," Tessa said, angling herself between her grandmother and doctor. "We already discussed this."

"We did, but I agree with Dr. Barnes. I want to stay a few more days."

The doctor's eyes shifted between the two of them.

"When can I take her home then?" she asked, irritated.

"As I said, Friday." Clearly, Dr. Barnes did not like repeating himself. "Will that work?"

"Yes, Dr. Barnes, and thank you." Rosa reached for his arm and squeezed it. "You take care, now. Many people depend on you, and that must be very stressful."

The doctor blinked, as if somebody understanding him were a rare event. He rubbed the scruff on his cheek, and his scowl faded. "Thank you, Rosa. I'll see you in a few days." His gaze landed on Tessa. "Goodbye, Ms. Mariano."

Tessa drove out of the parking garage and headed toward the bridge. She watched the minutes tick by as they crawled through traffic, making mental notes of everything awaiting her back in Clearwater, including Victor's cryptic "better if we talk" text message.

"You're preoccupied," Nonna said. "What's wrong?"

"It's nothing."

"It's not nothing. I know you don't like Dr. Barnes, but I thought he was much better today. I think I even saw him smile once."

"It's not about him. It's Victor."

"Oh. You mean the text he sent?"

Tessa took a breath. "Yes, that, and a conversation we had a couple of weeks ago."

She stretched her neck, cracking it to release the tension, and unloaded the entire story while they crossed the Golden Gate. Nonna's face showed concern as she learned about Victor's engagement, his possible but-not-yet-decided plan to move, and the ridiculous idea that Marco move with him.

Nonna's hand flew to her chest. "He wants to take Marco to San Diego?"

"That was the implication."

"Oh, Tessa, I can hardly believe it. And he's getting married? To whom?"

"Her name's *Crystal.* They've been together less than a year. And oh yeah, she's pregnant."

Nonna gasped. "You're kidding!"

"I'm not."

"Why didn't you tell me sooner?"

"Because I really wasn't all that upset," Tessa fibbed. She'd been frantic until Elaine talked her down. "Well, I was upset, but we had your operation to think about."

"That is no reason to keep secrets from me." Nonna pointed at her. "Especially not one so important."

"I'm sorry, I should've told you. Anyway, Victor and I haven't spoken since that day. But then I got his text this morning, and, well, now I'm nervous."

Her grandmother stared straight ahead, unblinking.

"You're making the face, Nonna."

"What face?"

"The *'I have something to say but I'm not gonna say it'* face." Tessa let out a puff of air. "So say it."

"I'm just thinking is all. Victor moving away, or at least moving on. Of course, it's not an ideal situation, but it is to be expected." Nonna gave her a sidelong glance. "You've been divorced a long time, and you can't blame him for not wanting to spend his life alone."

Tessa wondered if she was going to bring up her *hardened heart*, but thankfully her grandmother seemed to have forgotten the conversation they'd had while she was still loopy from the anesthesia.

Tessa lowered the temperature on the air conditioner. "I don't blame him for moving on."

"Whether you do or not is immaterial," Nonna said, closing the air vent on her side. "Marco is the priority. You've always put him first, and I know you always will."

Tessa nodded. Victor had accused her of putting her needs before those of others on several occasions. But she knew that wasn't true. "Of course, I will. My priorities are in very good order regardless of what my ex thinks."

Nonna cleared her throat. "Nevertheless, this turn of events may have thrown you off balance and undone the emotional progress you were making."

"That was a mouthful." Tessa suppressed a laugh, although it was hardly funny.

"Perhaps you should see a therapist," said Nonna.

"Good God, no. I had more than enough therapy at the wellness center, and I'm not about to start—dammit!" Tess flipped on the blinker and tried to cut across the freeway, but it was too late.

"I think we were supposed to get off back there." Nonna glanced over her shoulder.

"Yes we were." Tessa clenched her jaw and eyed the clock. "Now we have to circle back and get in all that traffic going in the other direction."

"I'm sorry," her grandmother said. "I upset you. We'll leave the subject alone for now."

"Thank you."

"Besides, you'll feel better after you talk to Victor. You'll have more information. Uncertainty creates stress. And if there's one thing you don't need, it's more stress." Her grandmother ended the statement with a firm nod.

After the brief detour, they made good time. Tessa parked in one of the handicapped spaces near the entrance. "I'll get your walker."

"Tessa, wait." Her grandmother put a hand on her forearm. "Don't be angry with me. You know I only want what's best for you and Marco. That's why I'm so concerned."

"It's okay, I'm not angry." Tessa patted Nonna's wrinkled hand. "And I only want what's best for you, too. That's why I'm so bossy."

Nonna gave her a weepy smile. "I'm concerned and you're bossy. We're a perfect pair."

"We certainly are." Tessa dropped a quick kiss on her grandmother's cheek and got out of the car.

She pulled the walker out of the back of her SUV and wheeled it along the sidewalk toward the passenger door. Tessa imagined herself in forty years shuffling behind a walker, living alone, depending on others.

She tried to push the image from her mind, but it refused to go.

12

That night after dinner, Tessa poured herself a glass of Pinot. Marco was in his room with the door closed, presumably doing homework, so it was a good time to call Victor back.

Her heart pounded while she waited for him to answer.

"Hello?" he said.

"It's me," she said, pacing around her kitchen island with phone in one hand and wine in the other.

"Thanks for calling."

Tessa rolled her eyes. "You're welcome. What's going on?"

"Oh, it's—it's about Crystal. I just wanted you to know she'll be picking Marco up for me tomorrow."

Irritation poked at her. She'd been on pins and needles all day thinking the matter was serious. "Okay, thanks for telling me, but you could've just texted the message."

Victor coughed and cleared his throat. "There's something else you should know which is why I wanted to talk to you."

Tessa stopped pacing and put her glass down. "I'm listening."

"Crystal's, well, she and I—we're having a baby."

"You are?" she said, feigning surprise. There was no reason to tell him she'd heard the juicy gossip from her lawyer.

"It, um, well it wasn't planned."

"You don't need to explain anything to me. In fact, I'd prefer you didn't." She drank some wine, barely tasting it. "What time should Marco be ready?"

"The usual, around five-thirty."

"I'll let him know." She was anxious to hang up.

"Okay," Victor said with a clipped tone. "Bye."

"Goodbye." Tessa ended the call, resisting the desire to throw her phone against the wall.

Buttercup pushed her nose into Tessa's stomach. She stroked her dog's soft face and kissed the top of her head.

On the way to her bedroom, she tapped on Marco's door and opened it a crack. He was at his desk hunched over his laptop. "Hey, honey."

Marco turned. "Hey, Mom."

Buttercup romped over and nosed her head under his arm.

"I just spoke to your dad. Crystal's going to pick you up tomorrow."

"Okay," he said, rubbing the dog under her jowls.

Tessa wished she could cuddle her boy, but those days had passed. Instead she gave him a peck on the cheek and a squeeze on the shoulder.

Upstairs in her sanctuary, Tessa took a hot bath and then crawled into bed, agitated but exhausted. She dangled her hand over the side, stroking Buttercup's silky fur and envisioning the day when it would be just the two of them. Then she broke one of her most strict rules and allowed the dog onto her bed.

The following afternoon, Tessa got home from work just after six. She hadn't purposely avoided the encounter with Crystal, and of course they'd have to meet eventually, but not tonight.

She dropped her bags on the counter, let Buttercup outside, and opened the refrigerator. The variety of leftovers held little appeal, and she considered driving to her favorite Japanese restaurant for sushi. When she shut the refrigerator, the sound of running water distracted her. Tessa hurried down the hall toward the guest bathroom worried there might be a leak. She stopped short when she heard the shower running in Marco's bathroom.

She knocked hard.

"Yeah?"

Tessa called through the closed door. "I thought you were getting picked up at five-thirty."

"They're running late. I'll be out in a few minutes."

"Okay." Tessa retreated. Now she'd have to meet her ex-husband's fiancé. Then again, she could take Buttercup for a quick walk or conveniently remember she'd left something at work.

The doorbell chimed, foiling any escape. She glanced in the entryway mirror, and a tired face looked back at her. "Oh, well."

Tessa opened the door. The woman standing there was hardly the Nicole Kidman lookalike she'd imagined.

Crystal had mousey brown hair wound into a low ponytail, and a gray sundress hung loosely over her body. In her hand, she held the wrist of little boy.

"Hello." Tessa forced a smile. "You must be Crystal."

"I'm so sorry. I was going to wait in the car, but, oh this is awkward, I need to use the bathroom." Her face scrunched, as if she were struggling to hold it.

Few things were more urgent than a pregnant woman needing to pee. "Come in. It's right down the hall."

"Thank you. Come on, Henry. Mommy has to use the potty."

"I wanna stay with her." The little boy pointed at Tessa.

"It's fine," Tessa said, surprised by his immediate comfort around a complete stranger. "Go ahead."

"Thanks." Crystal scurried to the bathroom.

Henry smiled up at Tessa. He had curly blond hair and dimples in both cheeks. "Do you live here?"

"I do," Tessa said.

"What's up there?" He pointed at the stairs.

"Just another room. How old are you?"

"Five." He showed her his right hand and spread his fingers out wide.

"Five? I thought you were at least six," she teased. He actually looked closer to four.

"I'm very big and strong." Henry put up his arms like a weightlifter and said, "Grrrrrr."

"Wow, you are strong, aren't you?"

"Yep." He ambled past her into the living room as if she'd invited him to take a look around. "I'm hungry."

"Do you want a snack?"

The little boy nodded and grinned, showing off the adorable dimples.

"Let's go to the kitchen," she said, corralling him away from her white furniture.

"Do you have candy?"

"Candy? I don't think so." Tessa picked him up and placed him on a stool at the island, hesitant to feed another woman's child without permission, especially so close to dinner time. "Let's ask your mom what kind of snack you can have when she comes out of the bathroom. But I'll give you a drink of water."

"I like juice."

"We'll start with water." Tessa dug through a bottom drawer where she kept a few remaining vestiges of Marco's childhood. "And look what I have for you to drink from." She held up an old sippy cup.

"That's 'Mickey Mouse'."

"Right," Tessa said, filling it with filtered water from the dispenser at the sink. "It used to be Marco's."

Henry's brown eyes widened. "You know Marco?"

"Of course I do. He's *my* little boy."

"He's not little." Henry put his pink lips on the spout and drank.

"Well, not anymore. But he used to be." Tessa sensed Henry was confused, and no wonder with many changes in his short life. "I'm Marco's mommy."

Henry pulled the spout out of his mouth with a pop. "You are?"

Thankfully, Crystal appeared. "Henry, remember we talked about this? Marco has his own mom."

Henry's face fell into a thoughtful frown. "So he gets two moms?"

"Oh dear." Crystal pressed her palms against her cheeks.

Tessa sighed. What a mess parents created when they split up. Marco's second-grade drawings were testament to that.

"Actually." Tessa leaned on the island and folded her hands. "It is kind of like that. I'm Marco's mom, and your mom will be his stepmom."

"Oh." His expression went from concern to delight. "So you can be my stepmom, and then I get two moms, too."

His response was bittersweet. "That's not quite how it works," Tessa said, although she understood his reasoning.

Crystal intervened with the distraction technique. "Henry, I have some toys for you." She opened her denim satchel and took out a few little cars.

"But I want a snack." He pointed at Tessa. "That mom said I could have a snack."

Crystal turned bright pink.

"I did," Tessa said. "Would it be okay?"

"Yes, if you don't mind." She put the cars in front of her son.

"I want chocolate!"

"It's a little close to dinner for chocolate," Tessa said.

Crystal seated herself on the stool next to Henry. She let out a loud, exhausted sigh. "I don't care."

Overly permissive. The curse of being a single parent. Tessa opened the pantry. All she had was a small box of La Maison chocolate ganache, her own favorite treat for when she really needed it. "No chocolate. But I do have c-h-i-p-s."

"Chips? I love chips."

"He can spell?" Tessa asked.

"I'm afraid so," Crystal replied. "It really makes communicating around adults difficult."

"Can I have chips, Mommy?"

"Sure." Crystal covered her mouth and yawned. "Sorry, I'm just so tired today."

Tessa put a small pile of potato chips on a napkin in front of Henry. "First trimester?" she asked.

Crystal broke eye-contact. "Second." She moved closer to Tessa and whispered, "The boys don't know yet."

Tessa figured as much, but it wouldn't be long before Crystal's belly grew rounder. "Victor should probably take care of that sooner rather than later."

"I know."

Tessa wanted a glass of wine in the worst way but thought it would be rude to drink in front of Crystal. She took a bottle of Perrier from the refrigerator and was about to pour two glasses when her son appeared in the kitchen.

"Marco!" Henry jumped off the stool and ran to him.

"Hey, buddy." Marco ruffled Henry's hair then glanced from his mother to Crystal. "I'm ready to go."

Crystal gave Tessa an awkward smile. "Nice to meet you, finally."

"And you," Tessa said. She felt a tiny hand slip into hers. "Oh, bye, Henry."

"Aren't you coming with us?" he asked.

Tessa's eyes burned, and a rush of emotion struck. "Not this time, Henry. I have other plans tonight." She escorted them to the front door.

"Bye, Mom." Marco brushed a kiss over her cheek, something he rarely did without prompting.

Tessa watched her son walk down the path with his soon-to-be stepmother and brother. Henry turned and waved. She raised her hand and waved back.

Once they were in the car and driving away, she closed the door with a quiet thud. She went to the kitchen, poured herself a glass of Chardonnay, and put some leftover Chinese food into the microwave.

Buttercup scratched on the door, and Tessa let her in. "Hello, girl."

The dog sniffed around the seat where Henry had been, then she sat in front of the cabinet where her food was kept. Tessa filled the dog bowl with kibble and set it on the floor.

The microwave pinged. She put her plate on the island, turned on the kitchen TV, and took a few bites. The greasy noodles stuck in her throat. She dumped them in the trash and looked at the clock above the window. Marco would be gone for at least two hours, so she clipped a leash to Buttercup's collar and took her out for a walk.

They strolled across the backyard onto the path down to the lake. Sitting on the grass, Tessa leaned on her sweet, strong dog and watched the sun dip into the water. In two days, she'd be bringing Nonna home from rehab. Maybe then she'd feel as if life could regain some semblance of normal.

13

*H*er grandmother chatted all the way back to Clearwater. Her progress in physical therapy had been extraordinary, according to the therapist.

"And I'm almost completely off pain medication, what do you think of that?"

"I think it's marvelous." Tessa squeezed Nonna's thigh. "And I'm thrilled to get you home."

When they pulled into the driveway, Tessa tingled with anticipation. A few days earlier, she'd hired a landscaper to replant the flower boxes with petunias, pansies, impatiens, and snap dragons in every shade. She couldn't wait to see Nonna's reaction.

She parked in front of the cottage, and her grandmother gasped.

"Oh my goodness! What a sight."

"I know how much you love lots of color."

"Oh, darling, I do." Nonna burst into tears.

"What's wrong?" Tessa asked. "Why are you crying?"

Her grandmother sniffled. "I'm just being emotional. You've done so much for me." She pulled a tissue from her purse and blew her nose. "And I, I'm sorry I have to depend on you so much."

"Please don't say that. There's nothing in the world I wouldn't do for you."

"I know that, which is why I'm crying." The old woman's shoulders trembled. "For so many years, I took care of you. I never imagined the tables would turn."

Tessa picked up Nonna's hand and kissed it. "It's only for a little while. Pretty soon you'll be back to driving and taking walks and planting your own garden and telling me what to do."

Nonna let out a shaky breath. "I hope you're right."

"Of course I am." Tessa opened her door. "Now let's get you inside."

The cozy house smelled musty. Tessa peeled back the curtains, opened the windows, and gathered the mail. She rolled Nonna's small suitcase inside and left it at the base of the stairs.

Her grandmother stood in the middle of the living room frowning at the hospital bed that had been delivered the day before. "I hate that there."

"Do you want it moved?" Tessa suspected it wasn't the location of the bed that bothered Nonna. It was the fact that she needed it.

"Doesn't matter." Nonna pushed her walker around the bed and went to the kitchen.

Tessa followed her. "I bought fresh-squeezed orange juice. I know you love that. And there's cottage cheese, bagels, fruit, and—"

"Don't you have to go to work?" Nonna asked, suddenly a bit cranky. "And what about Marco? It's Friday, doesn't he have a soccer game this afternoon?"

The answers to her questions were yes and yes, but Tessa danced around them. "I can stay until the caregiver gets here."

"What caregiver?"

Tessa puffed her cheeks then let the air out. "I told you I hired somebody. You're not ready to be alone."

"I forgot," Rosa said. "When's she coming?"

"About noon." Tessa checked the time. It was almost twelve. She needed to show the caregiver around and give her detailed instructions. With any luck, she could be at work by one.

"You can go." Nonna scooted her walker toward Tessa's legs, as if pushing her toward the door.

"But I need to meet the caregiver and make sure she knows what to do."

"I had my hip replaced, not my brain. I'm able to tell her what I need, myself." She continued moving the walker as Tessa backed up. "You hovering over me is—is bothersome."

Bothersome. Tessa cracked a smile at her grandmother's gentle word choice. She knew what a pain in the neck she could be. Still, she wasn't about to leave her grandmother alone.

A car rolled up the driveway, and Tessa looked out the window. A woman in a blue uniform got out. "Well, looks like she's here, but I'd like to—"

"Tessa." Nonna held up a hand to silence her. "Please don't treat me like a child."

The admonition hurt. "I'm sorry. I didn't mean to. I'll go, but can I at least call you later?"

"Of course you may." Her grandmother's voice softened. "Now off you go, darling."

Tessa kissed Nonna's cheek and left out the backdoor. She lingered just long enough to make sure the caregiver made it inside.

Cheering parents filled the bleachers at the soccer field, but Victor was not among them. Tessa kept glancing from Marco running up and down the field to the parking lot, hoping to see her ex-husband's car. Toward the end of the first half, Victor finally showed up. What made him think he could handle being the custodial parent when he couldn't even get to a soccer game on time?

"What's the score," he asked, lowering himself onto the bench beside her.

"Three to two," she said without looking at him. "We're behind."

Tessa felt his presence like an annoying gnat buzzing around her ear.

Because of the crowd, her arm brushed against him every time she moved, which distracted and irritated her.

They watched without speaking to each other.

With less than a minute left in the game, Marco dribbled the ball upfield and passed it to his teammate. The forward carried it toward the goal and kicked. It sailed into the air. Everybody jumped to their feet.

Tessa held her breath. The ball continued its flight, looking as if it were a perfect shot. But at the last second, the opposing goalie dove like an Olympian and knocked it out.

She collapsed back into her seat. The fans on the other side of the field erupted into cheers. Even from far away, Tessa could see the disappointment on Marco's face as he jogged toward his teammates.

"Well," Tessa said, stepping over the bleachers. "At least you were here in time to see Marco's team lose."

"Such a nice comment," Victor said. "I was held up at work."

True or not, getting held up at work was an excuse he used far too often. Victor tended to change jobs on a regular basis. He was in "sales," but what he was selling Tessa wasn't sure— computer parts or car parts or maybe carpet. Who knew?

"Marco's stuff is in my car. I'll go get it." Tessa climbed off the bleachers and headed across the grass.

"Tessa, wait." Victor followed her toward the parking lot,

dropping his sarcastic tone. "I just want to say thanks. Crystal said you were really nice the other day."

Tessa continued walking. Of course she was nice. The grown-ups had to keep things civil. They owed it to the children who were caught in the middle of their parents' dysfunction through no fault of their own. "Crystal seems nice, too. And her little boy's very cute."

"Yeah, Henry's a great kid. And he sure loves Marco."

Tessa had noticed that for sure. "Where's his father?" she asked.

Victor hemmed. "Not in the picture."

Tessa popped open the back of her SUV. "Vague answer, but okay."

"How's Nonna doing?" he asked, taking their son's backpack and duffle bag.

"She's not your Nonna anymore."

"I suppose not," he said, "but I still care about her."

Tessa let her guard down a notch. Before the divorce, Nonna and Victor had had a good relationship. "She's doing well. I got her home from rehab this morning, so she's settling in with the caregiver."

"A caregiver? She agreed to that?"

"Begrudgingly." Tessa closed the hatch and regarded her ex. They had more important things to discuss. "Not to change the subject, but when are you going to tell Marco about the baby?"

As if to make sure they were alone, Victor looked over his shoulder. "Yeah, I have to do that. I just haven't figured out how to explain it."

"He's almost fourteen," she said. "He knows how babies are made."

"Come on, you know that's not what I meant."

Tessa put on a Lululemon sweatshirt and zipped it up. "Just tell him the truth. At least you and Crystal are doing the right thing."

"You think we are?" Victor asked, sounding as if he sought her approval.

"I think you are. Time will tell."

They were interrupted when Marco yelled from across the parking lot as he ran toward them.

Tessa spoke quickly. "Bottom line is you'd better tell him soon, or he'll figure it out for himself."

14

*P*atty and Liza came out of the storeroom, each carrying a small cardboard box.

"Found them." Patty set hers on the counter. "Two dozen tins of Beluga caviar."

Tessa had closed the shop early for quarterly inventory. She insisted on turning over merchandise and checking expirations every season.

"Thank God. Where were they?"

"In the cooler," Liza said. "But not the one you said they were in."

Tessa lifted her hair off the back of her neck. "It's not like me to misplace things."

Natalie, who was sitting at the bar nibbling cheese samples and sipping a glass of merlot, laughed. "You're very distracted these days."

"I suppose." Tessa removed six tins of caviar from the box to place on display. The rest would go back in the cooler. "Are you girls hungry? Let's order pizza."

"None for me," Patty said. "Adam and I are meeting Cece and Brad at the lake for a barbecue."

Cece, a former ballerina and Natalie's dance director, was Patty's best friend.

"Okay," Tessa said. "Liza, what about you?"

Liza shook her head. "Thanks, but I'm going to a movie with Rebecca."

Tessa put an arm over Natalie's shoulders. "Just us two, then."

"I can't tonight."

"Are you kidding?" Tessa frowned at her friend. "You're always up for pizza on Sunday."

"I'm busy." Natalie's face disappeared into her wine glass.

"Busy with what?" Tessa put her hands on her hips.

"Yeah, what?" Patty chimed in. "This is Clearwater. You know we'll find out eventually."

Natalie balled up a napkin. "I have a date."

The other three women leaned forward like curious cats.

"With whom?" Tessa asked, surprised by her friend's reticence.

Natalie's fingers played upon her lips. "With Pierre."

"Seriously?" Tessa cocked her head.

Patty grabbed Natalie's arm and squeezed so hard it left a faint mark. "You mean Pierre Fabron? The dark and mysterious French chef who's building the massive wine cellar?"

"It's just dinner." Natalie swallowed the rest of her wine.

"Believe me." Tessa winked at Patty and Liza. "It won't be *just dinner.*"

"I can handle it." Natalie stood. "Anyway, I'd better head home. This face doesn't get pretty all by itself."

"I expect a full report tomorrow," Patty said. "Every single detail."

"We'll see." Natalie clicked her tongue on her way out the door.

Tessa smirked and waved her fingers. "Have fun," she said

with a lilt in her voice. A week ago, her friend had dismissed any thought of dating. But that was before she crossed paths with Pierre Fabron.

"I think they'll be great together." Patty did a little hop from foot to foot. "They're both so, I don't know, exotic."

"A Russian dancer and a French chef," Liza said. "How romantic!"

Romance, passion, love. Tessa couldn't even remember what that felt like. She went back to work and forgot about pizza.

Immersed in a spreadsheet on her laptop screen, she practically jumped out of her chair when the door flew open and smacked the wall.

"Mom!" Marco burst into the shop.

"Take it easy," Tessa said. "You nearly broke the glass." She walked over and locked the door.

"Sorry." Marco slumped as if embarrassed by his dramatic entrance.

"What are you doing here?" Tessa asked him. "I thought Dad was bringing you back after dinner."

"I, uh, I just wanted to come home."

Tessa noticed the small crease between his eyebrows. The same expression he wore as a toddler when he was put in time-out or denied candy or couldn't figure out a puzzle. It said everything.

She glanced at Liza and Patty, acknowledging their concerned looks, then guided Marco into the storeroom.

"What's the matter?" Tessa asked, although she already knew the answer.

"Dad and Crystal are having a baby. Did you know?"

Tessa bit into her upper lip. She nodded.

"I don't get it. Crystal has Henry, and Dad has me. Isn't— isn't that enough?" He dropped his duffle bag on the floor and kicked it hard.

He was angry and hurt, and Tessa had no ability to make the situation easier for him. She hoped Victor had seen Marco's reaction and was feeling terrible about it. "You know, honey, these things are complicated." Tessa cringed at how weak and useless her words sounded.

"Dad said the same thing. And he said it wasn't on purpose. Why didn't he, you know, use…" Marco stopped and averted his gaze. The subject of accidental pregnancies was not something a teenage boy wanted to discuss with his mother.

He dragged a sleeve across his eyes.

She tried to hug him, but he wriggled out of her embrace.

Anger burned inside her like faint sparks, ready to come back to life with the smallest amount of fuel. And Victor was the gasoline. He'd always been impulsive and immature. In their early twenties, his carefree ways were fun and easy. But once they had Marco, Tessa realized he would never grow up, never take responsibility. That's why she had to do it—make the money, rear the child, manage the home. If she didn't do it, it wouldn't get done. And as a response, because *Victor* was being neglected, he had an affair. Who could blame her for being resentful?

She tamped down the embers of her anger.

"I wish I could answer all your questions, but I can't. What you have to understand is that your dad loves you very much. And that won't change."

Marco wiped his eyes on his sleeve. "How do you know?"

"I just do. No matter what happens, your father will always love you." Tessa didn't know where she found the strength to set aside her own anger and say those words. Maybe because she knew it was what Marco needed to hear. More importantly, she knew it was true.

The creases in Marco's face deepened. Tessa's reassurance was not enough to allay her son's worry that he was about to be replaced.

"Can we just go home?"

"Sure. I'll meet you at the car in a few minutes."

Marco retrieved his duffle bag and went out the back.

Tessa put her hands on either side of her head and squeezed. If Victor were standing in front of her she would've punched him. How could he have been so stupid?

s soon as they got home, Marco threw himself onto the couch.

Tessa smoothed his hair. "I need to go check on Nonna, honey."

"Can't you just call her?"

"If I do that, she'll just say everything's fine whether it is or not. I need to see for myself."

"Okay." He pulled off his sweatshirt and dropped it on the floor. Buttercup sniffed it thoroughly then joined Marco on the sofa.

"When I get back, we'll eat and watch a movie or something." Tessa made the suggestion even though it was a school night. "How does that sound?"

"Fine." He picked up the remote and turned on the TV.

"I already ordered the pizza. Here's a tip for the delivery driver." She laid a five dollar bill on the coffee table. "Text me if you need anything. I won't be long, I promise."

Marco's eyes were stuck to the TV screen, but Tessa could tell his mind was somewhere else.

. . .

Nonna was sitting at her kitchen table with a cup of tea when Tessa walked in.

"Oh, hello, darling. I wasn't expecting you."

"I texted you this afternoon to tell you I'd be over." Tessa kissed her cheek. "Didn't you see it?"

"I didn't. I'm not even sure where my cell phone is at the moment." Her grandmother pointed at the old landline on the wall. "You can always call me the regular way. I actually prefer it."

"I know." Tessa peered down the hallway. "Where's your caregiver?"

Nonna set her cup on the table. "I had to let her go."

"What? Please tell me you're kidding."

"Of course I'm not. Who would kid about such a thing?"

Tessa sat next to Nonna. She smoothed a wrinkle in the flowered tablecloth, reminding herself to be patient. After all, she'd known from the start Nonna did not want a caregiver. "What happened? Did she do something wrong?"

"Not at all. She was nice and very efficient." Nonna dabbed her nose with a tissue. "I just didn't like having her around. She hovered over me too much. Even when I was just sitting and watching TV or reading my book."

"That was her job, Nonna, to look after you and be available in case you needed something."

"But I hardly need anything at all. The only thing I can't do at this point is go up the stairs or drive. Frankly, Tessa, it's a waste of money. And you know how I dislike waste of any kind."

"I know." Tessa rubbed her face. The weight of the day had exhausted her. "But there is no way you can stay alone. I won't allow it. You'll come to my house and stay in the guest room until—"

"I don't want to go to your house." Nonna tapped the handle on her teacup.

Tessa stiffened.

"The truth is, and I know you won't like this, but I was happier at the rehab hospital."

Tessa's eyes narrowed. "Now you're sounding crazy."

"It sounds crazy to you because you're not an eighty-five-year-old woman relying on others. I don't want to be a burden."

"I've told you a thousand times, Nonna, you could never be a burden."

"I beg to differ. But that's neither here nor there."

"What does that mean?" Tessa's patience was running thin.

"It means we will never agree on that particular point."

Tessa crossed her arms. "Okay fine. So what do you want to do? Call Dr. Barnes and ask him to arrange for you to spend a few more weeks in rehab?"

Nonna shook her head. "I have a better idea."

～

The next day, Tessa drove her grandmother to The Westridge, a senior living community twenty minutes outside of Clearwater.

"I can do all my therapy in the gym with a physical therapist, which means I'm not depending on you or anybody else to drive me. And it's included in my weekly rate along with three meals a day and all kinds of activities."

"Did you say weekly rate?"

"Yes, darling. It's a short-term commitment."

Short-term sounded good to Tessa. All she wanted was for Nonna to be the woman she was a few months ago. Tessa thrived when everything in life was normal, unchanged, and under her control—the exact opposite of how it was.

The GPS directed them onto Westridge Lane, a treelined road with houses set wide apart and white fencing around green fields. Horses grazed in some of the pastures, their heads bent into the grass.

"The area's lovely, don't you think?"

Tessa had to admit it was. "Have you been here before?"

"Several times. My friend Ruthie moved in a year ago, so I come to have lunch with her now and then. She was the one who suggested I inquire about short-term stays."

"I see." Tessa made a mental note to give Ruthie the evil eye if she bumped into her. "That was nice of her."

"Don't be snippy."

"I'm not being snippy."

While her grandmother buzzed about how much Ruthie loved the activities and services and caring staff, Tessa's thoughts wandered. Between Nonna letting go of the caregiver and Victor turning her life upside down, she was grasping for control like a drowning man reaching for a rope.

"Are you listening?" Nonna asked.

"Sorry. What'd you say?"

"I said I hope you understand that I'm doing this for both of us. If I have a problem, there are people here who will take care of me, and I won't need to call you."

Tessa didn't like any buffer between them. She wanted to be her grandmother's first call. "Maybe. I just can't stand not, not..."

Nonna brushed the back of her hand over Tessa's cheek. "Not being in control. You've always been that way, my girl, ever since your mother got sick."

Tessa blinked back tears.

She'd bargained with God to make her mother better, promising to be kind and patient and helpful.

Mama, I'll be good so you can get well. Please, Mama, please try.

But no matter how perfect she was, Mama got sicker. In the end, Tessa was powerless to control her mother's illness, unable to prevent her death.

Even so, she clung to the idea. Being in control gave her the best chance of preventing a disaster.

A private road led to a grand mansion right out of *Southern Living Magazine* with its enormous Oak trees, tidy hedges, and row upon row of white, yellow, and pink rosebushes. It was far from the sterile building she'd expected.

Tessa parked in front of the main entrance and removed her seatbelt. "There's something I've never told you. I've never told anyone."

Her grandmother tilted her head, eyes wide. "What is it?"

"After Mom died, I got this idea in my head that when bad things happen, it's my fault."

"Where on earth would you get an idea like that?"

"I don't know where it came from. Maybe because mom got sick because of me, that being pregnant messed up her kidneys. Which then led to my father leaving and everything spiraling out of control."

Nonna didn't respond right away, as if taking in Tessa's confession. "Well, that is a tremendous burden. But none of it is true."

"I've always wondered," Tessa said, sadness filling her soul, "what would've happened if I'd never been born, what the world would be like without me in it."

Her grandmother's clear eyes met hers. "My goodness, you do go to dark places, don't you?"

"Not always, but these last few months, yes. Therapy dredged up a lot of stuff. "

Nonna cupped Tessa's cheeks. "Let me tell you something. You, my darling, are the light of my life. And the very thought of a world without you in it makes my heart weep."

For a moment, Tessa couldn't breathe. Her hands shook, and her skin turned clammy. She threw open the car door and gulped in air. A warm breeze delivered the scent of roses, like a gift. She inhaled, closed her eyes, and pictured foamy waves rolling into the shoreline until her racing heart slowed.

"Tessa, your face is a bit pale. Are you okay?"

"Yes." She remained focused on the image of waves. "I just need a minute."

"Is it a headache? Are you getting another migraine?"

The episode passed, and Tessa forced herself to smile. "I'm okay. I just got a little—a little emotional."

"I understand, darling. Ruthie says it's common for people to feel ambivalent about bringing their loved ones here, even if it is only short term. You know, I hear they have an excellent therapist. Maybe we should talk to him."

Tessa grimaced. "No thank you. I've had enough therapy to last the rest of my life. Come on, let's go on in."

Tessa held Nonna's arm as she hobbled up the path with her walker.

They entered through automatic doors that opened into a sunlit lobby. Tessa noted the grand piano occupying one corner and the oil paintings of lakes and bridges gracing the walls. Sofa and chair arrangements created comfortable seating areas.

The director, Carol, a woman about Tessa's age in a white silk blouse and blue pencil skirt, greeted them. After a quick orientation of the lobby and front desk, Carol suggested a tour before going up to the apartment.

"Would you like to join us, Tessa?" she asked.

"Of course." Tessa liked the woman's no-nonsense approach, reminding her of a museum docent.

They glanced into the main dining room, library, and movie theater before circling back to the lobby.

"This is our calendar—speakers, classes, activities, outings." Carol handed them both a flyer. "No shortage of things to do, Rosa. And of course, you'll have your daily exercise and physical therapy."

Tessa scanned the schedule. Her grandmother could be busy from morning to night. "It's practically Club Med, isn't it?"

The woman smiled and nodded. "The Westridge is like an all-inclusive resort with the added benefit of medical attention. Our CEO grew up going to the Catskills every summer. It was his vision to recreate that experience." She cocked her head. "Hear the music?"

"Oh my goodness," Nonna said. "It's the Lennon Sisters, isn't it?"

"It certainly is. You will love Tuesday nights. We play *Name That Tune.*"

Nonna beamed. "I do love games."

"Now," Carol clasped her hand. "Let's go see your apartment."

Tessa felt like an interloper as she followed Carol and her grandmother into the elevator.

The apartment had a hospital bed with one nightstand, a small dresser, a flat-screen TV, and handicap bars along the walls.

"These units are for our guests recovering from surgery or hospitalization. There's a nursing station down the hall and twenty-four hour emergency access."

Tessa grew nauseated. The room, while nicely appointed, made her think of a nursing home. And Nonna did not belong there. "I'm going to run back to the car for your suitcase, okay?"

Her grandmother nodded and continued paying rapt attention to Carol the concierge.

A long hallway with a patterned carpet led to the elevator. Just as Tessa pushed the button, her cell buzzed with a text from Patty relaying a question from Angela Reid, the woman hosting the art show.

The doors parted, and Tessa stepped into the elevator, continuing to type her response.

"Ms. Mariano?"

Her head snapped up. "Yes?"

"I thought it was you." The speaker was a tall man standing behind a wheelchair. Between his Giant's baseball cap and aviator sunglasses, she couldn't tell if she knew him or not. With all the events Tessa hosted, she often was recognized by people she didn't know. The man removed his dark glasses.

Tessa's phone slipped out of her hand and smacked the floor.

16

"*D*r. Barnes?" She'd never seen him in anything but scrubs or his requisite white jacket.

He retrieved her phone and handed it to her. "Sorry I startled you."

Tessa slipped the phone into her purse. "Oh, no, I was just, um—it's okay."

The man in the wheelchair cleared his throat. "Who's this pretty lady?" he asked in a loud voice.

"She's a relative of one of my patients, Pop."

Pop? Somehow it never occurred to Tessa that Dr. Barnes was somebody's son.

"What'd you say? She's a patient?"

Dr. Barnes leaned down and spoke slowly. "No. The grand-daughter of one of my patients."

His beard was bushier than usual, and the baseball hat gave him a youthful look.

The elevator doors opened on the main floor. "After you," Dr. Barnes said, gesturing with an outstretched arm

"Thank you." Tessa stepped forward, almost bumping into the people waiting in the foyer. "Excuse me. Sorry."

Embarrassed, she moved out of the way while Dr. Barnes maneuvered the wheelchair out of the elevator.

"Is your grandmother all right?" he asked, pushing his father toward the lobby.

"Yes, she's doing well. Just staying here for a week or two. Her idea, not mine." Tessa wanted him to know she was not relinquishing her responsibility.

"Excuse me." The senior Barnes cleared his throat. "Come around here young lady, and let me introduce myself properly." He pushed himself against the arms of the wheelchair.

"Please," Tessa protested, "you don't have to stand."

"Yes, he does." Dr. Barnes grabbed his father's left arm. "He's an old-fashioned gentleman. And stubborn as hell. Okay, Pop, up you go."

Once on his feet, and holding onto his son for support, the old man gave a slight bow. "A pleasure to make your acquaintance. My name is Dr. Abraham Barnes. But you may call me Abe."

He was almost as tall as his son, with thick white hair and a well-groomed beard.

"I'm Tessa Mariano."

"A beautiful name for a beautiful woman."

"That's enough, Pop," Dr. Barnes said.

"So, you're a doctor, too?" Tessa asked, finding the senior Dr. Barnes delightful.

"Yes, my dear, but not like my boy. I was just a country doctor back in the days when we made house calls and took care of everything from sore throats to delivering babies." Abe returned to his wheelchair.

Tessa noticed a thin gold wedding band on his weathered left hand.

"Ms. Mariano," Dr. Barnes said. "May I speak to you in private for a moment?"

"Sure," she said, wondering if she was about to be reprimanded. For what, she had no idea, but the younger Dr. Barnes set her on edge.

"Sit tight, Pop. I'll be right back."

"Take your time, son. I'm not going anywhere."

They moved to a quiet corner beside the grand piano.

"Is something wrong?"

"Not at all. I just shouldn't discuss my patients in front of other people, and I wanted to ask about Rosa. I thought she was staying at home with a caregiver once she left rehab."

"Oh," Tessa said, "well she was, but it didn't work out. Apparently, the caregiver got on her nerves. I offered to take her to my house, but she refused and insisted on coming here for the duration of her recovery because her friend lives here and loves it." She let out a puff of air as if she'd just completed a speech.

The doctor rubbed his beard. "I understand."

Tessa wondered if the conversation was over, but he didn't make a move to return to his father who was observing them with a casual smile.

"I have to go get my grandmother's suitcase out of the car."

"Right." He gave her a nod. "Do you need any help?"

Tessa's eyes opened wide. "Oh, um, no. No thank you. It's just a small bag, you know the kind with wheels and a pullout handle."

The corners of his mouth edged up. "I'm familiar with suitcases. Anyway, I just want to tell you, I have a lot of older patients, and few are as fortunate as your grandmother. You're an excellent advocate for her."

Excellent advocate—an odd compliment, but sincere none-the-less. "It's the least I can do. Nonna raised me on her own after my mother died." Why she revealed that tidbit of her history, she didn't know. Especially to Dr. Barnes who probably couldn't care less.

"Really?" His face darkened. "That must've been—"

"Owen." Abe wheeled himself in their direction. "Maybe Tessa would like to join us for lunch."

"Oh, that's so kind of you, but as soon as I get my grandmother's suitcase to her apartment, I'm rushing back to work."

Dr. Barnes stepped behind his father's wheelchair. "Give Rosa my best and tell her I'll check in on her while she's here."

"I will. Thank you."

"It was nice to see you again, Ms. Mariano," he said, using his serious doctor voice.

Tessa angled her head. "You as well, Dr. Barnes."

And to her surprise, she meant it.

17

*I*t took over a week for Tessa to adjust to her new routine. She visited Nonna almost every day. As much as she hated to admit or even acknowledge it, she kept one eye open for Dr. Owen Barnes. It wasn't that she *wanted* to see him. She just wanted to be prepared in case he happened to appear. At least that's what she told herself.

Nonna took a bite of her chicken sandwich. "The food is very good, don't you think?" she asked, brushing a few crumbs off the front of her pink cotton dress.

"It is." Tessa pushed around the lettuce in her cobb salad. It had nice chunks of chicken, diced tomato, and chopped egg, but the blue cheese was sparse and the vinaigrette bland. "Is the dinner menu different?"

"Oh, yes. Dinner is like being in a fancy restaurant. We get our choice of nightly specials, and they set the tables with cloth napkins and china."

"That's impressive," Tessa said. "And I'm glad you're enjoying your stay."

Nonna nibbled a sweet potato fry. "But?"

"No *but,* I really mean it. Just don't enjoy it so much that you don't want to leave." Although she made it sound like a joke, she was serious. Her grandmother belonged at home, in the house where Tessa grew up. The house that held every memory of her childhood and of her mother.

A server stopped by the table. "Would you like your coffee now, Mrs. Mariano?"

"Why, yes. I like it—"

"Very hot with a drop of cream." The server pointed at her. "Right?"

Nonna's eyes crinkled with delight. "That's exactly right. Thank you."

"And for you, miss?" the server asked Tessa.

"None for me, thanks." Tessa was still limiting her caffeine. She took another bite of salad. "Quite a coincidence that Dr. Barnes's father lives here. Have you met him?"

"I haven't. I think he goes to the early dinner seating."

"He seems like a lovely man," Tessa said.

"That reminds me. I changed my appointment with Dr. Barnes. He'll see me in the clinic here for my next follow-up."

Tessa put down her fork. "He's seeing you here? Is that a good idea?"

"Why not? It's just a quick check-up."

Tessa frowned. "When's your new appointment? I'll need to check my schedule."

Nonna raised her chin. "First of all, you don't need to be here for it. And second of all, what's gotten into you? You're being a little snippy again."

"Sorry." She moved her plate to the side, annoyed the plan had been changed without anyone consulting her. After all, she was her grandmother's primary person. On the other hand, Nonna was more than capable of managing her life. "I didn't mean to snap. I just like to be on top of things."

"On top of things or *in charge* of things?" Nonna leaned forward with a stern expression.

Tessa didn't answer. Of course she liked to be in charge. She brushed some crumbs on the table cloth into a neat pile. "Just let me know when he's coming to see you. Okay?"

Her grandmother's attention was diverted by a gentleman approaching their table. Nonna patted her mouth with a napkin. "Oh, George, hello."

"Hello, Rosa." George had thinning gray hair and cheerful eyes. He wore dark slacks and a blue knit vest buttoned up over a white dress shirt.

After Nonna introduced her, Tessa sat back and observed with interest.

"Are you free this afternoon for bridge?" George asked. "We need a fourth."

"I am. And I'd love to play. Although it's been a while. I might be rusty."

"Not to worry. If you'd like, we could be partners." George smiled, showing off a nice set of teeth.

"That sounds wonderful," Nonna said. "Thank you."

"Very well then, see you at three in the game room. And lovely to meet you, Tessa." He nodded politely, walked across the dining room, and joined another gentleman at a table.

Tessa raised her eyebrows. "That was interesting."

Nonna waved a hand. "Just someone I met at dinner a couple nights ago. He organizes all the bridge games."

"He seems to like you. And he certainly is dapper." She helped herself to a few fries off of Nonna's plate. They were crisp and perfectly seasoned.

"He's nice to everyone. And he's married. His wife is in the memory care unit."

"Oh," Tessa said, chagrined. "That's terrible."

"It's very sad, but it's what happens when people get old. And for the most the part, we old folks accept it. Anyway, George is a dear man and very devoted to his wife. Except for bridge a few times a week and an occasional outing, he stays by her side."

Tessa couldn't even imagine a love so profound.

"Oh, and he does serve on the board here. He was the CEO of a huge trucking company. Very successful."

Tessa half expected her grandmother to spout out his net worth. "How do you learn so much about a person in only one week?"

"You've lost track of time, darling. I've been here nearly two weeks. Besides, when you live in a small community like this, you learn very quickly about the lives of others."

"I suppose." Tessa drank her iced tea and wiped her hands on her napkin.

"There are some interesting people here, too. Fascinating histories."

"I'm sure." Tessa scanned the faces around the room. Every resident was once young and vibrant with jobs and families and dreams. She thought about Abe Barnes with the gold band on his wrinkled finger, wondering if his wife was still alive. Is this what happened? One lives a long, full life only to be shuffled off into a home? Would it happen to her?

A wave of sadness struck hard, and the room felt as if it were shrinking. Tessa's face flushed with heat. "I'm sorry, Nonna, but I need to get back to work."

"Are you all right, dear?"

"I'm fine. I'll call you tonight, okay?"

"Please do. And tell Marco I'll see him on the weekend."

Tessa pushed her chair away from the table. "I hate to leave you sitting by yourself."

"Don't worry." Nonna beckoned someone across the dining room. "I see a friend over there. I'll have coffee with her."

"Okay. Love you." She kissed her grandmother's soft cheek and left the dining room at the fastest clip she could without breaking into a run.

18

"*P*lease put your phone down, Marco. We're having breakfast."

The two of them sat at a table outside of Nutmeg's. The morning chill carried the scent of dry leaves and plum blossoms. Halloween decorations were popping up along Main Street daily. The candy shop displayed caramel apples with orange sprinkles in the window. Hay bales and pumpkins filled the gazebo.

Marco dropped his cell into his lap and looked at her. "What?"

"I just want to spend a few pleasant minutes with you." Tessa sipped her latte. "I love Autumn in Clearwater. I think it's my favorite season." She plucked a pecan off the giant pumpkin muffin they were sharing and eyed her son who was leaning on his left elbow with his head on his hand. She might get a few minutes with him, but they weren't likely to be pleasant.

"Why'd you want Dad to meet us here?" Marco asked, playing with the mound of whipped cream on his hot chocolate. "Why couldn't we just do this whole family discussion thing at home?"

"Because I wanted a pumpkin muffin." The truth was

Nutmeg's felt like neutral territory. She cut the muffin into quarters. "Want some?"

"No thanks," he said.

"Is your stomach bothering you again?"

"I'm fine, Mom."

Ever since learning about Crystal's pregnancy, Marco had a constant crease between his eyebrows, wasn't sleeping well, and couldn't concentrate on his schoolwork. It was the same reaction he'd had when his parents separated.

"Do we have to talk about, you know, the whole baby thing?"

Tessa sighed. She didn't want to talk about it either, and she wished none of it were happening. "I know you don't want to deal with it. I know you're scared that it means—"

"I'm not scared about anything. I'm just, I'm just mad." He turned his body to the side and went back to his phone.

Tessa was incensed that Victor's actions and decisions had to upend Marco's life. And by extension, hers.

"Dad's gonna be late, isn't he?"

"I'm sure he'll get here any minute."

Despite all the dropped balls and frustrations her ex-husband caused over the years, Tessa did her best to not disrespect him in front of Marco. A boy needed to admire his father, to look up to him as a role model. When her son was younger, she could fudge the truth, make excuses for Victor's absence and inattention. But the older Marco got, the more perceptive he became. Little white lies no longer passed muster.

"Does he know I have to get to my soccer game?"

"I told him last night," she said. Whether he'd remember or not was questionable.

"Is he gonna come watch?" The furrow between Marco's brows deepened.

"I don't know, honey."

A horn beeped lightly, and Victor's car pulled into a parking spot. He hopped out with a jaunty wave. "Good morning." He sauntered over and kissed the top of Marco's head. "Sorry I'm late."

You usually are. Tessa finished her latte. "Do you want coffee?"

"Uh, no, I'm good." He sat in the chair next to Marco's.

Tessa folded and unfolded her hands. Although she had called the meeting, something she did only on rare, important occasions, she wasn't sure how to begin the conversation.

Her ex-husband crossed his legs. "So, what's on the agenda this time?"

The way he said *this time* stoked her ire. "The agenda is our son. Marco is having a hard time with the fact that you and Crystal are having a baby."

Marco's face paled. "Geez, Mom, did you really have to say it like that?"

"Hey, buddy, it's okay." Victor leaned closer to him. "We don't have to talk about it if you don't want to."

"Good, because I don't. Are you coming to my soccer game?"

"Can we get back on topic?" Tessa narrowed her gaze at Victor, but he ignored her.

"Sure I'll be there," he said. "It's at three, right?"

Marco's face fell. "No, it's at twelve."

"Twelve o'clock, huh?" Victor picked up his phone. "Lemme just see about something. I kinda have a thing that..." He stopped talking and started texting.

Tessa dropped her chin onto her hand.

The conversation was further derailed when Marco's cell chimed. He grabbed it and turned away from his parents, as if the text were top secret.

"Mom, Oliver wants me to come over so we can warm up before the game. Can I go?"

Tessa groaned. She couldn't compete with her son's best

friend, and her motivation to continue a serious discussion evaporated. "Fine. I'll drive you over."

"It's okay. I'll ride my bike. I left it at the shop yesterday. See you guys at soccer." He jumped up, threw his backpack over one shoulder, and sprinted off as if he couldn't escape fast enough.

Tessa scowled at her ex-husband. "Well, that didn't accomplish anything, did it?"

"What were you hoping to accomplish? I don't know why you arranged this meeting in the first place." Victor drummed the table with both hands. "I told Marco about the baby like you wanted me to."

"Like I wanted? As if *not* telling him was an option?" She closed her eyes and pinched the bridge of her nose.

"God, I hate it when you do that."

Tessa opened her eyes. "What?"

"That face. It's so—so irritating."

"Maybe it's irritating because I'm irritated."

The line of people waiting to get into Nutmeg's had grown. It extended out the door and onto the patio, invading their space. Tessa lowered her voice. "Would you just listen to me, please? For two weeks, Marco hasn't been sleeping, he's having nightmares, his stomach's upset, and his schoolwork's suffering. You know how anxious he gets."

"So that's why you summoned me?" Victor leaned closer. "You thought he'd just spill his guts. And I'd reassure him that nothing's going to change, and it'll all be hunky-dory." He threw his arms up. "You know that's not going to happen."

Her body tensed. "You're absolutely right. The only way Marco will believe nothing's going to change is for nothing to change. But that ship has sailed. I guess he'll just have to live with it."

Tessa rose and snatched her purse from the back of the chair. "I have to go to work."

"You always have to go to work. Maybe if you didn't work

so much, Marco wouldn't be so insecure. It's time you recognize the role you played in this mess."

A derisive laugh escaped her throat. "Are you serious?"

Victor's jaw tightened. "Damn right I am. Ten years ago you started a business, and that—*that's* what changed everything."

Tessa stood taller. What she did ten years ago she had to do because her husband was a grown man who behaved like a fraternity boy. His refusal to grow up forced her hand. After he lost his third job in as many years, Tessa had no choice but to find a way to support them.

"Somebody had to pay the bills. It was supposed to be a part-nership." Confidence and certainty fueled her. "You just couldn't hold up your end of the bargain."

"I've always owned my mistakes." He got up and shoved his chair against the table. "Unlike you."

"You're calling the fact that I worked night and day a mistake?"

"Your words, not mine." Victor elbowed past the line and headed toward his car.

Tessa followed. She wanted to strangle him, but she needed to smooth things over for Marco's sake. If Victor was angry, he'd miss the soccer game in his signature passive-aggressive move—punish her by disappointing their son. "Would you just wait a second?"

He pivoted. "Why? So you can berate me even more? I know I screwed up, okay?" Victor raked both hands through his dark hair. "I got my girlfriend pregnant, and now I'm trapped."

Tessa froze. She pictured Crystal's swollen belly and Henry's adorable dimples. "You're what?"

"I didn't mean trapped. I meant…" Victor winced, as if the word had stung him like a bee.

Tessa's chest rose and fell. "You know what? I feel sorry for you."

"Spare me, you do not."

"You're right. I don't feel sorry for you. I feel sorry for Crystal and Henry and Marco—anybody who has to depend on you. When it comes to letting people down, you never disappoint. At least you're consistent with that one thing."

Victor took a step back, his jaw twitching. Tessa could tell she'd touched a nerve. And now that she had the upper hand, she wasn't about to let it go.

"What on earth made you think I'd ever let Marco go live with you in San Diego or anywhere else for that matter? I'd have to be dead before I'd let that happen."

"Now I'm an unfit parent, huh? And it'd be better for our son to live like an orphan than live with me. Is that what you're saying?"

An orphan. A child without parents, just like Tessa.

She took several deep breaths and steadied her voice. "You're not an unfit father, but you're not a reliable one either. Marco is turning fourteen, and he loves you. But, and I'm not saying this to be cruel, he doesn't have confidence in you."

His lips were so tightly pressed they turned white, but he appeared to be listening.

"It's up to you to fix it, Victor, and you need to be around to do that." Tessa almost left it at that, but she couldn't contain herself. "I'm warning you though, do not try to take him away from me. Nobody, least of all you, will ever come between me and my son."

～

Victor arrived late to the game, but at least he showed up. They sat on opposite ends of the bleachers, the tension between them as thick as the sea of bodies that separated them. Tessa regretted her earlier outburst. She'd gone a bit too far threatening to bury him, but what was done was done. What was said was said.

When Marco scored a goal, Tessa attempted to catch the eye

of her son's father and share a moment of pride. Victor jumped up and cheered, but his focus remained straight ahead on the field, as if ignoring her deliberately.

After the game, Marco's team celebrated the rare win by slamming into each other, jumping and hollering. Tessa left the bleachers and headed off the field with Oliver's mom, Sandy.

"Finally, they won a game," Sandy said. "I was beginning to think it'd never happen."

"I was, too," Tessa said. Marco's goal and the team's win lightened her mood. She glanced back to see if Victor was still there. He was sitting on the bleachers, hunched over and texting.

"What are you looking at?"

Tessa snapped her attention back to Sandy. "Oh, sorry. Marco's dad is over there. We've got some, you know, issues to deal with."

"Ah, I get it. Ex-husbands are such a pain. Ever since Oliver's father moved to Oregon, I have total control over everything."

Total control—Tessa's dream come true. She wondered if Sandy's ex ever suggested a change in their custody arrangement.

"And I can tell you're in control when it comes to Marco. Victor seems to be the fun one." She opened the trunk of her car.

Tessa frowned. "I'm fun—occasionally." She hated being the strict parent all the time. If only Victor could support her more, *agree* with her more. Like the time she refused to let Marco go to a party where she knew there'd be no supervision, and Victor contradicted her, saying she was being overprotective.

"Whenever Oliver comes back from spending time with his father, my life is hell for at least a week. *Dad let me stay up late; Dad let me watch that show; Dad let me drink Coke for breakfast.*" Sandy shuddered. "I practically have to reprogram him, you know, like shutting down a computer and restarting it."

Loud laughter floated over from the field. Tessa heard her ex-husband's grating chuckle. He was standing with a few other dads, and one of them looked like he was telling jokes. She could tell by the way Victor bobbed his head with his mouth wide open that the laughter was genuine. The sound used to amuse her.

"See?" her friend said. "Put a bunch of men together and they behave like teenage boys."

"You're even more negative than I am, and I'm the one who had a fight with her ex this morning." Tessa checked the time. "I'd better go. I need to get to the shop."

"Oh, wait," Sandy said. "I almost forgot. Can Marco spend the night? Oliver pitched a tent in the backyard and wants to have a sleepover."

"He's with his dad tonight, so it's up to Victor." Tessa mulled it over for a minute. "You know what? I'd better say *no* because he'd probably say *yes*. And they need to spend some time together."

"Gotcha. I'll tell Oliver we'll do it another time." Sandy raised her arm and waved.

"Here they come now. Look how big they've gotten. Almost fourteen years old, hard to believe."

"Not our little boys anymore." Tessa grew somber. She hardly needed another reminder of how quickly time marched on.

"Great game, guys!" Sandy pumped her fists.

Tessa reached out to pull Marco into a hug, but she stopped herself. He'd made it clear that motherly affection in public was not okay. She understood, but she hated it.

Oliver, a skinny kid with a mouthful of braces and blond hair like his mother's, dropped his cleats and shin guards into the trunk. "Mom, guess what, Marco can sleep over."

"Yeah," Marco said, smiling at his mother. "Dad said I could."

Tessa rolled her eyes.

~

At the shop, Patty and Liza were busy changing window displays and unpacking new seasonal merchandise. The annual Fall Festival was a couple of weeks away, and Tessa was anxious to get a jump on the preparations.

The bells on the doorknob jingled non-stop for over an hour. Eventually, the crowd dwindled.

"Finally," Tessa said. "I've got more boxes in the storeroom to unpack. Who wants to help?"

"I will." Patty followed Tessa through the swinging door into the back.

"So, are you and Adam having date night tonight?" Tessa sliced through a strip of packing tape on a box.

"We were going to, but he canceled." Patty's lips formed a little pout.

"That's not like him." Tessa knew Adam well, and he was devoted to his adorable, redheaded girlfriend. "What happened?"

Patty shrugged. "Something with a batch of wine being off in color. He's on his way to see a chemist in Davis."

"Oh no, that's serious," Tessa said. "It could cost tens of thousands of dollars if an entire batch goes bad."

"I know. I just had something kind of exciting to tell him."

"Exciting?"

"Yes. Something I need to tell you, too."

Tessa stopped unpacking jars of apple-pumpkin butter. "Sounds like big news," she said with raised brows.

"It is." Patty's face broke into a big grin. "Liza and I are finally moving out of the loft." She pointed at the ceiling to the apartment above their heads. She and her sister had been living in the tiny studio for over four months.

"You are? I had no idea you were looking for a new place."

"We weren't, but it kind of fell in our laps. Cece heard about the place from one of the dance moms."

Tessa felt a prickle of loss. Although the girls had been living there for only a few months, she loved having them so close. On more than one occasion, their work day had spilled over into the night with the three of them hanging out upstairs like sorority sisters. When Marco went to Victor's or out with friends, Patty and Liza filled the void.

"Seems silly to move when you think about all the money you're saving by not paying rent." Tessa heard the note of desperation in her voice.

"I know." Patty tightened the tiny ponytail on the back of her head. "But honestly, I'm beginning to feel like a freeloader. You rescued me when I came to Clearwater, gave me a job, trained me, let me live upstairs with—"

"It wasn't charity. I needed you as much as you needed me."

At the time, Patty was unemployed and homeless after a flood destroyed her apartment. But Tessa had been in a predicament, too. Her summer employee had quit without notice. "It's been a mutually beneficial arrangement between us. And I think it's worked out well."

"I do, too," said Patty. "And thanks to you, Liza and I have saved enough money to rent one of those little cottages down near the lake. It's small, but there're two bedrooms and bathrooms and an updated kitchen. I can't wait for you to see it."

Tessa cleared her throat. "It sounds nice."

Patty cocked her head. "I'm sensing you don't want us to move."

"Don't be silly." Her shoulders curled forward. She usually was better at hiding her feelings. "It's just that…"

"Tessa, nothing's going to change just because I don't live at the shop anymore."

Nothing's going to change? Everything was changing. "I'm not sure that's true. Change begets change."

"I guess it does." Patty lowered her chin and blinked. "But

you have to know I'd never let you down. Not after all you've done for me."

Tessa's thoughts drifted back to five months ago when Patty was at her lowest. She'd turned her life around, which had been no small feat.

"I know you won't," Tessa said, pulling her protege into a hug. "You're one of the most dependable people I know."

"Thank you. That's a big compliment coming from you."

"Yes, it is." Tessa forced a lighter tone into her voice and fortified her tough exterior. "And you know how high my standards are."

"I sure do," said Patty with an emphatic nod. "And hey, we can hang out anytime you want."

Tessa chuckled. "I appreciate that. Anyway, since you're here to close up, I'm going home. I've got Angela Reid's art show tonight, and I have no idea what to wear." She gave Patty another tight hug. "You've come a long way. I'm proud of you."

Patty clung to her mentor and sniffled in her ear. "I love you, Tessa. I owe everything good in my life to you."

"Most things maybe, but not everything. Now I need to leave, and you need to get back to work."

She peeled Patty off and bid goodbye, leaving her shop in the hands of her very capable manager.

Once outside, Tessa shivered and pulled on her jacket. A gust of wind blew a pile of dry leaves into the air, scattering them in all directions.

Change begets change. And more change was on the way. She could feel it like a cold, misty fog rolling into town.

19

*T*essa lowered herself into a hot and heavenly bubble bath with votive candles burning along the edge under the window. Buttercup rested her head on the side of the tub, dipping her long tongue into the water and licking the bubbles.

Tessa gave her dog a light smack on the nose. "No, girl, too soapy."

When the water grew cool and her skin wrinkled, Tessa got out, wrapped herself in a fluffy white towel, and went into her walk-in closet.

She pulled out one dress after another, wishing she could just put on her robe, eat dinner, watch a movie, and go to bed.

"Oh, wait, I know." She shoved everything to one side. "There you are."

She held up a little black dress with off-the-shoulder cap sleeves and a ruffle at the hem, price tag still attached. "What do you think?" she asked her dog. "Perfect, right?"

Buttercup lifted her head as if nodding.

In the bathroom, Tessa spritzed her hair. She curled the ends and blew her wispy bangs to the side. Under the bright lights above the vanity, she applied serious make-up for the first time in ages—smoky eyes, layers of mascara, red lipstick—before slipping into her LBD and strappy sandals.

"Good enough," she said to her reflection in the full length mirror.

Buttercup got a kiss and a goodnight cookie as Tessa headed out the door.

Angela Reid's San Francisco residence was more like a museum than a home with its marble floors, minimal furnishings, and stark white walls dotted with artwork of differing shapes, sizes, and materials. Tessa had been to countless estates and mansions since she'd become a sommelier, but this place was the most impressive yet.

Natalie, Tessa's 'plus-one' for the night, stood beside her in the center of the massive entryway. "This is spectacular."

"It certainly is." Tessa sipped French champagne from a crystal flute, rare champagne she had procured at the request of their hostess. She suppressed a yawn.

"Are you feeling okay?" Natalie asked.

"I'm just tired." She took her friend by the hand. "And hungry. Let's look around and get some food."

They wandered through the gallery alongside tuxedoed men and women sparkling with jewels. White-gloved waiters passed trays of caviar puffed pastry, lobster stuffed mushrooms, and duck-liver pate on toast pointes.

"By the way," Natalie said. "You look stunning tonight. I love that dress."

"With you as my date, I had to step it up. Can't remember the last time I wore heels, though. My feet already hurt."

"At least you can wear them. With my beat-up ballet feet, I'm lucky I can wear anything other than sneakers."

Tessa glanced at her friend's red halter dress and silvery sandals with kitten heels. Between her slender body and long legs, she could make a belted trash bag look like a fashion designer's stroke of genius.

"You're attracting lots of stares," Tessa said.

"It's because I'm so tall." Natalie reached for her second demi-tasse cup of fennel zucchini soup with mini-croutons. "I'm far more interested in the food than I am in the men. Did you try this soup? It's delicious."

"I will, but first I need to check out the wine bar." Tessa put her empty flute on a passing try. "Want to come with me?"

"I'm going to take a look at those sculptures in the room where the violinist is, but I'll catch up."

Tessa left Natalie and drifted into the crowd of wealthy guests. Her four-inch heels clicked on the stone floor.

"Tessa." Angela Reid, statuesque in a teal silk suit, greeted her. "I'm so glad you could come."

She squeezed Tessa's hands in both of hers. The gesture, friendlier than a handshake but less personal than a hug, seemed contrived.

"Thank you for inviting me."

"Of course," Angela said, fingering the diamond choker around her neck. "You're my personal sommelier now. And that means you're a friend."

Tessa was choosy when it came to friends, and she doubted her hostess would make the cut. Angela's lack of warmth and obvious obsession with status made her an unlikely candidate in the small circle of people Tessa considered friends.

A passing waiter offered a tray of seared scallops on tiny teaspoons.

Angela ignored the offering, but Tessa did not pass up the treat.

"Thank you." She spooned the scallop into her mouth. It was seasoned and cooked to perfection. "Your home is truly magnificent, Angela."

The art collector scanned their surroundings. "It's nice, but not one of my favorites."

One of?

"My goodness." Tessa showed the right amount of awe. "Did you invent an app and sell it to Google?"

Her hostess laughed. "Nothing nearly that exciting." She waved to somebody in the crowd. "I come from money, which is both a blessing and a curse."

"Indeed it is," Tessa said, although she hardly knew that first hand. "I hope you're pleased with the wines we selected."

"Oh, beyond pleased." Angela looked over Tessa's shoulder. Something, or someone, had caught her attention. "Would you excuse me? I have to greet one of my featured artists. He offends easily, so I must pay special attention."

"Of course."

"Enjoy yourself." Angela appraised her. "By the way, you do clean up well."

Tessa watched her slip into the crowd. She would have to figure out how to turn Angela into an ongoing client without revealing how much she didn't like her.

Now that Tessa had made an appearance, it was time to find Natalie. Her feet hurt, she wanted to check in with Marco, and Buttercup had seemed particularly forlorn to be left all alone after dark.

She scanned the gallery searching for a spot of red in a sea of black. Although Natalie usually stood out in a crowd, she was nowhere to be seen. Tessa headed to the bar. If she had to wait for her friend, she might as well sip on a glass of award-winning wine while doing so.

Making her way through the tuxedo jungle, she helped herself to a skewer of three melon balls wrapped in prosciutto and ate as she walked. The salty meat and the sweet fruit made a delicious combination. At the bar, the four wines she had recommended were displayed. She opted for the Grenache blend, rich and full-bodied with a hint of cranberry.

She turned to continue her hunt for Natalie but stopped short. Wine sloshed up the side of the glass.

"Well, hello." Dr. Barnes stood in front of her. He looked as if he'd stepped off a movie set in a black tuxedo with satin lapels. His beard had been trimmed close to his smooth skin.

Tessa's heart pounded, but she met him with confidence and poise. "Small world."

For the first time, she noticed his eyes. They were greenish-gray, like jade, with gentle creases around the outer edges.

One corner of his mouth lifted. "For a moment I didn't recognize you."

Tessa brushed her bangs to the side. She took his comment as a compliment. "Well, bumping into each other at a social event is quite out of context."

"It is indeed."

The last time she'd seen him he looked like a regular guy going to a ball game. And now he looked like James Bond.

"How's your father?" she asked. "What a sweet, charming man he is."

"Fine. Thank you for asking."

Tessa sipped the Grenache. Part of her wanted to escape the awkward encounter, and part of her wanted to keep staring at him.

She opted for the latter. "Are you an art collector?"

"Me?" He laughed, and the lines around his eyes crinkled. "Not even close."

"Then you must be a friend of Angela's."

"Who's Angela?" he asked, his brows pressing toward each other.

"She's our hostess. And the owner of this lovely home." She waved her left hand with a flourish.

"Ah, I see." Dr. Barnes ran a finger inside the collar of his crisp white shirt. "I haven't met her yet."

"Owen, there you are." A tall blonde in a blue sequined cocktail dress joined them. She tucked her hand inside his arm and eyed Tessa. "Did you bump into someone you know?"

"I did."

That was all he said, and his date, or whatever she was, aimed a curious stare at Tessa.

"My grandmother's a patient of Dr. Barnes," she explained. "He gave her a new hip."

"How nice," the striking woman said.

Tessa tried to guess her age, but it was hard to tell with her plumped lips and frozen forehead. Her manicured hands sported several sparkly rings, but the fourth finger on her left hand was naked.

A moment of silence followed. Dr. Barnes made no move to introduce them, so Tessa changed the subject.

"I heard you'll be seeing my grandmother at Westridge for her next checkup. That's nice of you."

His date edged closer, tightening her hold on his arm.

"Not a problem," Dr. Barnes said.

"Nonna is very grateful for your care. And therefore, so am I." Tessa sounded—and felt—stilted. Carrying on a conversation with the handsome doctor was not easy.

"I know it's a long trip from Napa. Or is it Sonoma where Rosa lives?"

"It's all close," Tessa said, happy he'd finally strung two sentences together. "But technically, Clearwater's part of Sonoma."

The blonde cocked her head. "You're from Clearwater? Angela told me about that town. She bought all the wine from some little shop there. Sounds like she spent a fortune."

"Is that so?" Tessa remained nonplussed, waiting for her to continue.

"Though if you ask me," the woman said, holding up her glass, "this one's nothing special."

Tessa nearly choked. The Chardonnay from New Zealand was indeed special, with a rich, concentrated feel and the aromas of peach and mango.

"It takes a sophisticated palate to recognize a fine chardonnay."

The woman appeared to have no idea what to make of the comment, but Dr. Barnes stifled a smile.

Tessa returned her attention to him. "It was nice to see you. And I'll make sure to be there when my grandmother has her appointment."

He offered a slight nod, his eyes bright. "I expect you will."

20

*N*atalie removed her shoes and dropped them behind her seat. "You have to admit he's really handsome. Like James Bond handsome."

"Yeah, I thought that, too. But only because he had on a tuxedo." Tessa sped across the Golden Gate, as if distance would diminish her attraction to Dr. Owen Barnes. "But I never thought he was handsome before, not really. And I don't want him to be. I want him to be ugly."

Natalie laughed. "It doesn't matter what you want. The man is sexy-handsome, and you know it."

Tessa shook her head as if banishing the thought. "This is a ridiculous conversation. He's Nonna's doctor, that's it. I don't even like him."

Natalie turned on the seat-heater and settled into the soft leather. "Suit yourself. But I saw him as you were walking away. Even with that attractive blonde clinging to him, he watched you go."

"Come on," Tessa said. "You're making that up."

"Why would I do that when I know you don't like him?" Natalie poked Tessa's arm. "Or do you?"

"That's enough. Let's talk about you. Meet anyone interesting?"

"Actually, I did, an art collector from New York." Natalie glanced at her cell phone. "Look at that, he's already texting me."

"You gave him your number? Aren't you still seeing Pierre?"

"Not really. We went out a few more times after that first dinner, but I've decided he's a little boring."

"Boring?"

"Food, wine, and women—that's the extent of his interests."

Tessa stopped at a red light. "I could've told you that. I hope you didn't break his heart, though. He's one of my best clients, and he'll blame it on me."

"Pierre's got plenty of women in his little black book."

"I know, but his ego's quite fragile."

"Don't worry," Natalie said. "I'll make sure to preserve it. Besides, he worships you. He wouldn't stop talking about his new wine cellar and all the wines you're recommending. It practically put me to sleep."

Tessa frowned at her friend. "It pains me to hear you say that. Wines are a fascinating topic of conversation."

"I like to drink it, not talk about it. Anyway, with Pierre on the way out, I'm open to other men, which leads us right back to you and the handsome doctor."

"For goodness sake, stop bringing him up." Tessa merged onto the freeway. "Nothing's happening there. He might look good in a tuxedo, but beyond that—forget it. I've got more than enough to worry about. There's no room in my world for men right now."

And there probably never will be.

A few days after the event at Angela Reid's house, Nonna called to let Tessa know she'd be seeing Dr. Barnes that afternoon at three-thirty.

"That's not much notice." Tessa signaled to a customer that she'd be just a minute.

"His office called me this morning, darling. And I have to be flexible. After all, he's doing me the favor."

"I know, but they could've given us advance notice."

"You don't need to come. I know you're busy, and I hate to see you rushing around so much. Besides, it's going to be a quick visit, and I promise to call you afterwards with a full report."

Tessa wavered. The customer waiting threw an impatient glance in her direction. Taking an hour out of her afternoon for a five-minute interaction with Owen Barnes would be a waste of time. Still, she couldn't shake the feeling from the other night. That little burst of adrenaline had awakened something deep inside her.

"It's okay, Nonna, I'll be there. See you at three-thirty."

The next few hours were a whirlwind of activity. It was unusually busy for a Wednesday. Patty and Liza had started organizing for their move, so whenever there was a lull in customers, they dashed upstairs to pack. Then Sandy called to say she couldn't drive the boys to soccer practice.

"I'm sorry to drop this on you last minute, but my cat's sick so I have to bring her to the vet, and the only opening was this afternoon."

Tessa calculated how long everything would take. "It's fine. I'll take them to practice on my way to see my grandmother."

"You're a lifesaver. I'll get them after practice and bring Marco back to my house. He can have dinner with Oliver and me if you're running late."

"Thanks, I'll let you know."

"Okie-dokie, see you later." Sandy finished the call with quick kissing noises.

Tessa went into the storeroom in search of her manager. "Patty, where are you?"

"Up here." She stood at the top of the stairs that led to the loft, a broom in one hand and a rag in the other. "Just doing some last-minute cleaning. Whatcha need?"

The reminder that Patty and Liza were moving out in two days tugged on Tessa's emotions. She cleared her throat. "I have to leave earlier than I'd planned, so I need you to come back to the shop."

"No problem." Patty leaned the broom against the wall of the landing, dropped the rag, and started down the stairs. "When will you be back?"

"Couple hours, I think. I'm going to see Nonna after I drop Marco off at soccer."

"Okay." Patty halted on the last step, eye to eye with Tessa. "Why are you looking at me like that?"

Tessa licked her thumb and rubbed it on Patty's cheek as if she were a little girl. "You got some dirt there." She rubbed until the smudge was gone. "There you go, much better."

Patty flashed a smile. "Thank you."

Another pang of emotion struck, taking Tessa by surprise. "All right then, see you later." She scurried out the back door before Patty could notice her damp eyes.

Marco and Oliver stood under a tree in front of the school. They tossed their gear into the back of the SUV and scrambled into the car.

"We've been waiting for half an hour," Marco said, buckling his seat belt.

"What do you mean, it's barely three o'clock?"

A mumble came from the back seat. Tessa glanced in the rearview mirror at Oliver. "What did you say, honey?"

"I think it's three-twenty," he said.

Tessa checked the clock on her dashboard: *3:22 pm.* "Oh my God, you're right." She had no idea how she'd lost track of time. Not only would she be late dropping off the boys, she'd miss Nonna's appointment with Dr. Barnes.

"And I texted you a bunch of times, too, Mom."

"You did?" She pointed to her bag at his feet. "Grab that. See if you can find my phone."

Marco rummaged while Tessa drove out of the school parking lot toward the soccer field, which was in the opposite direction of Westridge.

"I can't find it, Mom. I don't think it's here."

"It has to be." She pressed the accelerator. "Call it. Maybe it slipped under the seat."

Tessa unleashed a deep breath, trying to keep anxiety at bay. She never ran late and had no patience for those who did. And her cellphone was her lifeline—for business, for Nonna, for Marco.

"It's ringing, but I don't hear your phone."

"Me neither," Oliver said, searching the floor of the back seat.

Marco hung up, but a minute later his cell rang. "It's you." He showed his mother the screen—a photo of her smiling face.

"How could it be me? Answer it."

Marco took the call and tapped the speaker. "Hello?"

"Hey Marco, it's Liza."

"Liza, it's me. You have my phone?"

"Yeah, it's right here on the counter by the register. Is everything okay?"

Tessa counted her breaths so she wouldn't hyperventilate. She had no recollection of putting her phone on the counter. "It's fine. I'm glad you found it. Just leave it there. I'll see you when I get back."

"Sounds good. I'm helping a customer, so I'd better run. Bye everyone."

Tessa, Marco, and Oliver all said, "Bye, Liza."

Tessa turned the corner. "Well, at least I know where it is."

"We're still gonna be late for practice, Mom," Marco said.

"I know, I'm sorry. I'm driving as fast as I can."

The wail of a siren sounded, and flashing lights came up from behind.

"Oh shit! I mean shoot."

"My mom says *shit* all the time," Oliver said.

Marco moaned. "Now we're gonna be even later."

Tessa pulled to the side, closed her eyes, and mouthed a silent mantra. *Calm as the setting sun; calm as the setting sun; calm as...*

A knock on the window startled her. And the face of Officer Glen Duffy made her want to scratch her own eyes out.

He tapped again, and she lowered the window.

Glen leaned in. "Looks like you're right on schedule."

Tessa glared at him. "What's that supposed to mean?"

"I pull you over about once a month, so this'll be your October infraction."

Tessa tightened her hands around the steering wheel. "I'd like to tell you something. May I get out of the car?"

"No." He put a hand on his holster. "You never get out of the car unless instructed to do so."

Marco leaned forward, pushing against his seatbelt. "We're really late to soccer practice, Officer Duffy."

"Oh, hey, Marco, didn't you see you there."

Oliver squirmed in the backseat. "I'm here, too."

Glen peered over Tessa's said. "That you, Oliver?"

Tessa opened her door and nudged it against the officer's legs. "Don't shoot me. I just have to tell you something."

He stepped back. "Okay, but no sudden movements. Keep your hands where I can see them."

If Tessa weren't so furious, she'd have laughed at his *mall-cop* performance.

She closed the car door and put her hands up. "I didn't want to say anything in front of Marco. But I'm on my way to see my grandmother. She's in a—a nursing home, and there's been a, well, a kind of an emergency." Tessa could justify stretching the truth, even if it was a very long stretch.

"Rosa's in a nursing home? I didn't know that."

"Yes, and I have to get over there. And I left my cell phone at the shop. And the boys are late for soccer practice." Her voice cracked a tiny bit, as if she were about to cry.

Glen narrowed his eyes. "Are you telling me the truth?"

"A hundred percent, I swear. So if you have to give me a ticket, I understand. Just let me go, and I'll come to the station and pick it up. Or you can bring it to the shop. Or put it in the system, and I'll pay it when it comes in the mail. Just please, please let me get on the road."

The officer grumbled and crossed his arms. "Fine, go. But I won't let you off so easy next time."

"Thank you." Tessa managed to squeeze out the words. She returned to her car and drove away, making sure she stayed under the speed limit until Glen Duffy was out of sight.

By the time she dropped the boys off at soccer and headed toward Westridge, her agitation level had reached new heights.

Her grandmother would be worried sick about her. Tessa wished she'd thought to have Marco call Nonna and let her know she'd be late.

But what was really distressing her was that she'd missed a chance to see Owen Barnes.

And that she cared about seeing him distressed her even more.

21

*T*essa swung her car into a parking space. She dashed into the lobby and skipped down one flight of stairs to the lower level where the medical clinic was located.

Nonna was perched on the seat of her walker, her face etched with worry. "Oh, Tessa, you're here. What happened?"

"It's a long story, Nonna. I'm sorry."

"You never run late. I was certain you'd been in an accident. And I called you three times. Thank goodness Liza finally answered." Her grandmother touched a tissue to her nose.

"I'm really sorry. My day has been nuts. Did you see Dr. Barnes yet?"

Even with the stop forced upon her by Officer Duffy, Tessa was only twenty minutes late.

"Yes, we just finished up a few minutes ago." Nonna pushed herself out of her seat. "I had my check-up, and everything's fine. I don't need to see him again for two months."

"Two months?"

"Yes, two months. Anyway, I'm sorry you rushed over here for no reason, but I'm happy to see your beautiful face." She brushed a hand against Tessa's cheek. "Why do you look upset? I told you, everything's fine."

"I—I just had a few questions for the doctor. And I'm annoyed with myself for being late. That's all."

Nonna put her hands on her walker and started moving forward. She threw a pensive glance in Tessa's direction.

"What's that look for?" Tessa asked.

Her eyes crinkled in the corners. "Dr. Barnes did ask if you were coming to the appointment. He seemed a bit disappointed you weren't there."

"You're making that up." Tessa followed her grandmother toward the elevator.

"I'm not making anything up. He also mentioned that you'd run into each other at some fancy party last weekend." Nonna pressed the button to call the elevator. The doors opened. She entered, turned, and positioned her walker in front of Tessa.

"What are you doing? Let me in."

Her grandmother didn't budge. "He's probably still here. I think he was headed to get coffee. If you have questions, you might find him at the coffee bar in the rose garden."

"But I was going to go with you to your apartment."

"I'm off to the game room to play bridge, so you run along." She backed up with a little wave, her eyes bright and sparkly. "Bye-bye, darling."

The elevator doors closed in Tessa's face. She stared at them, dumbfounded, then checked the time. Did Nonna just suggest she go in search of Owen Barnes?

"Unbelievable." Tessa took four steps in one direction, spun around, then walked in the other, her mind in a whirl.

There were a million things she needed to do at the shop. She ought to just get in her car and head straight back to work. On the other hand, she did have one or two questions about her grandmother that only Dr. Barnes could answer. What they were, she didn't know yet, but they existed.

She ducked into the ladies room and refreshed her face—a touch of blush and a swipe of color on her lips. She washed her hands, patted her chest and neck with a damp paper towel, and used a tiny squirt of the lavender hand cream beside the sink. Her leopard print blouse hung around her hips. She tucked it into her black jeans, then changed her mind and pulled it out. "Oh come on," she said, tucking it in again.

Tessa hurried out of the lobby and toward the rose garden.

At the end of a long pathway, she found the walk-up coffee bar set inside a vine-covered trellis. People, mostly old people, milled about.

Through the crowd, she spotted him. He had on his white physician's coat over a blue dress shirt and khaki pants. Four days ago he looked like James Bond, and now, like Cinderella after the ball, he'd returned to his old self. But even in tattered rags, Cinderella was beautiful...

Tessa straightened her back and strode over. "Dr. Barnes, hello."

His head snapped to the side. "Oh, Ms. Mariano, how are you?"

"Fine," she said, drawn in again by his greenish-gray eyes. "My grandmother said you might be here, and I was hoping to ask you a few questions about her, if you don't mind."

"I don't mind." A shallow frown appeared on his forehead. "She was quite concerned about you being late."

Tessa clasped and unclasped her hands. "Yes, I pride myself on my punctuality, but I had to drive my son to soccer practice." She left out the part about Officer Duffy pulling her over.

The line moved, and they took a step forward. "You have a son?"

She nodded. "I do. He's thirteen."

"Thirteen." Dr. Barnes blinked. "A good age."

"It is, I guess. Although he's almost fourteen, and teenage boys can be complicated."

"I suppose they can."

She wondered what he meant by *I suppose*. She knew so little about him, only that he had a sweet father.

"Well, at least I got here in time," she said, trying to sound as if her questions were of the utmost importance.

The barista at the coffee bar motioned to him. "What can I get you, sir?"

He removed his wallet from his pocket and glanced at Tessa. "Would you like something?"

"Oh, um, you don't have to—"

"It's just coffee."

Tessa gulped. "Well, thank you, then. I'll buy next time."

The words fell out before she could stop them. It was an ordinary response, one she used with Natalie or Elaine at Nutmeg's, knowing there always would be a next time. Her face flushed, but it appeared Dr. Barnes hadn't noticed her gaffe.

He set his credit card on the bar. "I'll have a double espresso, please, one sugar." He gestured toward Tessa. "What would you like?"

"Espresso, as well. Thank you." She'd regret the heavy caffeine later, but it sounded delicious. And she was happy to have something in common with him, even if it was only her taste in coffee.

As they waited, Tessa considered what topic she might bring up. As far as she knew they had nothing in common or any connection other than her grandmother. Oh wait, there was one thing.

"Did you enjoy the event the other night?" Tessa asked, recalling how dashing he looked in his tuxedo.

"Not especially."

She gave him a sidelong glance. "No? Why not?"

"Not my scene exactly. How about you?"

"Me? Oh, well, it was okay," she said. "Very impressive home."

"I'd have to agree with that. You looked very lovely, by the way."

The compliment unnerved her. She hoped it didn't appear as if she'd been fishing for it. But it pleased her that he'd noticed.

"Thank you. As did you—and your date." Maybe the comment would segue into a bit of information about the beautiful blond.

But the barista halted the conversation. "Your coffee, sir." He put their espressos on the bar.

They carried their coffees across the patio and sat at a small table in the corner surrounded by vines and roses.

Dr. Barnes dropped a brown sugar cube into his cup and got right down to business. "So, Rosa is coming along well. Surgery went exactly as planned."

Tessa lowered her sugar cube into her coffee and stirred it with the tiny spoon. "I guess it's time for me to admit you were right. My grandmother's hip was a textbook case."

"Textbook, yes, I use that term often." He rubbed his eyebrows, suppressing a yawn. "Forgive me. I've been up since five this morning. Hence the late afternoon coffee. Anyway, you have questions for me?"

"I do." She scooted her chair in and crossed her legs. "How long does she have to keep going to therapy?"

"Another two months or so. I'll reevaluate when I see her again." He sipped his espresso. "Sometimes patients get tired of going to therapy and quit too soon, so please make sure that doesn't happen."

Tessa laughed. "It won't. My grandmother is a dedicated rule follower." She tried to come up with another question of critical importance. "What else do I need to be aware of?" *Ugh, what a lame question.*

"Well, in addition to…"

As he spoke, she fell into a daze. His voice was rich and deep. Everything about him that irritated her early on no longer mattered. Like a fine red wine that had aged, his sharp edges had smoothed.

"...so other than that, Rosa can return to all her normal activities." Dr. Barnes lifted the tiny espresso cup and held it between his fingers.

"Good, um, very good." Tessa hoped her response was appropriate, considering she'd hardly heard a word he said. She took a moment to taste her coffee. It was hot and strong and earthy. "What about driving? When can she go back to that?"

"As soon as she feels comfortable doing so."

"And, um, when can I move her home?"

"It's entirely up to her." He paused, and a flash of amusement crossed his face. "Or you."

Tessa brushed her bangs out of her eyes. "You noticed our dynamic, did you?"

"I picked up on it." He finished his coffee and set the cup and saucer off to the side.

They regarded each other for a moment without speaking. Tessa's stomach fluttered.

"Don't worry." Dr. Barnes patted her hand, catching her off guard. "Your grandmother's fine, and she knows what to do. I don't anticipate any problems. Of course, like any person her age, she has to be cautious. A fall could land her back in the hospital, and that's the last place I want her to be."

Tessa shuddered at the thought of another hospitalization. "Absolutely."

He pulled a business card out of his jacket pocket and unscrewed the cap on a fountain pen. "Here's my cell number. If you think of any other questions, feel free to call."

Tessa didn't know what struck her more—that he was giving her his cell number or that he owned a fountain pen.

"That's a beautiful pen." Tessa pointed at it, admiring the sleek black resin barrel with gold-coated rings. "I have one very similar. It belonged to my grandfather."

"Really?" He settled back into his chair. "Do you use it?"

"I used to, but it ran out of ink." She extended an open palm. "May I?"

He placed the pen in her hand, and Tessa sensed he was entrusting her with something precious. She removed the cap and signed her name on the back of his business card, putting just the right amount of pressure on the nib.

"You have an elegant signature," he said.

She looked up at him. "It's an elegant pen."

Dr. Barnes swallowed, and his Adams apple rose and fell. "My father taught me to love fountain pens. He gave me this one when I graduated medical school."

Dr. Abraham Barnes, a whole new topic. Excellent.

"How is your father?" She handed back the pen.

"He's doing better."

"Had he been ill?"

He slipped the pen into his shirt pocket. "He had a minor stroke a few weeks ago. In fact, it was the day you brought Rosa in for her follow-up visit. The nurse at Westridge had just called to tell me he'd been transported to the hospital."

Tessa recalled the appointment and remembered how annoyed she was. She hoped he didn't remember.

"Your grandmother said something very kind to me that day. It was about how stressful an emergency could be. It stuck with me for some reason." He rubbed the stubble on his cheek. "Rosa is an extraordinary woman."

"She is." Tessa regretted how harshly she had judged Owen Barnes at their first meeting. And now, the chemistry was undeniable.

In Tessa's line of work, men flirted with her all the time. She had become an expert in deflecting such attention, declining their invitations without offending. With them, she was in total control.

This felt different. Her attraction to Owen Barnes's physical appearance was secondary to her attraction to *him*. As hard as it was to admit, she liked him. She cared about him. And that made her vulnerable.

She touched the pearl cluster in her earlobe.

Clouds moved across the sky, and a cool breeze blew a napkin to the ground. They reached for it at the same time, backed away, and reached again.

"I got it," Owen said with a laugh. He straightened up and glanced at his watch. "Thank you for having coffee with me."

"My pleasure, Dr. Barnes." Tessa stood. "And thank you for answering my questions."

"You're welcome."

Tessa picked up the business card with his cell number written on it. "If I have any questions, I'll give you a call. Otherwise, see you in two months."

"Until then, Ms. Mariano." He stood and offered his hand.

The firm squeeze, his warm palm, and his eyes gazing into hers—Tessa caught her breath. She felt eighteen again.

22

---

*B*etween the caffeine from the double espresso and her school-girl crush on Owen Barnes, Tessa's brain refused to shut down, keeping her awake into the wee hours.

When she awoke the next morning, she turned onto her back and stared at the ceiling, recalling the taste of sweet espresso, the smell of fragrant roses, and the cadence of his smooth voice.

But as the weekend approached, Tessa talked herself down from the clouds. She reviewed every bit of conversation, his body language, his polite words and decided their encounter, while pleasant, was no more than a cup of coffee and a professional update on her grandmother's health.

She forced him out of her mind, sharpened her focus, and concentrated on work.

For the next few days, she directed Patty and Liza as they unpacked the new fall products and decorated with autumn décor. She scheduled the cleaning service to deep clean the shop, her house, and Nonna's house, too. Then she called the florist and ordered bunches of cut flowers for her grandmother's homecoming.

On Saturday, Pierre called to discuss the variety of wines

she'd selected for his new cellar. To her relief, the French chef was in a delightful mood and not the least bit offended by Natalie. In his mind, he had ended the brief romance, claiming the beautiful ballerina was not his type. And there was more good news. The wine cellar would be finished ahead of schedule, and the contractor Tessa had recommended was excellent. Then he approved every one of her suggestions for wine and placed an order for over two hundred bottles.

Later in the afternoon, she studied her calendar and sent Victor an updated schedule for Marco—soccer games, back-to-school night, and orthodontist appointments.

She checked items off her to-do list one by one, gaining a sense of accomplishment and control.

On her way home Saturday evening, she stopped by Patty and Liza's new cottage with a gigantic gift basket of gourmet treats and a bottle of Patty's favorite Prosecco. It had been her most productive day in ages. So busy in fact, she *almost* forgot about Owen Barnes.

∽

The day Tessa had been looking forward to for weeks finally arrived. Early that morning, she and Marco had gone to Nonna's house where they divided the flowers into vases and put them in every room.

Tessa opened the front door of her grandmother's cottage, and the perfume of dozens of flowers greeted them.

"Oh my goodness, it looks like a wedding reception in here!" Nonna left her walker by the door and went around sniffing every bunch. "It's beautiful, and it feels so good to be home."

"It sure does." Tessa followed her into the kitchen where Marco was making lunch.

"There's my favorite boy in the whole world." She hugged her great-grandson and smothered him with kisses. "I've missed you so much. And my goodness, did you grow in the past few weeks? You're taller than I am now."

"I've been taller than you for a year, Nonna. I hope I get as tall as my dad."

"Speaking of your dad," Nonna said, "I understand he and his fiancé are going to have a baby."

"Nonna!" Tessa's aura of serenity popped like a champagne cork. "Why would you bring that up now?"

"Because, darling, it's a family matter that must be addressed. If Marco has feelings about it, he should be comfortable sharing them."

It had been a week since the meeting at Nutmeg's where Tessa had tried to cajole her ex-husband and son into discussing the situation. That had ended in disaster.

Marco spooned some blueberries into a cup and topped it with a dollop of plain yogurt. "Me and you can talk later, Nonna."

"You and *I*, Marco." Tessa corrected his grammar. "And if you want to talk about it, we can."

Her son flipped back the mop of hair hanging in his face. "It just upsets you, Mom."

Tessa regarded her son. "It only upsets me if it upsets you, honey."

"Well it doesn't," he said sharply.

"What do you mean? A week ago you practically—"

"Now, now dear." Nonna placed a hand on Tessa's lower back and applied a small amount of pressure. "Why don't you let me have some time alone with Marco? He and I have hardly seen each other since my surgery."

"You want me to leave?" Tessa asked, incredulous.

"Well, yes I do. Marco and I could spend the afternoon together. It's a beautiful day. We can even walk the old path like we used to."

The old path…Tessa recalled how much Marco loved

running up and down it when he was little, picking wildflowers, gathering bugs, collecting sticks.

"That sounds good," Marco said.

"That sounds bad." Tessa nixed the idea. "I know you're more confident walking now, Nonna, but the path is bumpy. You could trip."

"Then we'll do something else." Nonna pressed on Tessa's back a little harder, coaxing her out of the kitchen.

Tessa pouted. "I don't even get to have lunch?"

Her grandmother gave her a firm nudge. "Go. Take some time for yourself."

Time for herself? What a concept. She'd already told Patty she wouldn't be at the shop today, so the afternoon really was free.

"Well, okay. I guess I'll go home and start the Bolognese for dinner tonight."

Cooking always soothed her. The rich aroma of pancetta and onion sizzling in olive oil filled the house, reminding Tessa of the days when she and Nonna lived all alone. Every Sunday had been family pasta night. Sometimes it was just the two of them, and sometimes it included Aunt Sophia's family.

After her mother died and her father left, Tessa was consumed by bitterness and grief. But over the years, Nonna's steadfast love and patience rescued her. Tessa owed everything to the woman whose guidance, wisdom, and honesty kept her from giving up on herself.

When the sauce was finished, she tasted it, added a bit of salt, and tasted it again. "Mmm, perfect."

Buttercup sat up straight, a string of drool hanging from her jowls.

"Sorry girl, none for you."

Tessa wiped the dogs face with a paper towel and gave her a

treat. She cleaned her kitchen, made the garlic bread, and set the table for her family of three.

Then she went upstairs and took a nap.

That evening, Nonna ate with gusto. "This is delicious, darling. I've certainly missed your cooking."

Tessa sipped her Cabernet. "You're the one who taught me how to make the sauce."

"Yes, I did. This recipe goes back generations, all the way to my grandmother in the old country. Marco, you should learn to make it, carry on the tradition."

"Maybe." He licked his thumb and helped himself to another serving.

Tessa was relieved to see his appetite had returned. Maybe spending time alone with Nonna had been a good idea. He was comfortable telling her things he might not tell his mother.

"Did you two enjoy your afternoon together?"

"We certainly did." Nonna squeezed Marco's hand.

"Where'd you go?"

"To Nutmeg's for Halloween cookies." Marco grinned at his great-grandma.

"Did you get me one?" Tessa asked.

"Of course we did. Marco picked out one for each of us."

Tessa's heart warmed. Their Halloween cookie tradition lived on. "So how was it driving? Must have felt strange getting behind the wheel after five weeks."

"Not at all," Nonna said. "I rather enjoyed it. But I do think I left the cookies in the back seat. Marco, can you get them?"

He wolfed down the last few bites on his plate. "Sure."

Tessa watched her sweet boy go off in search of cookies. As soon as he was out the door, she quizzed her grandmother.

"What did you find out? What did he say?"

Nonna pushed her plate to the side. "Not a lot. I could tell he's working things out in his mind. He's very observant, and he knows plenty."

"You're being too vague. Tell me something specific."

Nonna tapped her lips with one finger. "He knows his father made a mistake and that the baby was not intended. So I got the sense he's thinking deeply about the choices we make and the consequences of our actions. Not an easy lesson, you know."

Tessa nodded. "Maybe observing someone else's mistakes is a good way to learn it." She hoped Marco would be smarter than his father when it came to such things. "Do you think he knows anything about—about the custody issue? I mean, I have no idea if Victor's even mentioned it to him. I don't even know if he's still thinking about it."

Nonna shook her head. "It didn't come up. Marco did say he likes Crystal, though, and the little boy. But my goodness, Tessa, you've been stressing about it for over a month now. Why don't you just ask him?"

Tessa puffed up her cheeks. Why, indeed? "You're right, I should. I just wish I had more information or at least a better idea of—of why he…" she dropped her head into her hands and groaned.

"Indecisiveness does not suit you at all," Nonna said.

"Truer words have never been spoken." She threw her napkin onto her plate. "Anyway, you've made me feel a little better about Marco, so for that I thank you."

Nonna rubbed the back of Tessa's hand. "I'm glad. That's what I'm here for."

Tessa stood and went behind her grandmother's chair. She draped her arms over her shoulders and kissed her cheek. "I love you."

"I love you too, bambolina."

Tessa leaned into Nonna's neck. She caught a fleeting whiff of floral perfume and took comfort in the familiar scent.

It was late when Tessa crawled into bed. She nestled into the crisp white sheets and tucked the fluffy down comforter around her body. The lamp beside her bed threw off a warm yellow glow.

She rolled over and switched off the light. The pillow case was smooth and cool under her cheek. Her eyelids grew heavy, and she surrendered to the blissful sensation of falling into a deep sleep.

Just as she drifted off, a buzzing sound shook her awake. She grabbed her phone, squinting at the light coming off the screen. It was a text from her lawyer:

News about Victor. Call me.

Tessa bolted upright. She called Elaine, but it went straight to voicemail. She sent a text and stared at the screen. She texted several more times. Nothing.

Tessa tried to shake off her anxiety. *News about Victor*—that could mean anything. But if it warranted a late night message from Elaine, it definitely meant something.

23

*I*n the morning, the cloudy sky reflected the inside of Tessa's head. She stumbled downstairs and made a full pot of coffee.

The drip-drip-drip took forever. Tessa removed the carafe from the burner and stuffed a towel in its place to catch the flow. She poured coffee into a mug and over-flowed it. The stream of hot liquid ran over the edge of the counter and onto the floor. "Dammit!"

She threw a towel over the puddle and checked the time, watching the minutes until seven o'clock.

As soon as the big hand hit the twelve, she dialed. It rang four times before her lawyer answered.

"Good morning!" Elaine said, far too cheerfully.

"Are you kidding me?" Tessa eschewed polite niceties. "I've been up all night."

"I can tell. I woke up to half-a-dozen texts from you."

"You told me to call, so I did, and then you didn't answer."

"Well, I had to go to bed eventually," Elaine said. "I texted you at nine, and I figured you'd call me right away."

"Nine?" Tessa inhaled, trying to stay calm. "It was almost midnight."

Elaine groaned, as if dragging herself out of bed. "Oh, you know how crazy the network traffic can be. The text must have been delayed. Anyway, there's no reason to panic. Can I come by the shop this morning?"

"Yes, that's fine, but first tell me what—"

"Mom?"

Tessa spun around.

Marco stood in the kitchen, rubbing his eyes. He had on boxer shorts and a white tee-shirt, and his hair stuck out in all directions.

Tessa hung up on Elaine without saying goodbye.

"Good morning, honey," she said, faking a carefree tone. "How'd you sleep?"

"Fine. Can I have French toast for breakfast?"

"Of course." Tessa picked up the coffee-soaked towel and tossed it into the sink. "I'll make it while you get dressed for school."

"Okay."

As Marco shuffled out of the kitchen, Tessa texted her lawyer:

I'll be at the shop by eight-thirty. Come then.

The bells on the doorknob jingled at eight-thirty on the nose. Elaine Cooper entered in her signature pantsuit, orange this time. She closed the door with a firm push and hollered. "Tessa?"

"I'm right here," Tessa said from her seat at the counter. "Wow, you look like a walking pillar of pumpkins."

"Thank you, I think."

"Yes, definitely a compliment. Now, talk to me."

Elaine sat on the stool next to Tessa. "What, no coffee?"

"I already had two cups." She showed Elaine her trembling

hand. "But I'll make you one after you tell me what's going on. Your text last night really threw me."

"Yeah, sorry about that. Here's the scoop. I was at a function last night, part social, part business. You know how those things are—unbelievably boring."

"I'm sure." Tessa wished she'd get to the point. "Go on."

"Right, okay." Elaine crossed her legs. "Here's what happened. I ran into an old friend, sort of a friend, we've crossed paths a million times. Evidently, he's Victor's lawyer now. The old guy—you remember him, that jerk—retired about a year ago."

Tessa would never forget the old lawyer who represented Victor in the divorce, that condescending egotist.

Elaine flattened her hands on the counter, and Tessa's focus sharpened. The big news was about to drop.

"So my friend, more of an acquaintance but you know what I mean, said something that made me think. Very subtle, but telling." Elaine paused and leaned forward. "Is anyone else here?"

"Just Pat—oh, wait." With a slight jolt, Tessa remembered that Patty and Liza had moved out over the weekend. "Nobody's here."

"Okay, good. So I don't have to whisper." Elaine removed her jacket. "Would you hang this up for me? I have to be in court this afternoon, and I don't want it to wrinkle."

Tessa took the jacket and draped it on the coat rack by the door. Elaine was the smartest person she knew, but her brain bounced so quickly she was as distracted as a fruit fly.

When Tessa returned to her seat, Elaine said, "I love orange, but it might be a little loud for court. What do you think?"

"I think I want to know what the lawyer said. That's what I think."

Elaine blinked. "Yes, right, so—we were standing around chatting and drinking wine. Ugh, horrible wine by the way, I meant to tell you that. And then he said, and I quote, '*We have something in common.*' So I asked him what that meant, and he said, '*You represent Tessa Mariano, don't you?*' I said yes, I do. And he said, '*I represent her ex-husband.*'"

Elaine stopped and eyed Tessa as if she should grasp the significance of the news.

"What does that mean?"

"It means something new has happened. The fact that he was aware of our association indicates he's had recent contact with Victor or with your divorce decree. Which, by the way, wouldn't even be a blip on my radar if not for our last discussion." Elaine reached into a basket on the counter containing small packages of Italian biscotti. "May I?"

"Sure." Tessa glanced at the clock on the wall. She had to open the shop in less than an hour.

Elaine unwrapped a cookie and tasted it. "Mmm, yummy. Can I have my coffee now?"

"I suppose." Tessa went behind the counter, turned on the Nespresso machine, and made a quick Americano.

"Here." She set the white mug in front of Elaine. "Can you drink and talk at the same time?"

"Of course I can." She sipped. "Ah, perfect. Where was I?"

"A blip on your radar." Tessa pushed her hands through her hair and squeezed her head. "Come on, Elaine, you're torturing me."

"I have a question. The day you and I met at Nutmeg's—that was about six weeks ago, right?"

"I think so."

"Since then, have you had any more conversations with Victor about a change in custody?"

Tessa drummed a finger on the counter. As far as she could remember, the only time it came up again was the day they argued right before Marco's soccer game. And she had been the one to bring it up. "Not really."

"Not really? That means yes."

"We had an argument a week ago, and I—I might have said something stupid."

"What did you say?"

Tessa gazed out the window, trying to recall her exact words. "It was something about why would I ever consider letting Marco live with him." She paused, reluctant to admit the next sentence.

"There's more," Elaine said. "I can tell."

"Fine." Tessa heaved a sigh. "I told him I'd have to be dead before I'd let it happen. It was a terrible thing to say, I know. But I was so mad."

Elaine waved a hand in front of her face as if swatting a bug. "Oh for God's sake, I've heard ten times worse, so don't worry about that." She dunked a cookie in her coffee. "Here's the thing. I'd like to figure out what precipitated Victor's request in the first place. I mean, after seven years and the two of you accommodating each other's schedules pretty darn well, why now?" She held out her hands, palms up. "I mean, does he *really* want Marco to live with him?"

Tessa had no idea what Victor really wanted. "Why would he ask if he didn't?"

Elaine crossed her arms. "You want a list of reasons? Because I know them all."

"Victor loves Marco," Tessa said. "But he's not the kind of man who welcomes additional responsibility. He definitely wasn't planning on another baby—he told me that." She didn't mention his use of the word *trapped,* and even though he'd back-peddled on it, Tessa sensed he meant it.

Elaine stood and started pacing. "What about work? Does he have a job these days?"

"Yeah, he's in sales."

"Does he make good money?"

"I think so. Good enough, why?"

Elaine put her hands on the back of the stool and squeezed the wood. "Because maybe he's trying to get out of paying child support."

"He hardly pays it, anyway."

Elaine's mouth dropped open. "Whoa. What does that mean?"

Tessa felt like a kid in trouble. "Sometimes he sends it, sometimes he doesn't. It's not like I need it to take care of Marco."

"That's not the point." Elaine raised her voice. "You're entitled to it, and he's legally obligated to pay it."

"Is it that big of a deal? His payments were never on time, even when I needed them desperately. And reminding him only created more friction. Anyway, whatever he paid went into Marco's college fund. But, who cares? The amount is insignificant."

"To you maybe, but not to him."

Her assertion gave Tessa pause. A few hundred dollars might not mean much to her, but it could mean a hell of a lot to Victor, especially with him starting a new family.

"Do you know offhand how many payments he's missed?" Elaine pulled a yellow legal tablet and a pen out of her bag.

"Over seven years? I have no idea. But I know I haven't received one in months, probably not since the beginning of the year."

"And you haven't said a thing to him about it?"

Tessa's lips formed a thin line. She shook her head. "No."

"You should have told me," Elaine said, scribbling numbers on her yellow paper with remarkable speed. "He probably owes you at least several thousand dollars, which we can petition to collect."

"I'm not going to take him to court over a few thousand dollars."

"Which he probably knows." Elaine tapped the side of her head. "What I wonder is why he's never petitioned the court to reduce his obligation. The fact that you haven't done anything about his lack of payment could be used as evidence that you don't need to collect support."

"Well, I don't. And he knows I don't. He saw the remodel I did on the house, he said he's been following my career, he even said…" Tessa rewound her brain and went back to the morning he'd showed up to tell her about his engagement.

"He even said what?" Elaine leaned in closer.

"He said, *I know you're rich now.*"

Elaine looked like a detective solving a mystery, the wheels in her brain spinning.

"Here's what I think. This isn't about the money he owes you. It's about the money you'll owe him if he gets custody of your son."

24

*T*essa could hardly breathe the rest of the day. If money was Victor's motivation, she could work with that. And she wasn't above bribery, at least not when it was for a greater good. If her ex-husband needed money and she needed him not to pursue custody of their son, why not? They'd both get what they wanted.

But what if Marco found out his father had used him as a bargaining chip? He'd be devastated.

The anxiety and exhaustion Tessa had worked so hard to overcome at the wellness center rushed back in like a storm.

Elaine had instructed her not to do or say anything until they got new information. And doing nothing wasn't something Tessa excelled at. Waiting around for Victor to make a move was like watching a chess game in slow-motion.

~

On Saturday, Tessa and Nonna went to Town Square Park for an early morning stroll. Dry leaves littering the path crunched under their feet.

Tessa tucked her hands into the pockets of her black wool jacket. "Are you warm enough, Nonna?" she asked, eyeing her grandmother's worn coat.

"I'm fine, darling," she said, tapping her cane on the ground.

"I think you could use a new coat."

"This old coat has gotten me through at least thirty winters. It'll last a few more. No reason to spend money on new clothes at this stage of the game."

"Please don't say things like that. I'm already hanging on tenterhooks, and you joking about your own demise doesn't help."

Across the lawn, a father pitched a ball to his son. The boy, perhaps eight or nine, swung hard but missed. The father called to him, "That's okay, son, try again."

As they circled around the gazebo, Tessa told her grandmother about her meeting with Elaine.

"You really think Victor wants custody in order to get money from you?" Nonna asked. "I mean, that is so—so unseemly."

"Part of me doesn't believe it, but Elaine said based on my income, he'd collect at least a few thousand a month in child support." It made Tessa sick to think her child could be bartered.

"You know I'm always on your side," Nonna said. "But we have to acknowledge Victor's stress, too. The fact that he owes you money could be weighing on him, especially now with a new baby on the way."

Tessa mulled over her grandmother's idea then dismissed it. "I don't care about his stress—for God's sake, he created the mess he's in all on his own."

She ran through every scenario she could think of and kept coming back to the one that was best for Marco—Victor wanting custody so he could be with his son. But in her gut, she only half-believed it.

"Does Marco know anything about this?" Nonna asked.

"I don't think so. I mean, I haven't said a thing. And I doubt

Victor has. He dropped enough of a bomb on Marco with news about getting married and having a baby."

"He certainly did," Nonna said with an edge of disapproval.

Tessa caught a whiff of pumpkin muffins baking at Nutmeg's. They passed a crew setting up booths for tomorrow's fall festival. In less than two weeks it would be Halloween, another reminder of the seasons going round.

"You know what though?" Nonna continued. "Marco will be fourteen soon. Doesn't he have some say in the matter?"

Tessa heard the satisfying smack of a ball hitting wood. She saw the boy fling the bat and circle the makeshift bases as his father cheered and shouted that he'd hit a homerun. *A boy needs his father.*

"Maybe, but I can't imagine putting him in that position. It's not right." Tessa let the air out of her lungs. If she were being honest with herself, she'd admit to what really worried her—that Marco, given the choice, might choose Victor. "My hope is that Marco never needs to know about this—this conflict. And if that means I pay Victor off, so be it."

Nonna halted and faced her. "I've always been honest with you, haven't I?"

Tessa nodded. Her grandmother was the only one who was honest with her about her mother's illness.

Too smart for her own good, her father used to say. *And relentless.*

Month after month, as her mother's condition worsened, nine-year-old Tessa had insisted on going to the doctor appointments so she could ask questions. But the doctor's responses were little more than platitudes and false reassurances.

In the weeks before her mother died, Tessa had begged her father to talk to her about death. She stamped her feet in front of him and yanked his arm, tears streaming down her cheeks. *"What will happen when Mommy dies? You have to tell me. I need to know what to do!"*

Her father shook her off. *"I don't know what you should do. I don't know what anybody should do."*

But Nonna answered every question with patience and honesty. Sometimes Tessa challenged and argued and demanded, but her grandmother was steadfast.

My precious bambolina, Nonna had said, I will always tell you the truth as I know it. For the rest of my life, I will be honest with you no matter what.

That was over thirty years ago, and Nonna had never once broken her pledge.

She stroked Tessa's hair. "The most important thing is that Marco has two parents who love him. I know you're worried about losing your son, but I promise you that will never happen. Marco loves you so much, and that will not change."

Tessa closed her eyes, and tears dripped onto her cheeks. Her grandmother wiped them away with her thumbs. Then she wrapped her arms around Tessa and held her until there were no tears left to fall.

25

The *Mariano's Cheese and Wine* booth at the Fall Festival occupied a prime location in front of the gazebo and directly across from the shop. Tessa, Patty, Liza, and Marco dragged red wagons filled with food and wine across the street into the park, where they set up under a white tent.

Tessa kept a close eye on Marco, watching for any sign of anxiety, but he seemed to have bounced back to his old self.

The festival kicked off at noon with pumpkin carving, bobbing for apples, and a pie eating contest. The park, warmed by the sun high overhead, was packed with locals and tourists. A guitarist on the gazebo played country music.

"Mom, can I go now?" Marco asked. "I'm supposed to meet Oliver at the pie table to watch the eaters stuff their faces."

"Sure, but remember I need your help setting up for the wine tasting tonight."

"I'll be back in time."

As soon as he disappeared into the crowd, Patty said, "He seems to be doing better." She tied an apron over her short denim dress and slipped her hands into plastic gloves.

"He is." Tessa said. "Nonna spent the afternoon with him last weekend. I'm not sure what was said, but whatever it was seems to have helped."

"Nobody can cure a problem better than Nonna." Patty opened a package of crackers and arranged them on a platter with cheese, dried fruit, and olive tapenade. "I wish I had a grandma like her."

"Yeah, I won the grandmother lottery for sure." Ever since their walk the previous day, Tessa felt a renewal of strength and focus.

"Have you tried this new triple-cream brie?" Patty handed Tessa some on a cracker with a dab of balsamic fig spread. "I think it's my new favorite."

"Every new cheese is your new favorite." Tessa bit into it. It was mild, creamy, buttery. And the sweet fig brought out the cheese's velvety texture. "Mmm, that is good. You've become a real expert at pairing, too."

"You taught me everything I know. I'm serious—you literally did."

"A teacher is only as good as her student. And you, my friend, are a—"

"Mom! We need you!"

Tessa peered into the crowd, and saw Marco sprinting toward her. She clutched her chest. The front of his shirt was covered in blood.

She dropped the cheese and cracker and stepped over the partition around her booth.

"Marco, what happened? You're bleeding."

"It's not me," he said, panting hard. "It's Henry. He fell and knocked out a tooth."

Henry was there?

"And his chin is bleeding, too. Can you come help?"

"Well, where's his mother?"

"She's not here. Dad brought Henry himself. Come on."

"Oh, geez." Tessa grabbed a stack of napkins and followed

her son toward the playground.

"They're over by the merry-go-round," Marco said, visibly concerned about his little soon-to-be stepbrother.

Tessa spotted Victor on a bench with Henry on his lap. The image was bittersweet. If not for the blond curls, it could've been a young Marco sitting on his father's lap. As she got closer, she heard Henry's soft whimpers.

Marco sat next to them and squeezed the little boy's knee. "Hey, buddy, you remember my mom?"

Victor flashed a pained look in her direction. "He knocked out both his lower teeth."

Tessa leaned closer. "Henry, can I take a look?"

He opened his mouth just a tiny bit. "It hurts," he said. He had blood on his hands, his face, even in his hair. The sockets where the tiny teeth had been were oozing, and a nasty scrape marred his perfect chin.

"Were the teeth loose, Henry?" Tessa asked, dabbing his face with a napkin.

"A little."

"I should probably take him home," Victor said.

"No." Henry's lip trembled. "I don't wanna go home."

"You know what," Tessa said. "There's a first aid station over by my booth. Why don't we go over there and let them clean you up?"

"Okay." Henry clasped his thin arms around her neck.

Tessa hadn't expected him to even remember her, and here he was clinging to her like a little rhesus monkey. As she stood up straight, his legs wrapped around her hips.

Henry nestled his face into the side of her neck, his tears and saliva wet against her skin.

She looked over his shoulder at Victor, pointed to her lower teeth, and whispered, "Where are they?"

Victor and Marco shook their heads and raised their shoulders in unison.

Oh, no, Tessa thought. Henry's first baby teeth. Crystal would be heartbroken.

"Find them," she mouthed.

Her son and ex-husband went in search of two needles in an enormous haystack, and Tessa carried Henry all the way across the park to the first aid station.

The nurse, who probably wasn't a nurse, put a Superman bandage on Henry's scrape. Blood slowly seeped through the pad.

"You think it's deep?" Tessa whispered, hoping the non-nurse knew what she was doing.

"Hard to tell, but my mom says faces bleed a lot." She opened a fresh bandage. She padded it with a bit of gauze and covered the scrape. Then she wiped his face and hands with a damp cloth.

"Can you get that little bit out of his hair?" Tessa pointed to a few curls near his forehead. "Right there?"

"Sure." She cleaned his curls, gave him a juice box, and said he was good as new.

Tessa clasped Henry's soft hand, and together they wound their way through the congested park.

"Feeling better now?" Tessa asked.

"Uh-huh. I'm hungry."

"I'll try to find something you can eat. Where's your mommy today?"

"Just at home, because she has to sleep, because she has to work later."

Now there was an interesting bit of information. "Mommy works at night?"

"Sometimes. And she works in my school. And she said I could get a puppy." He took a breath before continuing his chatter. "And we're getting a baby. So I get to have two brothers. Marco's big. I'm medium. And the baby will be very little until he grows some."

Hmm, the baby was a boy—at least according to Henry.

He stopped and pointed. "Look!"

At the Nutmeg's stand, a bunch of kids were in line for cookies—pumpkins, ghosts, and witches on broomsticks.

"May I please have a cookie?" Henry asked Tessa, impressing her with his politeness.

"How about we get you one to take home?"

"Okay." Henry smiled then grimaced. "Ow, that hurted."

"I'll bet it did." Tessa stepped up to the cookie stand with Henry. "Well, look who's here, my friend Rebecca."

"Tessa!" The dog-walking, house-sitting, animal-rescuing, cookie-baking, part-time barista threw her long, frizzy braid over her shoulder and gave her a tight hug. "I haven't seen you in ages."

"I saw you the other day after Buttercup's walk." Tessa maneuvered herself out of Rebecca's arms.

"Oh, yeah, I forgot." She laughed. "I've been so busy with all my jobs, I totally can't keep track of anything. And oh my gosh, who's this little cutie?"

"I'm Marco's brudder."

"Seriously?" Her eyes doubled in size and her mouth dropped. "You adopted a little boy?"

Tessa rubbed her forehead. "Henry is the son of my ex-husband's fiancé."

Rebecca's face fell. "Marco's dad is getting married? Man, that's too bad. I kinda had a crush on him."

"Oh Rebecca, that's ridiculous. He's nearly old enough to be your father."

"The operative word being *nearly*," said Rebecca. "Besides look at all those actresses who marry men twenty years older."

"You're not an actress. And we'll discuss your taste in men another time." Tessa gestured toward the cookies. "Now, how about a cookie?"

"Oh, yeah. What'll it be, cutie-pie, ghost, witch, or

pumpkin?"

Henry studied his choices. "Ghost—no wait, pumpkin."

Rebecca handed him the cookie in a small white bag. "There you go."

Tessa and Henry said goodbye and continued their stroll through the festival grounds. A puppet show taking place behind a wooden stage with curtains caught Henry's attention. A bear and a squirrel were trying to get a cat out of a tree. The cat meowed, and Henry giggled, his eyes widening with delight. Tessa recalled how endearing it was to see a child captivated by something as simple as a puppet show.

Her cell buzzed with a text from Patty:

Getting busy here. You coming back?

Tessa cupped a hand over her eyes, shielding them from the sun, and saw a small crowd had gathered near her booth.

"We've got to go, Henry."

"But I wanna watch the puppet show."

"I have to get back to my booth." She picked up his hand. "I have work to do."

Henry pouted, his lower lip trembling. "But I wanna stay here." He snatched his hand away.

The puppet show continued with no sign of wrapping up.

"Sorry, but I can't leave you here by yourself." She put her hands under his arms and tried to lift him, but he wriggled out of her grasp.

"No, I don't wanna go."

Tessa had no choice but to scoop him up from behind and half carry, half drag him across the park.

He whined and struggled, but she held tight and did her best to keep moving. "Henry, please, if you'd just—"

A man stopped in front of her. "Looks like you could use some help," he said.

"Thanks, but I'm..." Tessa halted. The baseball cap, the aviator sunglasses—what was Dr. Barnes doing in Clearwater?

26

An amused smile crossed his face. "I thought you said your son was thirteen."

The statement baffled Tessa until she felt Henry squeeze her hand.

"Oh, this isn't my son, this is—never mind." She pushed her hair out of her face.

"Is that blood?" He pointed to the side of her neck, and his finger brushed against her skin.

"Probably." Tessa rubbed the spot on her neck with her sleeve. Her linen skirt was a wrinkled mess, her white sneakers grass-stained and dirty. "Henry just lost a tooth."

"I lost theseth two teeth," the little boy said, opening his mouth.

Owen, in jeans and a black tee-shirt that hugged his broad shoulders, crouched. "I see that. And what's going on under this Superman bandage?"

Henry let go of Tessa's hand. "I banged my chin on the mewwy-go-round."

"Mind if I take a look?" Owen asked.

"Okay." He raised his chin and jutted it out.

Gently, the doctor peeled away the bandage.

Tessa winced. "Do you think it needs s-t-i-t-c-h-e-s?"

"Stitchesth?" Henry said. "I want stitchesth. My friend got 'em in his head."

Tessa had forgotten how smart the child was.

"No stitches," Owen said, rising up. "But it needs a little cleaning and a better bandage. I have a cool kit with all kinds of stuff in my car. You want to see?"

"Uh-huh!" Henry raised his arms expectantly.

Owen hesitated. "Oh, you want to go with me?"

Henry nodded, and Owen lifted him onto his hip. Tessa couldn't believe this was the same man who had infuriated her the first time they'd met. Or the same kid who was having a meltdown two minutes ago.

"Before I walk off with this kid, do you actually know him?"

Not really, she thought. It was only the second time she and Henry had met. But he'd attached to her willingly, warming her heart.

"Sort of. Henry's my ex-husband's soon-to-be stepson."

"Ah, got it. Is his mother around, because if—"

"Henry!" Crystal ran toward them, her crocheted satchel bouncing against her leg. She stopped to catch her breath.

"Take it easy," Tessa said. "He's okay."

"That's my mommy. She hasth a baby in her tummy."

"Does she?" Owen's eyebrows lifted.

Crystal lumbered over to them, breathing hard, glancing from Owen to Tessa and back to Owen. "Who's this holding my son?"

"This is Dr. Barnes," Tessa said, disbelieving the entire scene. "He's my grandmother's orthopedic surgeon."

"I see." Crystal wound her chaotic hair into a knot on top of her head.

"I'd like to put a couple of butterfly bandages on Henry's chin, if it's okay with you."

Crystal examined her son's face, and Tessa was impressed by how calm she remained, considering the severity of the cut.

"Good idea, and it also looks like—"

"Mom!" Marco hollered. "We found Henry's teeth!"

The next thing Tessa knew, Victor was at Crystal's side. "Babe, I told you everything was fine. He rubbed her back with a tenderness that surprised Tessa. He'd never been gentle and attentive with her, at least not that she could remember.

"Your ex-husband, I presume?" Owen asked.

Tessa nodded, her lips forming a weak smile. "It's complicated."

"It usually is. And the kid holding the teeth is your son?"

Tessa glanced at her handsome son. "Yes. That's Marco."

"Excuse me." Victor sauntered over and parked himself chest to chest with Owen. "Do we know you?"

Tessa didn't know what he meant by *we,* but she sensed he'd lumped her into it.

Owen remained unfazed, and Henry was still perched on his hip. "I'm Rosa's doctor and a friend of Tessa's. I'm going to get my first-aid kit and fix up Henry's chin."

"You're a real doctor then? Not some holistic guru or anything?"

Tessa and Crystal exchanged an expression of disbelief.

"I'm an MD, if that's what you mean."

"All right that's enough," Tessa said, moving between the two men. "I've got to get back to work."

"And I've got to get to a bathroom," Crystal glanced side to side. "There's got to be one in the park somewhere."

"There's a bathroom in my shop," Tessa said. "Victor knows where it is. And Marco, you go find a little bag for Henry's teeth."

The three who had received orders took off.

Owen set the boy down in front of Tessa. "You're good at being in charge, aren't you?"

"I don't mean to be bossy," she said, "but sometimes that's what it takes to get things done."

"No need to explain that to me. I've been bossy a time or two myself." He winked at her. "Be right back."

Tessa watched him jog across the lawn, admiring his narrow hips.

"Where's he going?" Henry asked.

"Dr. Barnes went to get your bandage. Now, we have to hurry because people are waiting for me. Can you walk fast?"

"I can run. Wanna see?"

"No, no, don't run." Tessa grasped his hand. The last thing she needed was for him to fall and damage himself further.

They walked through the park swinging their arms. Henry skipped along and chattered incessantly about his chin, his teeth, and his new big brother Marco. Soon Marco would have two little brothers, extended family for the rest of his life.

How much easier it would have been to deal with her mother's death if she'd had a sibling—somebody experiencing the same heartbreak, somebody to help shoulder the loss and carry the grief.

At the Mariano's booth, Patty was describing the different cheeses to a few visitors.

Tessa waved at her, then lifted Henry over the partition.

"What's this?" Patty asked. "Lost child?"

"Don't even ask." Tessa plunked the little boy down on the grass. "Your mommy will be here in a minute, Henry. Don't move, okay?"

"Okay. Can I eat my cookie?"

"Sure." She'd forgotten he even had one.

Crystal and Victor showed up and relieved her of babysitting duty. A moment later, Owen appeared. He carried an old-fashioned doctor's bag, the brown leather cracked and faded.

"Lemme show you what's in my bag."

Owen removed a stethoscope and let Henry listen to his own

heartbeat. Tessa was tempted to snap a photo—they were a Norman Rockwell painting come to life—but taking a picture of two people she hardly knew might be a little creepy.

"Alrighty, let's get that chin of yours patched up." Owen cleaned the scrape with a swab.

"Ow, it hurts."

"Yeah, I'm sorry," Owen said. "Just a little more."

Victor shifted from foot to foot, a pained expression on his face, while Crystal leaned over the doctor's shoulder asking questions and pointing out specks of dirt.

Patty squeezed Tessa's arm. "I'm liking your doctor friend. Natalie said he rocked a tux like nobody's business."

"Oh, please," Tessa said. A flash of Owen in his black tuxedo passed through her mind. "And he's not really my friend; he's Nonna's doctor, and I know almost nothing about him."

Tessa tried to recall every place she'd encountered him. His office and then the hospital where he was the epitome of authority; The event in San Francisco where he was the date of an attractive blonde who had no taste in wine; The Westridge where he was somebody's child, a caring and loving son who looked after his father, visited his patients, and drank double espresso with one sugar.

"Mom?"

She snapped out of her daydream.

"Here's Henry's teeth." Marco handed her a tiny bag.

"Oh, right, thank you."

"Can I go now? Oliver's waiting for me."

"Yes, honey, go. Have fun."

"I will. See you later." He observed the activity around Henry for a moment then turned to his father. "Hey, Dad, can I talk to you for a second?"

"Sure," Victor said. He slung an arm over his son's shoulders and guided him out of earshot.

Tessa strained her ears to catch a word or two, but nothing intelligible reached her.

They spoke only a minute, and the interaction ended with Victor giving Marco a hug and a hearty pat on the back.

Their son hurried off to meet his friend.

"Pssst." Tessa motioned with a curled finger. "Come here."

Victor complied.

"What was that about?" she asked.

"Nothing important."

"Yes it was, I could tell by Marco's stance. He slouches when he's upset."

Victor cracked his knuckles. "I'm allowed to have a private conversation with my son. Or are you trying to prevent that, too?"

Tessa narrowed her eyes. There was only one thing she was trying to prevent, and she wasn't about to discuss that in the middle of the park. His sarcasm miffed her. Why he'd become contentious after she'd taken care of Henry for him, she couldn't comprehend. Leave it to Victor to turn a step forward into two steps back.

"Have it your way."

She tried to push past him, but he blocked her.

"Hey, is there something going on between you and that doctor?"

"Don't be ridiculous." Tessa responded too fast, sounding defensive. She subdued her tone. "He's Nonna's surgeon, that's it."

"That's a non-answer if I ever heard one."

"Why are you challenging me?" Tessa wanted to shake him she was so frustrated. "I just solved a problem that *you* created. You should be thanking me, not asking me irrelevant questions."

A vein in his neck pulsed. "The men you date is not irrelevant."

"Jesus, Victor, I'm not dating him. But if I were, it wouldn't be any of your business."

Victor crossed his arms. "We have a son together, Tessa. Everything you do is my business."

27

The Fall Festival wrapped up late in the afternoon. Most of the booths had been broken down, but not Mariano's. In the roped-off tasting area, fifty people milled about the event benefitting Natalie's dance school.

Cece and Natalie were the official hosts. Dressed in ballet costumes with sequined bodices and tulle skirts, they circulated among the dance parents beneath a canopy of twinkling white lights. Tall cocktail tables had been set with candles and a board laden with foods for pairing—dried fruits, dark chocolate, Greek olives, apple slices, aged cheddar, smoked gouda, salted nuts.

While Patty and Adam poured, flirting with each other at every opportunity, Tessa mingled with her guests. She did her best to be present, but Victor's words preoccupied her. They shared a child—their actions and choices would impact each other forever.

As for Owen, he'd left the park after tending to Henry's chin, saying he'd return later. Why he'd been at the festival, Tessa had no idea. And why he was coming back was even more mysterious.

Tessa wandered from table to table. The attendees were interested in tasting and pairing at first, asking all kinds of smart questions. But the more wine they consumed, the more jovial they became, making for a relaxed atmosphere.

Cece stopped her as she walked by. "Tessa, tonight is amazing. Everything's so beautiful—you really outdid yourself."

"And thanks to you," Natalie said, "we granted more scholarships this year than ever before."

"You know it's my pleasure." Tessa poured three glasses of Syrah.

"To our favorite benefactor." Natalie raised her glass, and they toasted to the success of the evening.

"By the way." Natalie poked Tessa on the arm. "I heard *Dr. James Bond* came around earlier. What was that about?"

Tessa peered into the park. "I'm not sure."

Cece fluffed her long brown curls. "I hear he's got a crush on you."

"And I think it's mutual." Natalie chimed in.

"That's ridiculous," Tessa said, although she did feel a little flutter in her stomach. "I admit he looked good in that tuxedo, but I'm much too old for a—"

"Tessa," Adam said, "I need you for a second."

"Thank goodness. These girls are talking like they're back in high school. What do you need? Are we low on something?"

"No," Adam said, his eyes dancing. "Some guy's asking for you. Said his name's Owen."

Natalie and Cece tittered like little girls.

"Shush," Tessa said to them. "Where is he?"

Adam motioned with his head. "Over there. Why don't you take off? Patty and I can handle the rest of the tastings. And our two ballerinas here will take care of everything else."

"Are you sure?"

"Absolutely." Adam winked at her. "You deserve a break."

"Thanks. You're a doll."

"Yeah," he said, stretching out the word. "That's what everybody says."

Tessa gave him an affectionate squeeze and strolled toward the rope. Owen, standing on the other side, offered his hand.

"You came back," she said, resting her hand in his while she stepped over.

"I said I would."

Tessa's hand lingered in his for a split second before she let go.

They walked toward the edge of the park, less crowded now that families with children had gone home. The sky had turned pink and orange, and the aroma of caramel corn hung in the air. Teenagers sat around the gazebo listening to music, dancing, and laughing.

The question of why Dr. Barnes had shown up at the Fall Festival remained unanswered, and Tessa expected him to offer an explanation. When he didn't, she asked, "Is this your first time in Clearwater?"

"Sort of. A friend of mine lives about a half-hour from here, so I've driven through a few times. Never actually been in the town before, though. It's charming."

As if in response, the streetlamps along Main Street flickered to life.

When they reached the sidewalk, Tessa pointed across the street. "That's where I work."

Owen read the name imprinted on the window. "*Mariano's Cheese and Wine*. Sounds interesting."

"Would you like to see it? I happen to have the key." She patted her pocket as if it were hiding in there.

"I would love to see it."

Despite the easy banter, Tessa's insides were jumping as they crossed the street. She opened the door, jingling the bells, and Owen followed her inside.

"Wow," he said, moving toward the wine racks. He took a

bottle off the shelf, studied the label, put it back. "You have quite a selection."

She was drawn to his side. "It is a *wine shop*, you know."

His eyes settled on hers. "I brought you something." He removed a small plastic tube from his pocket and held it up between his thumb and index finger. "I hope it's the right one."

She blinked. "Should I know what that is?"

"It's an ink cartridge for your fountain pen."

"How did—" She broke off and remembered the day they drank espresso, how he'd used a fountain pen to write his number on the back of his card.

"Is the pen here?"

Tessa shook her head. "It's at home."

His eyes seemed to turn greener. "If you have trouble switching the cartridge, let me know. I'll walk you through it."

Warmth spread from her chest to her face. "Dr. Barnes, what are—"

"Tessa, I think it's time you called me Owen."

She inhaled. Her pulse in her neck thumped. "What are you doing here?"

"May I tell you over a glass of wine?"

She tucked some hair behind her ear and regained her composure. "I have one I think you'll enjoy." She slid the ladder along the wall and climbed a few rungs. Based on his taste for espresso, she knew he'd like a wine that was bold and slightly acidic. Her hand stopped on one of her favorite Cabernets.

Holding the bottle in one hand, she stepped off the ladder and turned. Her face hit his chest.

"Oh, I didn't know you were right there."

He didn't move. "Sorry," he said. "I, um, it looked a little precarious there. Didn't want you to fall."

She had only two choices—step to the side or stay there and see what he'd do.

Tessa stepped to the side. "I never fall." The words were out before she considered their potential double meaning.

"This Cab is from a local winery," she said, deflecting. She removed a corkscrew from a drawer and pulled the cork with a satisfying pop. "It needs to breathe a bit, so we'll have to wait."

"I don't mind waiting." Owen slid onto a stool at the bar.

Tessa sat beside him.

He put the ink cartridge on the counter beside his phone. "You probably know Rosa sings your praises to all who will listen. The last time I saw her she informed me you're quite famous."

"Famous?" Tessa chuckled. "That's just Nonna being Nonna."

"I don't think so." He placed an elbow over the back of his stool. "I googled your name."

"Why?" she asked, surprised he'd reveal something like that.

"Why does anybody google anyone? I wanted to know more."

Her stomach flipped over.

"Turns out, you're a woman of many talents."

Air filled Tessa's lungs, and her chest rose. "So you came all the way to Clearwater to find out?"

One side of his mouth flicked up. "Kind of. I learned, courtesy of an article I stumbled upon, that you are, and I quote, *a skilled sommelier with natural instinct, sophisticated palate, and entrepreneurial brilliance.*"

Tessa reddened. "A bit over the top, but I can't deny it."

"Nor should you. There's no shame in being the best at what you do."

"Perhaps that's something we have in common." She was enjoying their flirtatious repartee.

Owen gave an easy nod. "Perhaps."

Tessa tapped her feet on the legs of her stool. "So, Owen, are you going to tell me how you ended up here, so far off the beaten path?"

"Well, thanks to Google, I found more articles that mentioned the great sommelier, Tessa Mariano, and one was all about today's festival. So, I decided to take a drive, check out Clearwater, and see if I might run into you."

It was no accident then, he'd come to see her. "And run into me you did."

"Yes. Must admit I hadn't expected to find you dragging a little kid away from a puppet show."

Tessa laughed. "Not my finest moment."

"On the contrary," Owen said, becoming serious. "Seems to me you saved the day."

Had she? It didn't feel that way at the end, especially after the argument with Victor.

Tessa fidgeted with the hem of her skirt and refocused before the unpleasant recollection dampened her mood. "And the ink? How do you explain that?"

"Ah, yes, the ink. You told me your pen was dry, and I have plenty of cartridges." He slid it toward her with one finger.

Tessa picked it up. A small gesture with big meaning. Most people would never have remembered. "Thank you."

"You're welcome." His gaze mesmerized her.

"Let's try the wine," she said, breaking the intensity of the moment.

"I'd love to." He filled the two stemmed glasses.

They both sipped. Tessa closed her eyes and held the liquid in her mouth, savoring the notes—black currants, pepper, vanilla.

When she opened her eyes, he was watching her. She swallowed.

"Do you like it?" she asked.

"Yes. Very much."

Her fingers stiffened around her glass as he drew close. His lips brushed against hers so lightly they didn't really touch, leaving every nerve around her mouth tingling with anticipation.

His phone vibrated on the counter, and the moment evaporated like a drop of water in fire.

He read the message, and a worried frown crossed his face. "Duty calls, I'm afraid."

Tessa licked her un-kissed lips. "I understand."

Owen stood. He slipped his phone into his pocket. "May I give you a call?"

"Of course." She wasn't sure why he wanted to call— perhaps to check on Henry's chin or find out if the ink cartridge worked.

Or maybe he wanted to call in order to pick up where they were leaving off.

28

A few days passed with no call, which surprised her. Five days went by, which puzzled her. A week went by, which annoyed her. But there was nothing she could do about it, because she wasn't about to call him. Then she had the bright idea to try replacing the ink cartridge in her fountain pen. Maybe it would be a complicated procedure, requiring her to seek his expertise.

But her self-sufficiency, not to mention a simple you-tube video, made replacing the cartridge quick and easy. Besides, the damsel-in-distress act did not suit her.

She told herself to snap out of it and renewed her stance that she had no time, energy, or desire to entertain the notion of going out with any man, least of all her grandmother's doctor.

~

With Halloween on the horizon, Clearwater was awash in pumpkins, scarecrows, and sidewalk planters bursting with orange marigolds and black-eyed Susans.

Tessa and Natalie sat across from each other enjoying an early Sunday breakfast at Nutmegs.

Trevor the barista, clad in a skeleton costume, refilled their water glasses. "Hi, Natalie."

Natalie looked up from her phone. "Hi, Trevor."

"Doing anything special for Halloween?" he asked.

Tessa rested her chin in her hand, hoping Natalie would be gentle with the love-struck young man. Despite the ten-year age difference, the poor guy had been crazy about the beautiful ballerina since he was a kid.

"No. And please don't ask me out, because you already know the answer."

"There's always a chance you'll change your mind."

"I'm sorry, Trevor, there's not." Natalie addressed him with gentle firmness. "I'm almost thirty-five. You need to fall in love with somebody closer to your own age."

"Nah," he said, wiping a drop of coffee off their table. "You're the one for me. Someday I'll be more than just the guy who brings you sticky buns and pours your coffee."

He marched off with admirable confidence.

"You gotta give him credit. He's as loyal as my dog." Tessa patted Buttercup's velvety head. The St. Bernard sat beside her with the rigid attention of a bodyguard.

"He sure is." Natalie scrolled through her phone and sighed.

"What are you so busy looking at?" Tessa asked.

She put her phone face down. "Just this dating app I'm trying."

Tessa's eyes widened. "You've got to be kidding."

The ballet teacher crossed her long legs and ate a piece of sticky bun. "Thought I'd give it a shot."

"Sorry the art collector guy didn't work out." Tessa felt somewhat responsible for their meeting since she'd taken Natalie to the event. "Was he really that obnoxious?"

"He was. I suspected he was a pompous know-it-all from the start. Should've listened to my gut." She licked her fingers.

Tessa leaned on her elbows. "See that? First impressions are always right."

"Not always. Look at the dashing Dr. Barnes. You changed your mind about him."

"Which appears to have been a mistake." Tessa shook her head. "Can't believe I never heard from him."

"Maybe he lost your number."

"Are you kidding?" Tessa popped a caramelized pecan into her mouth. "My number is on a hundred medical forms he has access to. If he wanted to call me, he would have. I'm going back to my original opinion of him."

"I don't think you should write him off just yet. According to Nonna, he's a rare find."

"How do you know that?" Tessa asked.

"I bumped into her at the supermarket the other day. She went on and on about him. And you know your grandmother is *always* right."

"That she is. But she's also more forgiving than the average person." Tessa took another slice off the sticky bun. "You want anymore?"

"Yes." Natalie picked up the remaining piece and bit into it. "What's happened to us?" she said, her mouth full. "A month ago we both swore off men. Now I'm on some stupid dating app, you're infatuated with Nonna's doctor, and both of us are watching our phones like a couple of teenagers."

"Pathetic," Tessa said.

"Pa-the-tic," Natalie repeated. She wiped crumbs off her lips. "I need to go. We're holding auditions for *The Nutcracker* this afternoon. It's not even Halloween yet, and I gotta be thinking about Christmas."

Tessa swallowed the last of her coffee. "I need to go, too. I'm dropping Buttercup off with Rebecca, picking up Marco, and then going to work. Thanks for breakfast. No doubt, it'll end up being the highlight of my day."

"Mine, too." Natalie gave Buttercup a kiss and a nuzzle. "Maybe I should get myself a dog."

Tessa parked in front of Victor's house and texted Marco.

I'm here.

While she waited for him to come out, she called Patty and told her to take the day off.

"Are you sure? I thought you needed me to open at eleven."

"I'll be back in time. Besides, you worked last Sunday at the festival, and I don't want you to burn out on me. Holidays are right around the corner, and we'll be working night and day."

Patty laughed. "Okay, thanks. See you tomorrow then."

Just as Tessa ended the call, she received a text from Marco.

I'm out with Dad and Henry. Be back soon. Crystal's in the house.

"Oh come on, really?" Tessa clicked her fingernails on the steering wheel. Why hadn't Victor let her know to come later? He had no respect for her time or the demands of her job.

She grabbed her purse, got out of the car, and slammed the door. A gust of wind blew through the oak tree on the lawn, showering her with dry leaves and bits of bark.

The path to the house was cracked and uneven from tree roots pushing up through the concrete. Tessa stepped over them with caution. Victor had bought the yellow ranch house just over a year ago—about the time his child support payments sputtered out.

On the porch were two white wicker chairs with bright blue cushions. A shiny two-wheeler with training wheels leaned against the house. Tessa caught a whiff of fresh paint.

She rang the bell and waited. When nobody answered, she opened the screen and knocked on the front door. Nothing.

"Hello? Crystal?"

Finally, the door opened. "Oh, Tessa, I'm sorry I kept you waiting."

"Did I wake you?" Tessa asked, although she knew she had.

"No, I was just—nothing, please come in."

Tessa entered. She'd been in the house only once before, right after Victor had moved in. The living room furniture was pushed into the center and covered with plastic. "Looks like you're doing some work," she said.

"Just a little painting, that's all. The living room and one of the bedrooms."

Tessa wondered if Victor was fixing up the house to sell it.

"When did you and Henry move in?" she asked

"About three weeks ago."

Crystal's tone was light, so Tessa figured she didn't mind the question.

"They'll be back soon, I'm sure." Crystal rubbed her rounded belly. "Would you like tea?"

"Um, okay. Thank you."

Tessa followed her into the kitchen, passing through the family room with a large sectional couch, widescreen TV, and a plastic bin full of cars and trucks.

Crystal put a kettle on the stove. The countertops were covered with boxes and stacks of dishes.

"Sorry about the mess. I'm unpacking my kitchen stuff. Trying to figure out what to keep and what to get rid of."

Tessa took off her jacket and hung it on the back of a chair. If they were thinking about moving soon, there'd be no reason to unpack. Getting rid of stuff, however, was a good thing to do before moving. Her detective work was not pointing toward a definitive explanation of anything.

"So, where are the boys?"

"They went to breakfast. Victor thought I needed a little more sleep. I was up a lot last night." She withdrew two mugs from a cabinet, including one with a photo of Buttercup on it. "I had this made for Marco. Cute, huh?"

"Very." The image of Buttercup panting, practically smiling at the camera, made Tessa smile. What a thoughtful thing for Crystal to do. "I'm sure Marco loves it."

The kettle whistled. Crystal removed it from the stovetop and poured water over the tea bags. Tessa noticed a ring on her left hand, a small, sparkly diamond in a simple Tiffany setting. It hadn't been there before.

"Thank you again for looking after Henry last weekend. He really banged himself up."

"How's his chin?"

"Almost healed." Crystal carried the mugs to the table. "Your doctor friend knew what he was doing."

"I'm glad it worked out," Tessa said, refraining from any comment about the man who said he'd call and then didn't. "How does Henry like living here?"

"Loves it. We were in an apartment, so having a backyard is a big improvement."

Tessa sat beside the bay window and looked out. An enormous swing set with a fort, ladder, and yellow slide occupied half the yard. "That's quite a swing set."

Crystal lowered herself into a chair. "A gift from my parents, it just arrived a few days ago. You should've seen Marco pushing Henry on the swing last night. They were out there until after dark."

Tessa pictured her son playing with his little brother and being part of a family that did not include her. "Do your parents live nearby?"

"San Diego." Crystal pulled her ponytail over her shoulder and smoothed it with both hands. "That's where I'm from."

Tessa caught her breath. San Diego, of course. Crystal's

hometown. It made perfect sense she'd want to be near her family. Who better to help care for a new baby than one's own mother?

Tessa plucked the tea bag out of her mug and set it on the saucer. "You and I don't know much about each other, do we?"

"I suppose not." Crystal's eyes shifted. She swept a bit of salt off the table.

"Henry mentioned you sometimes work at night. What do you do?"

"I'm a vet tech at an animal hospital. So I pull the night shift now and then."

"Sounds like a rewarding job."

"It is."

Silence. Tessa tasted her tea. Her gaze drifted to the clock on the wall.

"I'm sorry they're still not back," Crystal said. "I know how busy you are."

The poor woman had said *I'm sorry* at least three times since Tessa arrived.

"It's not your fault. And you don't need to keep apologizing."

Crystal laughed. "Right, yeah, I tend to do that a lot, especially when I'm nervous."

"Am I making you nervous? I honestly don't mean to."

"No. Well, maybe a little."

"Now I'm sorry." Tessa offered a guilty smile. She pushed her chair away from the table and stood. "I'll go wait in the car. I'm sure they'll be back soon, and you probably need to rest." She picked up her jacket.

"Wait." Crystal rose from her chair. "Please don't go."

Tessa put her jacket down and tilted her head. "Is there something you want to talk about?"

Crystal's blue eyes filled with tears, her mouth quivering. "There is, but I'm not sure how to say it."

Tessa squeezed the back of the chair. She had a horrible feeling it was about Victor angling to take custody away from her. "Just go ahead and say it."

"It's about, well, it's that I don't..." She covered her face. "I don't think I should marry Victor."

29

*T*essa stared in disbelief, not only because of what Crystal said but also because she said it to her. Didn't she have any girlfriends? Couldn't she call her mother?

The proclamation had blindsided Tessa. She could not have been more unprepared. Despite her ability to dispense excellent, common-sense advice on any number of topics, she was at a loss.

Tessa channeled her inner Nonna, summoning every bit of wisdom she had absorbed over a lifetime of being the granddaughter of Rosa Mariano. If she couldn't be Nonna, the least she could be was her best *Tessa*. But words failed her.

"I'm not sure what to say."

Crystal blinked, and big tears dropped onto her cheeks. She wrapped her arms around the baby inside of her. Tessa teared up herself, racking her brain for words that could be both sympathetic and sensible. Nothing.

A car horn went beep-beep-beep.

"They're back." Crystal's face scrunched and turned red as a berry. "They can't see me like this."

Tessa jumped to her feet. "I'll take care of it. You go calm down and freshen up."

"Okay." Crystal dashed out of the kitchen. Tessa seated herself at the table, tea in hand, seconds before Victor, Marco, and Henry clamored into the house.

Henry's face broke into a smile when he saw her, and she instinctively held open her arms for the little boy. "Hi, Henry."

He fell against her lap. His head went back, and he opened his mouth wide. "Look! My teeth are growing."

Two tiny white nubs had popped through.

"They sure are. Those are going to be some big teeth soon."

"Yeah." Henry tugged on her hand. "You want to see my new swing set?"

Victor pulled Henry off of Tessa. "Slow down there, buddy. Marco and his mom have to go."

"Hi, Mom," Marco said. "Sorry we're late. It's kinda my fault."

Tessa knew it wasn't, but he'd become adept at heading off arguments between his parents.

"Where's Mommy?" Henry asked.

"In the bathroom. She'll be right out, honey." Tessa couldn't decide if she should wait or flee the scene. If she were gone when Crystal returned, she could wash her hands of the problem. Whatever was going on between Victor and his fiancé did not involve her.

Marco stood in the doorway between the family room and kitchen with his backpack slung over one shoulder. "I'm ready to go."

Tessa's mind flip-flopped. Whatever was going on did indeed involve her. Victor's words resonated: *We have a son together... what you do is my business.*

They were inextricably linked, all five of them.

"I just need to tell Crystal something."

"What do you need to tell her?" Victor sounded suspicious.

"Just that—" Tessa grasped for a story. Her eyes landed on the wet tea bag she'd left on the saucer. "It's about tea."

"Tea?" Victor cocked his head.

She straightened her shoulders. "Yes, Victor, tea."

"What about tea?" Crystal appeared, her cheeks fresh and rosy.

"Mommy!" Henry threw himself against his mother's legs, and she picked him up with a little groan.

"The tea I told you about." Tessa turned to Victor. "It's a special herbal tea for pregnancy."

"Oh right," Crystal said. "The tea."

It was a game of ping-pong, and the ball bounced back at Tessa. "I'll check and let you know if I'm able to order it. You can call me later today. Okay?"

"Yes. Thank you." Crystal's eyes welled.

"And about your eyes being red and itchy." Tessa caught the ping-pong ball and told another fib. "It's probably an allergy. Cool compresses will help."

She retrieved her jacket from the chair, gave Henry's leg a little squeeze, and pulled Marco out the door by the strap on his backpack.

As soon as they got in the car, Tessa quizzed her son.

"What happened this morning? You knew I was picking you up early."

Marco tugged on his seatbelt strap. "Dad and Crystal had a fight."

She wondered what it was about, but Marco offered no additional information. She treaded lightly "And that's why you went out to breakfast?"

"Not exactly." Marco removed his cell phone from his pocket and started texting.

Tessa drove away with growing frustration. Getting Marco to talk was harder than pushing Buttercup off the couch. "Can you give me a little more explanation?"

He let out an exasperated sigh. "We were all going to break-fast, but then Dad said something about Henry's grandparents buying him too much stuff. And then Crystal got upset and said she didn't want to go out, and I said I didn't want to go either. Then Henry had a tantrum, so I changed my mind and said I'd go." Marco leaned his head against the window. "We left late, everything took longer than it should've, and Henry can be a real brat sometimes."

Tessa had seen that herself at the fall festival. Still, he was an adorable little boy. "Sometimes little kids are difficult." She poked Marco's arm. "Believe me, you threw plenty of tantrums."

Marco shrugged and went back to texting.

After dropping Marco off at home, Tessa drove straight to the shop. She put the *open* sign in the window, hung her jacket on the coat rack, and exhaled. The cleaning crew had been in early that morning and left behind the fresh scent of lemon polish. The wooden counters and tabletops gleamed.

Tessa took the cheese samples out of the refrigerator and unwrapped a box of crackers. She added olives, cornichons, and roasted red peppers. After setting up a display of new products, she finally sat down with her laptop. At least a dozen new emails in the last couple of hours, including one from Pierre asking if she had confirmed a delivery for his new wine cellar. "Oh, shoot." She dashed a quick email to the manager at the winery asking him to call her ASAP. Nobody seemed to care that it was Sunday.

The bells on the doorknob jingled, and Tessa readied herself for a customer.

"Nonna, what are you doing here?"

Her grandmother closed the door. "Did you forget we were having lunch?"

Tessa had zero recollection of making the plan. "No, no, I just thought we were, um, eating later."

"You forgot, didn't you?"

She pushed on her temples. Her mind was in a whirl. "I might have."

"Darling, you look like you're getting a headache."

"I'm not." Tessa massaged the back of her head with both hands. "At least I don't think I am."

"Have you been keeping up with your meditation? It's very important you know."

Meditation? Who has time to meditate?

"Of course. I do it every morning."

"No, you don't."

Tessa blanched. "You're right, as usual. And I'm sorry I forgot lunch. There was a whole scene when I picked up Marco from Victor's house."

"Oh no, about the custody issue?"

"Actually something else, but it's not important," Tessa said without conviction. Crystal and Victor's problems were becoming her problems on a regular basis lately. She entwined her arm with Nonna's. Her grandmother's soft lavender sweater felt like a cozy blanket against her skin. "Come sit. We'll have charcuterie for lunch."

One of Mariano's most popular items was the premade charcuterie plate, a favorite for taking to the park or down to the lake with a bottle of wine or Prosecco. Tessa unwrapped one and set it on the table with napkins and cocktail forks.

"This is lovely." Nonna helped herself to some Italian salami and a slice of crusty bread. "I do hope you're avoiding stress, darling. You're barely two months past your, you know, your—"

"My *breakdown*. Yes I know."

"I wasn't going to say breakdown. I know it was more of, well, an anxious episode."

Tessa scoffed. "Which is really a euphemism for breakdown, isn't it?"

Nonna patted her mouth with her napkin. "It doesn't matter what it's called. All that matters is you being well, which is why you must avoid stress and exhaustion. You know, I worry about you just like you worry about me."

Tessa reached across the table and squeezed her grandmother's hand. "We worry about each other. We can't help it."

"You're right about that," Nonna said. "Which leads me to another topic. I might need to see Dr. Barnes next week."

Tessa dropped her little fork on the floor. "I thought you weren't going back until after Thanksgiving."

"That's what I thought, but I called the office a few days ago because I felt a twinge in my hip. I thought I should let the doctor know."

"And?"

Nonna studied her face. "Goodness, you're a bit flushed."

Tessa patted her cheeks. "I'm fine. So you called about your hip. And, um, he said to come in?"

"I didn't speak with him. He wasn't there. But his nurse suggested I make an appointment just in case. He's supposed to call me tomorrow."

Tessa could only imagine how awkward it would be to see Owen. He'd practically kissed her. And then he said he'd call but didn't. Just the thought of facing him made her hyperventilate. "Next week is pretty booked for me."

"Don't worry. If you're busy, I'll drive myself."

Tessa's cheeks puffed up. "I don't think that's a good idea. It's a long drive, and there's traffic, and what if there is a problem in your joint? No, you can't drive yourself. I'll have to—"

Her cell phone rang, but she didn't recognize the number. "Hold on a sec, this might be the winery. Hello, this is Tessa."

"Hi, it's me, Crystal."

"Oh, hi. Hold on." Tessa held up a finger and whispered, "I'll be right back."

She went through the swinging door into the storeroom. "I'm here. How are you doing?"

"Am I bothering you? Is this a good time?"

Tessa squeezed her forehead. If trying to help Crystal wasn't stepping into a pit of quicksand, she didn't know what was. "Actually, I'm with my grandmother. Do you want to get together? Maybe when Henry's in school?"

"Yes, that would be—" She hiccupped. "Good."

"Don't cry." Tessa felt terrible. What an awful mess the woman was in. "Just text me when and where. I'll make it work."

Crystal sniffed. "I will. Thank you. See you soon."

"Bye-bye." Tessa tapped the end-call button, missed and tapped it again. It would be a miracle if she didn't have another *anxious episode.*

When she returned to the shop, Nonna was eating more.

"Well, your appetite is good, I'm happy to say."

"The physical therapist has me doing so much exercise now, I'm eating like a horse."

Tessa sat. She put Crystal out of her mind and returned to the problem of her grandmother's appointment with Owen. Maybe she could drive Nonna to the appointment but avoid seeing him. There was always business to do in the city, or she could stay in the car and work.

On the other hand, why should she be uncomfortable? He was the one who tried to kiss her and then didn't call when he said he would. He should be embarrassed to see her, not the other way around.

The thought of making him squirm gave her a bit of a thrill. "Nonna, you're not driving yourself into the city. If you have to see Ow—Dr. Barnes, I'll take you."

"Well, as long as it doesn't interfere with—"

Her cell chimed.

"Goodness, your phone doesn't stop, does it?"

"It's probably Marco letting me know what time to pick him up." She turned her phone over and the screen lit up.

Tessa, it's Owen Barnes. I apologize for not contacting you sooner. If you're free tomorrow night, I'd like to take you to dinner.

30

*T*essa's fantasy of making him squirm dissolved.

"Is it Marco?" Nonna asked.

Tessa's head snapped up. "Oh, no. It's nothing." *It's not nothing. It's something, something big.* "I'll take care of it later."

Much later. He'd made her wait an entire week, so she could make him wait an hour or two. But wasn't she a little old for playing games? Tessa already knew what her answer would be, so a quick response would show decisiveness and organization. Then again, she didn't want to appear overly eager.

Bells jingled, and a young couple entered the shop.

"I'll be right with you," Tessa said. "Sorry I've been so busy, Nonna."

"Not to worry." Her grandmother stacked the plates. "I have a few errands to run, so I'll be on my way. If you need me to pick up Marco later, let me know."

"Thanks. And you let me know about your appointment." She ushered Nonna to the door and kissed her goodbye.

The young couple stood in front of the wine racks holding hands and whispering to one another.

"Are you looking for something in particular?" Tessa asked.

"We're going down to the lake," the man said. "Thought we'd have a little picnic."

Tessa clasped her hands. "I have just the thing."

They bought two charcuterie trays and a crisp, dry Riesling. As soon as they left, she reread Owen's message and responded:

I'm free tomorrow night. Dinner would be lovely.

~

Marco looked up from his homework. "Where are you going?"

"Just to dinner." Tessa tucked her license, cell phone, and lipstick into a small shoulder bag.

She'd tried on a dozen outfits searching for one that was sophisticated and flattering, yet comfortable. She settled on black pants, a leather bolero jacket, and red Prada pumps.

"What about my dinner?" Marco asked. "I'm starving."

Buttercup, who was lying under his feet, raised her head and whined in agreement.

"There's leftover pasta in the refrigerator, and I made you a salad if you want it. And I got a new container of rocky-road. Be sure to let the dog out at some point. And don't forget to lock the door. I'm not expecting anybody to call or stop by, so don't answer the—"

"Mom, I'm almost fourteen. I'll be fine."

"Okay, but text me if you need me." Tessa kissed his cheek and patted Buttercup's head. "I'll check in on you in a couple of hours, so be sure to answer my call."

Tessa arrived at the restaurant ten minutes early. Owen had offered to pick her up, but she insisted on driving herself. With all the disruptions in Marco's life, he didn't need to see her going out on a date. If it really was a date. It felt like a date, although she hadn't been on one in so long she hardly knew what one should feel like.

The restaurant, known for fresh fish and an eclectic menu, had a rustic farmhouse atmosphere with rough wood flooring and iron light fixtures.

"I'm a little early," she said to the host. "Reservation for Barnes at six."

"The table's ready. Would you like to be seated now?"

"Please." She followed him to a table near one of several fireplaces.

Before she even had a chance to remove her jacket, a waiter was by her side holding bottled water in both hands. "Flat or sparkling, Ms. Mariano?"

Tessa glanced up. It wasn't unusual for her to be recognized in restaurants, but having never been to this particular place, she'd not expected it.

"Flat, please."

He poured with aplomb. "Would you like to see our wine list?"

"Yes. Thank you."

The waiter motioned with a curled finger. A moment later, a young man in a navy blue blazer appeared and handed her a leather menu. "It's a great honor to serve you, Ms. Mariano. I'm the wine steward, and I, well, I am such a big fan of yours."

Tessa was flattered, although the last thing she wanted was to draw attention to herself. "That's very kind of you."

"I've been to a number of your seminars, and about a year ago I attended a tasting at your shop." The steward took a big breath. "I wonder if I might ask you a few questions about my wine list."

"Of course," she said. Dispensing a little free advice never bothered Tessa. Evaluating wine lists was one of her favorite hobbies.

"Thank you so much." He pulled out a chair and sat. "I'm

concerned we don't have enough choices from wineries outside of Northern California. I, myself, am quite enamored with a few reds from Washington. What do you think?"

His eyes were wide, as if Tessa were about to reveal the location of hidden treasure.

"I think…" She scanned the list, noticing a number of wines she loved along with a few unimpressive ones. She tempered her inclination to criticize. The eager, young steward would be crushed if she didn't tread lightly. Tessa caught a glimpse of the nametag pinned to his lapel. "Do you have a pen, Stephen?"

"Yes, ma'am." He clicked the button on a ballpoint and handed it to her.

Tessa looked at the cheap plastic pen with a bank logo on it. The professional in her took over. "Don't take this the wrong way, but you might want to get a better pen. My grandfather used to say a gentleman always carries a handkerchief and a nice pen."

"I'm so embarrassed," he said. "Let me go get another one."

"That's not necessary." She patted his hand to put the poor fellow at ease. "Now, these are excellent, especially these two." She circled five of the wines and put checkmarks by the two that impressed her the most.

"Thank you."

"However, I assume they don't sell well, do they?"

"They don't. How did you know?"

"Too expensive." She wrote in a new price for each bottle, subtracting about fifteen percent. "Profit margin's important, but it's meaningless if nobody's buying."

"Wow. You're right."

Just common sense, she thought.

"Your selection for moderately priced wines is sufficient. I'd suggest adding one or two more in the sixty dollar range." She pointed to a Cabernet from Gilroy. "This Cab is a hidden gem. Good work."

Stephen grinned like a kid with straight A's.

"Now these," she said, drawing lines through two others on the list. "How much do you have in stock?"

"A few cases of each, maybe more."

"I love this winery, but these aren't their best. I'd discount or even donate them. My favorites are their 2017 Chardonnay and 2016 Pinot Noir, both Sonoma Coast AVA."

Stephen hung on her every word. "I love the Sonoma Coast region."

Tessa wrote the name of the winery manager on the menu. "Call tomorrow. Tell her we met and that I suggested those two. She'll be thrilled. Now, if you want to add something from Washington State, look into the—"

"Hello."

Stephen jumped to his feet. "Dr. Barnes, hello."

Immersed in wine talk, Tessa had almost forgotten Owen was coming.

She flushed. "Hello."

Owen, in a tweed sport coat and a blue button-down shirt, took a seat.

Stephen turned his head from him to her and back to him. "You're dining together?"

"We are." Owen had a way of being aloof but polite at the same time.

"Ms. Mariano," Stephen said, folding the wine list and putting it in his pocket. "I can't thank you enough."

"My pleasure."

The wine steward buttoned his jacket. "To show my appreciation, may I bring a bottle of wine on the house?"

"That would be lovely," Tessa said.

"Might I suggest the Cabernet Franc?"

It was one of the wines she had circled. Tessa motioned toward Owen, but he returned the gesture and said, "I defer to the expert."

Tessa gave Stephen a little nod. "A perfect choice."

As the wine steward left, Owen scooted his chair closer to the table. "You do make friends wherever you go, don't you?"

"Just those who want advice about wines." Tessa resisted the urge to touch his face. He'd shaved his beard close to the skin, and his cologne was an intoxicating mix of sandalwood and patchouli.

"Please forgive me for not calling sooner. My father was hospitalized last week."

"Oh, no." Tessa forgave him instantly. "Is he all right?"

"He's better. I finally got him out of the hospital and back to Westridge. It was a mild case of pneumonia, but in an older person even a mild case is serious." Owen unfolded his napkin and placed it in his lap. "This aging parent thing is not easy, as you know."

"Yes, I do." Tessa felt their connection tighten. "I heard you spoke with my grandmother today. She said the twinge in her hip is nothing to worry about."

"Rosa's fine. I asked her a few questions, and everything she described is perfectly normal."

"Dr. Barnes, Ms. Mariano, your wine." Steven set a decanter on the table and showed them the bottle. "I hope this is everything you expect it to be." He decanted the wine and set it on the table. "I'll be back to pour in twelve minutes."

"Thank you." Tessa returned her attention to Owen.

"Your dad seems like a dear man. I enjoyed meeting him that one time."

"He enjoyed meeting you, too, and made a point of telling me several times."

"Very kind of him." She suppressed a smile, pleased to hear she'd come up in conversation following the brief interaction.

Owen picked up the decanter. "Do we have to wait twelve minutes for the wine?"

"My answer depends on who I am tonight. Sommelier Tessa would say we do. She'd recommend at least fifteen minutes."

Owen raised his chin. "I see. And what would Tessa Mariano, the lovely woman I'm taking to dinner, say?"

Her throat went dry. "Pour."

As the dark purple liquid filled their glasses, a smile appeared around his lips.

Tessa's foot jiggled under the table. She had never been good at dating. In fact, she didn't really like it. It was one of the reasons she had married so young. Twenty years ago, she and Victor were an adorable, compatible couple. Getting married meant never having to go on a date again. And after the divorce, dating was the farthest thing from her mind. She slipped on occasion and agreed to a set-up, but those dates never failed to disappoint. A movie with Marco was more fun, a bubble bath with candles and wine more relaxing.

She tapped her fingernails on the base of her glass. "I don't normally go out on dates." The confession embarrassed her, but Owen deftly brought her through it.

"I find that hard to believe."

"Why's that?" She twirled a few strands of hair and toyed with her earring, a white gold hoop encrusted with dark blue sapphires.

"Because you're smart, entertaining, and very attractive." Owen put his elbows on the table and leaned forward. "Although…"

"Although?" Tessa asked.

"It might be ill-advised if I were to complete that sentence."

She loved the way he talked. His grammar was impeccable, his words genuine, his tone resonant.

"You can't leave me hanging like that."

"Then I'll choose my words carefully. But first, may we taste the wine?"

Tessa lifted her glass, and Owen followed suit.

"To fine wines," he said.

They tapped their glasses and sipped. Tessa's taste buds opened to the notes of sugar plum, graphite, and star anise. She took another sip, thoroughly impressed. "What do you think?" she asked Owen.

He drank again. "I'm no expert, but I'd say it's good. Excellent, in fact."

His assessment pleased her. "I'd have to agree."

Owen swept a hand across his brow as if relieved. "Phew. I got it right."

Tessa could tell he knew more about wine than he was letting on. "So," she said, setting her glass on the table. "Although what?"

"Although—" He paused. "I think some men might find you intimidating."

Tessa laughed. "My grandmother has told me that on several occasions. She says I can be prickly."

"Prickly? An interesting adjective."

Stephen stopped beside their table. He went pale to see the wine in their glasses. "Oh, Ms. Mariano, you already poured the Cab Franc?"

"I did," Owen said. "With Ms. Mariano's approval of course. Thank you for the wine, and would you please ask our waiter to bring menus?"

"Of course, Dr. Barnes."

Tessa watched the young wine steward hurry off. "And you think *I'm* intimidating? He practically ran away from you."

Owen laughed, and the flames dancing in the fireplace reflected in his eyes.

They chatted. They drank. The waiter delivered menus to the table, but neither of them noticed. Owen refilled her glass.

The waiter returned and asked if they were ready to order.

"Give us just a minute," Owen said, opening his menu.

Tessa opened hers and scanned the entrees. "So many good

choices. I'll bet the…" Her cell buzzed. "I'm sorry, but I have to answer. My son's home alone."

"I understand. No apology needed."

The screen flashed and her grandmother's smiling face appeared. They'd spoken earlier in the day, so it was unusual for her to be calling again so soon. "Hi, Nonna." She glanced at Owen, and he smiled.

"Are you at home, darling?" There was a tremor in her voice.

"No, what's the matter?"

"I—I've been in a car accident."

31

*O*wen insisted he leave his car at the restaurant and drive her car, which Tessa appreciated.

The moment they arrived and Owen parked the car, Tessa flew out the door. Her grandmother was sitting in the back seat of Officer Glen Duffy's patrol vehicle.

"Nonna, oh my God. Are you okay?"

"I'm okay, darling. Just shaken up. Glen made me sit here until you arrived."

"For your own safety, Mrs. Mariano."

Tessa warmed to the officer who made her life miserable whenever he could. "I appreciate that, Glen."

"I'd like to stand up," said Nonna. "I just need to—Dr. Barnes?"

Owen moved in closer. "Rosa, sit tight for a minute. Let me check you over."

"Excuse me," Glen said. "Are you an EMT or something?"

"I'm Rosa's doctor, Officer. If it's all right with you, I want to do a brief exam to see if she sustained any injury that's not visible. Or have you called for paramedics?"

"No. Both parties said they were fine."

"Wait. I'm confused." Nonna hauled herself out of the car using Owen's arm for support. "Why are you here? Did Tessa call you?"

"I didn't, Nonna. He was with me when you called."

The frown on her grandmother's face softened, and a curious smile took its place. "With you? What exactly does that mean?'

"Rosa, we'll explain later. Let me check your neck and back."

Tessa left her grandmother in the capable care of her doctor and surveyed the damage. Nonna's trunk and bumper were crunched, but the car appeared drivable.

"You can leave it here overnight if you want," Glen said. "The kid who caused the accident is across the street with his dad. You want to talk to him?"

They were standing under a street light. Tessa saw the teenager drag his sleeve across his eyes. His father said something and then pulled his tearful son into his arms.

"I don't need to," Tessa said, thinking how distraught Marco would be under the circumstances. "Can you just make sure he's okay?"

"Yeah. I'll take care of it." He gave her shoulder a reassuring pat.

After Owen declared Rosa uninjured and Glen confirmed the proper information had been exchanged, Tessa put her grandmother in the back seat of her SUV.

Still shaky, she accepted Owen's offer to drive again.

Throughout the ten minute ride back to her house, Nonna questioned them about why they were together.

"Okay, Nonna, you're right. Dr. Barnes and I were at dinner. There I said it."

"So you were on a date?" Nonna's voice rose on the word 'date'.

Owen snickered. "We were on a date, Rosa."

"Oh, dear, you had to cut it short because of me."

"Don't worry. All that matters is that nobody was hurt." Tessa gave Owen directions to her grandmother's street. "And by the way, Nonna, where were you going on a Monday night?"

"I told you this afternoon. I joined the bridge club at the senior center. We play two evenings a week."

"Oh, right, I completely forgot." Tessa glanced at Owen, who was looking straight ahead like a chauffeur—listening but not reacting. She wondered what was going on in his head.

When they arrived at Nonna's cottage, Owen shut off the motor and turned to Nonna. "Stay there, Rosa. Let me get the door for you."

He helped her out of the car, holding onto her arm. She peered up at him with her most charming smile. "You devil you, asking my granddaughter out without even telling me." Nonna glanced over her shoulder at Tessa who pretended to not hear.

"I didn't want you to get your hopes up, Rosa. What if she'd turned me down?"

"I would've told her she was a fool."

Tessa marched past them. "I hear you, Nonna."

The cottage smelled like fresh-baked bread. "Were you baking today?" Tessa asked.

"Oh, yes, my first time since the surgery. I have a loaf of crusty sourdough for you."

Leave it to Nonna to be baking bread as soon as she could stand for more than ten minutes.

Tessa hung her grandmother's coat in the hall closet. "I'll pick up your car tomorrow and get it to the body shop."

"Thank you, darling. Let me get you the bread, and then off you go. Perhaps you two can salvage what's left of the evening."

"Are you crazy? We just came back here for an overnight bag. I'm taking you home with me."

"You are not." Nonna walked toward the kitchen with Tessa on her heels. "I'm fine. It was just a little fender-bender, although that poor boy who caused it was beside himself. Which reminds me, where's Marco?"

"He's at home." Tessa looked at her watch. It was almost nine. She was supposed to check on him hours ago. "I need to text him."

When he didn't text back immediately, Tessa called, but it went straight to his voicemail. Her heart skipped a beat. She dialed her house number. It rang five times before she heard her own voice—*You've reached Tessa and Marco. Leave a message and we'll call you back.*

"No answer." She was ninety percent certain her son was fine. But the panicky ten percent was far more powerful than the logical ninety. "I should get home."

Nonna squeezed Tessa's elbow. "I'm sure everything is fine, darling."

"I'm sure it is," Tessa said, although numerous disastrous scenarios ran through her head. "Where'd I put my keys?"

"I got 'em." Owen held them up between two fingers. "Let's go."

Tessa allowed him to drive again, grateful for his calm presence. "One more block, and you'll turn right."

Owen came to an abrupt halt at the stop sign that was set to be removed. "Funny place for a stop sign."

"I know, right?"

They agreed on almost everything. "I'm sorry our dinner was interrupted. What a disaster this night turned into." Her voice hitched. Between Nonna's accident and her worry about Marco, her nerves were frayed and her stomach in knots.

Owen pulled out a cloth handkerchief from his pocket. "Here. It's clean."

"You carry a handkerchief?"

Tessa couldn't believe it. Then again, she could. His appeal soared.

"Another lesson from my dad."

She held the soft fabric to her nose and inhaled the fresh scent. Abe Barnes must have been a wonderful father.

Tessa studied Owen's profile—the strong jaw and straight nose. She wondered if he had children. Maybe an ex-wife. Or even two. Or maybe he was unencumbered, free and easy, no baggage at all.

As they approached her house, Tessa saw light pouring out of every window. At least the place wasn't on fire.

When Tessa opened the front door, Buttercup came flying out of Marco's room. As soon as she saw Owen, she skidded on the slippery floor and came to a hard stop in front of him.

"This is one big dog," Owen said, his hands in the air.

"Don't worry, she's a sweetheart. I'll be right back."

She peered into Marco's room. He was sprawled out on his bed sound asleep, one leg hanging over the side.

Sweet relief washed over her. Tessa exhaled. She turned off the light and closed the door.

In the living room, Owen was sitting on the couch with Buttercup's front end on his lap. "Everything okay?" he asked.

"Yes, he's fine. Sound asleep." She laughed. "Did my dog force you into this position?"

"Not at all. I encouraged it."

"I find that hard to believe. She's very forward." Tessa spotted a brown lunch bag on the coffee table. "What's that?"

"Rosa's bread. She gave it to me as we were leaving."

Tessa sat next to him and opened the bag. She tore off a piece of crust and handed it to him.

He chewed and swallowed. "Oh, wow, I wish Rosa were my grandmother."

"Everybody says that."

Tessa inhaled, enjoying the calm. Nonna was fine. Marco was fine. And a handsome doctor was being held captive in her living room by her St. Bernard.

"You look surprisingly comfortable with a dog in your lap."

"Feels kind of like one of those weighted blankets." He stroked the dog's head. "Only heavier."

"We never had dinner, did we?" Tessa said.

"We did not." Owen's eyes crinkled at the edges.

"I'm going to whip up some pasta. When you get yourself out from under Buttercup, join me in the kitchen."

She left to the sound of Owen trying to push the dog off his lap.

32

They sat next to each other at the island in her kitchen. Even the way he ate was sexy. How he licked sauce from the corner of his mouth, buttered bread, swallowed wine.

"Are you watching me eat?" he asked.

"I just want to make sure you like it."

"I do. It's delicious."

"Bolognese is one of my specialties."

He finished off the wine in his glass. "You have others?"

"A few." Tessa gave him a sideways glance. She hadn't flirted with a man in forever and was surprised she remembered how.

He wiped his hands on the cloth bistro napkin and leaned back. "We seem to have salvaged our evening as your grandmother suggested."

"We did indeed." Tessa lifted the wine bottle. "More?"

"Please."

She tilted the bottle but stopped mid-pour. "Oh no, I just remembered I've got to drive you back to your car."

"Absolutely not," he said. "I'll call an Uber."

"Are you sure? I really don't mind."

"I'm sure." He removed his phone from his pocket.

"Wait." She removed his phone from his hand and placed it on the counter. "Don't call yet. Let's take the wine into the living and light a fire in the fireplace."

He arched one brow. "I won't say no to that."

They stood at the same time, their bodies so close she could feel the warmth of his skin. Owen put his hand on the side of her neck, and his thumb brushed over her cheek. "I've wanted to kiss you for a long time."

His words were as enticing as his touch. Tessa moistened her lips and tipped her head back. She heard the thumping of her own heart.

"Mom, are you home?"

They both jumped back, and Tessa banged her knee on the edge of the island. "Yes, Marco, in here." She mouthed *I'm sorry* to Owen while rubbing her kneecap.

Her sleepy son shuffled into the kitchen. Only a faded pair of boxer shorts covered his slender body. He rubbed his eyes and squinted at them.

"You remember Dr. Barnes, don't you?" Every blood vessel Tessa's face expanded and rose to the surface. She left Owen's side and went to her son's. "He took care of Henry's chin at the Fall Festival last week. And he's Nonna's hip doctor."

"Hi, Marco, how are you?"

"Um, fine."

Tessa felt like a little kid getting caught doing something she shouldn't have done.

"Dr. Barnes," Tessa said with formality. "Thank you again for your help tonight."

"Of course." Owen flowed into his doctor persona without missing a beat. "Your grandmother should be fine, but call me if—"

"What happened to Nonna?" Marco's head swung from Owen to Tessa and back to Owen. "Is she hurt?"

Tessa rested a hand on his back, his skin cool and smooth. "Nonna's fine, honey. She had a minor car accident, but nobody was hurt. So, nothing to worry about, okay?"

"I guess." The crease between his eyebrows deepened.

"Alrighty then." Tessa handed Owen his cell phone. "I'll call your office tomorrow if I—if my grandmother needs anything."

"Perfect. And thank you for discussing the wine business with me. I'd like to attend that tasting this weekend—if it's happening, that is."

It took Tessa a moment to realize he was asking her out again, playing the same game she'd played with Crystal.

"I'll check into it and let you know."

She glanced at Marco who hadn't moved.

Owen slipped on his jacket. "I'll let myself out. Goodnight."

"Goodnight."

Tessa waited a beat, listening to the front door open and then close. She took a deep breath and turned to Marco.

"Are you hungry?" she asked as if the scene that had just occurred wasn't the least bit out of the ordinary. "How about some milk?"

Marco eyed the dishes on the island. "Did he have dinner here?"

Tessa stacked the plates as if tampering with the evidence.

"Well, as it turned out, he did." She poured a glass of milk and handed it to him. "We went to a restaurant, but before we had a chance to eat, Nonna called about the accident."

Marco drank down the milk and wiped a drip off his chin with the back of his hand. "I don't get it. Why did he go with you to see Nonna?"

"Well, because Dr. Barnes is her doctor, and he was concerned. He wanted to make sure she was all right."

"Oh." Marco tucked his hands in the waistband of his boxers.

He was on the verge of manhood, but still a little boy in many ways. "So are you like friends or something?"

"I suppose."

"Is he gonna be your boyfriend?" Marco blinked, void of expression.

"Boyfriend?" Tessa wasn't prepared for such a direct question. She brushed off the idea. "No, I don't think so."

"Why not? Dad's always had a girlfriend, and now he's getting married."

"Are you saying you *want* me to have a boyfriend?" Tessa asked, incredulous.

Marco rocked on his feet. "No. I mean—I don't know."

Tessa could tell how uncomfortable he was trying to figure out why his father had always been in relationships and she hadn't. The obvious answer was that Victor's priority was his love-life while her priority was Marco, but she couldn't tell her son that.

"I'm much too busy for a boyfriend. And my life is more than full with you and Nonna and work…" The words sounded familiar—she'd said them before. "Anyway, Dr. Barnes is a nice man, and he cares about Nonna. That's the only thing that matters to me."

Marco scratched the back of his head. "Okay." He placed his glass in the sink. "G'night, Mom."

"Goodnight, honey." Tessa took his face in her hands and kissed his forehead. "I love you."

"Me too," he said, tolerating her affection.

As he traipsed back to his room, she felt the push-pull tug between them. The slow, painful process of their inevitable separation had begun in earnest. And it was Marco's job to navigate his journey toward adulthood.

A sudden sense of loss seized her heart and squeezed it hard.

.   .   .

Owen's text came in an hour later.

Despite another interrupted kiss, I haven't given up. See you this weekend, I hope.

She carried her phone upstairs, reading the message and vacillating over her response. How could she even entertain the idea of dating when Marco's life had been turned upside down by his father.

Tessa got into bed, reread his text, and responded with the only answer she could come up with:

I'll let you know.

33

*N*atalie slipped an arm through Tessa's as they walked into the park with their coffees from Nutmeg's. Morning sun filtered through the trees, and dry leaves fluttered to the ground.

"So when are you going to text him again? I mean, you can't leave him hanging."

"I said I'd let him know." Tessa defended her indecisiveness. Although apprehension was one of her least favorite emotions. "I need to think it through."

"No, you don't. You know you want to see him again, so quit pretending you're not sure."

"That sounds like something I would say."

Natalie laughed. "Thank you, that's what I'm shooting for, because nobody is more persuasive than you."

"I am that." Tessa sipped her coffee. "Anyway, I can't let some silly crush distract me from my priorities—Marco, Nonna, and work. That's it."

"Now you're just making excuses," Natalie said with increasing impatience. "Marco's almost fourteen, he's not a little kid. Nonna has practically ordered you to pursue a relationship.

And your work, well, work doesn't snuggle with us on cold nights."

"Geez." Tessa was surprised by her friend's harsh tone. "This sounds like a classic case of psychological displacement."

"What's that supposed to mean?" Natalie put her shoulders back.

"It means you're making excuses, too. And you're afraid of ending up alone because you wasted your prime dating years with a man who was never going to marry you." Tessa was on a roll, well aware that she and Natalie both had made choices in their lives for deep-seated reasons. "So don't get snippy with me when the person you're really mad at is yourself."

Natalie lowered herself onto a nearby bench, unable to meet Tessa's gaze. She looked like a scolded puppy.

Tessa sat beside her friend and squeezed her knee. "Sorry, I got a little worked up."

"I did, too. And you're right—I am mad at myself. I stuck with him for six years thinking things might change, even though I knew they wouldn't. I'm not even sure I wanted them to."

"That's pretty insightful," Tessa said.

Natalie finished her coffee and tossed the cup into a trash can. "I'm scared I blew it, you know? I might never get another chance at love."

Tessa considered her own wrong decisions, poor choices, and missed opportunities.

"You're only thirty-four, Natalie. It's not too late for you, I promise." Tessa spoke with conviction. "And it's not too late for me, either. At least that's what Nonna thinks."

"And Nonna's always right." Natalie offered a hopeful smile. "Right?"

Tessa felt a wave of calm as she pondered her grandmother's foresight and common sense approach to every dilemma. "She's definitely the wisest person I know."

Natalie bumped her shoulder against Tessa's. "So what would she say about Owen Barnes?"

"About Owen?" Tessa pondered for only a second. "She'd say he's a good man and that good men are hard to find."

"Well then, there's the answer to your dilemma," Natalie said with confidence.

Tessa wished it were that simple.

A constant flow of customers kept Tessa, Patty, and Liza on their toes all morning. With Halloween only a few days away, the town was abuzz with the official start of the holiday season. By the weekend, it would be full-speed ahead into Thanksgiving.

Tessa's cell chimed with a text from Crystal giving her the address of where to meet that afternoon. She had hoped Crystal might cancel, but no such luck. For the millionth time she wondered how she'd allowed herself to be dragged into her ex's fiancé's love life. It had no-good-deed plastered all over it.

Her phone chimed again with another text, this one from Officer Duffy telling her she needed to get her grandmother's car moved.

"Oh, shit." Tessa smacked her forehead.

"What's wrong?" Patty asked.

"I forgot about Nonna's car. I'll be right back."

She scooted into the storeroom to call the body shop and arrange for the car to be picked up. Then she texted Officer Duffy to let him know she'd handled it.

She tipped her head side to side, trying to release the stiffness in her neck. It signaled the beginning of a headache, something else she didn't have time for.

Tessa retreated into her cellar, a hidden room off the storeroom where she kept most of her personal wine collection along with family heirlooms and photos of her ancestors in Italy.

She dimmed the lights and set the timer on her phone. For a

solid ten minutes she relaxed with a cold pack on her head. Her thoughts drifted to Owen, his care and affection toward Nonna, dedication to his father, concern for Henry's chin, the ink cartridge for her fountain pen...

The timer chimed, ending her daydream.

She scrolled to his text from the night before and answered:

Yes to this weekend. Is Sunday good for you?

Owen's answer came within seconds:

Sunday is perfect.

There. At least she'd made that decision.

In the shop, Liza was helping a customer, and Patty was preparing another beautiful tray of samples.

"I need to duck out for a bit," Tessa told her.

"What is going on with you?" Patty put down the cheese slicer. "You're all over the place."

"I know." Tessa rubbed her temples. The headache had subsided. "I'll be back in a couple hours."

"Hours? Halloween's in two days. We have so much to do." Patty had become such a good manager, she thought she could manage her boss.

It made Tessa proud. "I've trained you well, haven't I?"

"Well, yeah." She pushed her red hair out of her face.

Tessa grasped both of Patty's hands. "This is why I hired you and Liza—so that I'm not tethered to this shop day and night. Which if I remember correctly, was your idea in the first place."

Patty grinned. "A brilliant idea, if I do say so myself."

"Exactly. I've got to run. Don't forget, the giant pumpkin will be delivered this afternoon. You know where it goes, right? To the left of the door."

"I know. You've told me ten times."

"How did I ever function without you?" Tessa slipped on her black jacket and went to face the next challenge on her list.

34

The veterinary hospital where Crystal worked was at the far end of a strip mall with a bike shop, a few restaurants, and a nail salon.

Crystal was standing out front. She looked professional in green scrubs and white sneakers, her hair tied back in a low ponytail.

Tessa parked and climbed out of her SUV. "Hello."

"Hi. You look so nice," Crystal said, pulling her ponytail over her shoulder.

"I came from work," Tessa said, as if to explain her outfit— dark pants and a silk blouse, practically her uniform. "I try to look decent when I'm at the shop. Never know who might pop in."

"Well, you always look nice when I see you," Crystal said. "Have you had lunch?"

With the day she'd had so far, Tessa couldn't remember. "I think I did, but I could use a little snack."

"Great, I'm starving. But then I'm always starving."

She started walking, and Tessa moved along beside her.

Crystal's pregnancy hardly showed under the baggy shirt. "How far along are you?"

"Almost five months." She patted her stomach. "And growing bigger by the day. Do you like milkshakes?"

"Sure." Tessa replied with an easy smile. "Doesn't everyone?"

"There's a diner on the corner with old-fashioned shakes. I think the baby likes them, because he always settles down after I have one."

"Sounds good to me."

Tessa relaxed a little. If Crystal weren't her ex-husband's fiancé, it would feel like going to lunch with a friend. Something about the woman appealed to her. She seemed honest and transparent. But Tessa remained wary. If she didn't trust Victor—and Crystal was an extension of him—could she trust her?

Tessa opened the door to the diner and let Crystal enter ahead of her.

"Hi, Dee, how ya doing?" Crystal waved to a middle-aged woman standing behind the counter.

"Hey sweetie, have a seat. Be right with you."

Tessa followed Crystal to a table and slid into a pink vinyl booth. Juke box music played in the background. Dee, wearing a red striped dress and white apron, brought water and took their order.

"By the way," Dee said, "Coco's still limping. I might need to bring her back in."

"Let me check her first, see if I can save you another office visit. I'll swing by on my way home tonight."

"You're the best." Dee tucked her pen behind her ear. "I'll get those milkshakes started."

Tessa studied Crystal's face—hardly any make-up, a few freckles on unblemished skin, a slightly crooked front tooth. She seemed approachable, authentic.

"Nice of you to make a house call," Tessa said.

"Dee just lost her husband. That dog is all she has now."

"You're a thoughtful person, which is important to me if you're going to become my son's stepmother." Tessa posed the question in the form of a statement. Was Crystal really having second thoughts about marrying Victor?

"I'm sorry I dragged you into my problems." Crystal pulled some napkins out of the metal holder and set them in a neat pile. "But I feel like, well, like you might be able to help me."

"I'll try," Tessa said in all sincerity.

Crystal's lips formed a thin line. "It's not that I don't want to marry Victor, because I do. But I think, I'm—I'm worried he doesn't want to marry me." Her voice cracked.

Tessa didn't know if he did or didn't. All she knew was that he'd said *trapped*. But then he took it back. "Why do you think that?"

"Because I…" She glanced out the window then returned her gaze to Tessa. "Because I think he might still be in love with you."

Tessa eyed the woman sitting across the table. The idea that Victor might still be in love with her was ludicrous. She wasn't even sure he'd loved her in the first place. They'd married too young without ever having discussed the unromantic issues of adult life. At twenty-one, nobody worried about the worse part of *for better or worse*.

She offered Crystal a reassuring smile. "I promise you, Victor is not in love with me. Not even a little."

"I figured you'd say that." She shifted and crossed her arms over her baby. "But either way, I'll never measure up to you."

"Oh, Crystal, please—"

"I mean it. The first time I met Victor, he talked about you."

Tessa found that hard to believe, but she didn't say so. "Doesn't sound much like first-date conversation."

"It wasn't a date. We met in line at Trader Joes and started talking about a bottle of wine. That's when he mentioned his ex-wife was a famous sommelier." She motioned with an outstretched hand. "He seemed proud, which was refreshing. Most divorced men love to complain about their former wives."

Probably true, Tessa thought. She certainly complained about Victor now and then.

Dee delivered their chocolate milkshakes along with a tuna melt and a basket of French fries.

Crystal thanked her and pushed the fries to the middle of the table. "Have some."

Tessa ate one. It was hot and crispy. She tried the milkshake, cool and creamy, reminiscent of summers long ago, when life was carefree and anything was possible. "You were right about the milkshake. Delicious."

Crystal sucked on her straw. "It's my guilty pleasure, but once the baby's born, I'll have to cut back."

Tessa ate a few more fries and licked ketchup off her fingers, thinking about the purpose of the meeting. What if she supported Crystal's concerns about Victor, encouraged her doubts? After all, he hadn't been a good husband the first time around. And what if they broke up? Crystal would be a single mother for the second time. Henry would lose the big brother he obviously adored. Marco might never get to know his half-brother.

"I hope you don't mind my asking, but where's Henry's father?"

The sun slipped behind the clouds, darkening the window. Crystal steadied her gaze on Tessa. "I've made a few mistakes, did things I'm not proud of."

"Nobody gets through life without regrets," Tessa said.

"There's a difference between having regrets and being ashamed."

Tessa blinked. It sounded like something her grandmother would say. As far as regrets, she had many, both big and small. But shame? None. Never.

Crystal picked up her sandwich and took a bite out of the

middle. A string of melted cheese attached to her lower lip. She wiped her mouth and said, "I can't afford to make another mistake."

Tessa leaned on her elbows. She folded her hands and let Crystal's words settle like dust.

This moment, and the question hanging between them, was monumental. Crystal's decision would impact their lives and their sons' lives for years, decades, generations. And she was asking Tessa to help her make it.

Noises from the kitchen grew louder. Patrons spoke with raised voices. Jukebox music blared. The ambient sounds melded and filled Tessa's head.

"What are you ashamed of?" Tessa asked gently.

Crystal rubbed her round belly. "This is my third unplanned pregnancy."

"Your third?" Tessa said, not hiding her surprise. Hadn't she heard of birth control?

"First time I was sixteen. My mother took charge of everything like it was 1955. She sent me to my aunt in Connecticut and told her friends I was attending a prestigious East Coast boarding school." Crystal looked out the window again, as if seeing something nobody else could see. "Somewhere in the world there's an eighteen-year-old girl with no idea who her birth mother is."

Tessa reached for her earring, a Tahitian pearl surrounded by tiny diamonds.

"You have the most exquisite earrings," Crystal said. "I noticed that the first time I met you."

Tessa touched both earlobes. "Earrings remind me of my mom," she said without thinking. The sudden shift in conversation jolted her, and a long ago memory surfaced.

They'd gone to the jewelry store where nine-year-old Tessa sat on the stool squeezing her mother's hand, while the jeweler poked holes in her earlobes.

"Did it hurt, darling?"

"No, Mommy. Not even a bit."

Her mother stroked her hair. "Such a brave girl you are. You will always be my strong, brave girl."

Now, decades later, earrings were much more than mere accessories. They reminded Tessa that she had become the woman her mother knew she could be.

"I know your mom passed away when you were young. I'm sorry."

Crystal's empathy was sincere and heartfelt. She understood loss as well as Tessa did.

"It must have been hard to give up your baby," Tessa said, steering the conversation back to Crystal's life and away from hers.

"It was unbearable. But I was in no way prepared to be a teenaged mother. Anyway, after a few years, I got back on track. Went to college and then started veterinary school at Davis."

"Veterinary school? That's impressive."

"You're surprised, aren't you?"

"Not really," Tessa said. And in all honesty, she wasn't.

"I'm book smart, but common sense smart, not so much. Henry's father was one of my professors. It was a brief affair, and he never even knew I was pregnant."

Crystal's history flowed out of her like rushing water.

"Abortion wasn't an option in my family. And I couldn't bear to give up another child. Long story short, staying in school with a baby was impossible. So here I am, a single mother with half a degree in veterinary medicine."

They had more in common than Tessa could have imagined. Seven years ago, she was a single mother struggling to make ends meet, too.

"Henry is a remarkable child."

"He's the best thing I ever did. And if not for Henry, I would never have met Victor."

"I thought you said you met at the grocery store."

"We did, but it was Henry who met Victor. He was sitting in the cart while I was checking out, and Victor was behind us. The two of them struck up a conversation, and Victor was so sweet to him. Answered all his questions. I'd never seen Henry so engaged."

Tessa pictured her ex with an amused grin, focused and attentive. He'd always liked little kids.

"Up until then, the only man in Henry's life was my dad, and he's, well, he's old." Crystal giggled, sounding like a young girl, and it made Tessa laugh.

"How old?"

"In his eighties. My mom's his fourth wife, but that's a whole other story." Crystal downed the rest of her milkshake. "The fact is, Henry brought Victor into my life. And then Victor brought us Marco. And Marco brought us..." She blinked, and plump tear drops fell. "Marco brought us you."

"Me?" Tessa flushed. "I don't know what you mean. We hardly know each other."

"I know you. Marco and Victor talk about you a lot. Even before we met, I knew I'd like you."

Tessa said nothing. Crystal's regard for her seemed blown out of proportion.

"What you've accomplished, especially as a single mother, is astounding. You're a true inspiration. I have to confess, I googled you."

Again, somebody had googled her. So much googling going on. And when did *google* become an actual verb? Tessa pulled her mind back to the issue at hand.

"I think you've overestimated me."

"I don't think so." Crystal shook her head. "But either way, can you understand why I worry I won't measure up? I—I don't want to marry a man who will always be comparing me to the woman he lost."

The woman he lost? Tessa doubted Victor had used those words. Even so, they gave her a surge of confidence. With just a hint that Victor still harbored feelings for Tessa, Crystal probably would break the engagement.

Tessa clenched her hands, her teeth, her toes. She could alter the trajectory of everyone's life.

Crystal had relinquished control and was handing it to Tessa like an unwanted gift.

35

*H*alloween arrived with all the fanfare befitting a holiday-loving small town. Main Street had been closed to traffic and the shops and businesses surrounding Town Square Park had their doors opened wide to welcome trick-or-treaters. Parents allowed their children free rein to run ahead and dash in and out of the park.

Mariano's had a steady stream of visitors with a special treat for the parents. Tessa used the occasion to promote a few new wines and get rid of some she'd discontinued.

Patty had the night off, so Liza and Rebecca, both dressed as pirates, were in charge of distributing candy to kids while Tessa poured wine.

"Oh, man, I love this Pinot," said a father whose two children were tugging on his hand. "Set aside a few bottles for me, Tessa. I'll come by tomorrow and get them."

"You got it," she said. "Have fun."

He went out just as Cece came in with her little boy, Noah. He was not quite two, but as tall as a three-year-old. He ran to Tessa with arms raised.

"You're so cute." She scooped him up. "I love your pumpkin costume"

"Cheesth," Noah said.

Tessa squeezed him, feeling his squishy diaper. "Cheese, huh? Well, you've come to the right place."

"His favorite food," said Cece.

Tessa passed the baby to his mother. "Wine?" she asked, giving Noah a square of cheddar.

"Thanks, but I've got to keep moving with Mr. Squirmy-pants here." She set him down, and he hightailed it over to Liza and Rebecca. "Off he goes, I'd better run."

Tessa waved as the little pumpkin toddled away. It seemed like yesterday Marco was wearing a pumpkin costume with a fat diaper underneath.

The hubbub lasted until after dark. At half past seven, the streets reopened to traffic, families went home, and the shops locked up.

Tessa handed the pirates some cash. "Thanks for working tonight."

Rebecca, in usual fashion, threw her arms around her. "Oh my God, it was so much fun! I would've done it for free. But thanks for the money. I sure can use it."

"You're welcome," Tessa said. "I hear Adam's throwing a bash at Hawk and Winters."

"That's where we're headed," said Liza. "You should come."

"You totally should." Rebecca pranced like a Labrador getting ready for a walk. "It's gonna be so fun. Food and music and dancing." She shimmied her shoulders.

"No party for me. But thanks for asking." Drinking and dancing was the last thing she felt like doing.

As soon as they left, Tessa turned the lock and pulled down the shade. She tossed her witch's hat into the storeroom and went to her car. The festivity of the night faded as her worries returned. Two days ago, she left Crystal hanging with a meaningless *let me think about it.* And she was still thinking, indecision weighing on her.

She drove toward home, stopping cautiously at the unneeded stop sign. The driver in the car behind her pressed his horn, startling her.

Tessa started forward, but changed directions and went to see her grandmother.

Nonna sat on her porch with a huge bowl of candy in her lap.

"Why are you sitting outside?" Tessa climbed the steps and sat beside her on the old swing.

"It's a beautiful fall night, and the older kids are still roaming. In fact, Marco and Oliver just came by. They looked so cute dressed up as Sherlock Holmes and Watson."

"They did, didn't they?" Tessa took the bowl from her grandmother and fished for her favorites. She ate a Milky Way and then an Almond Joy.

"What's the matter?" Nonna asked.

"Nothing." Tessa poked around the candy bars. "Are there any KitKats in here?"

Nonna pulled the bowl off Tessa's lap and stood. "Let's go inside. I have a pot of chili on the stove waiting to be reheated."

"Oh, that sounds good. Corn bread, too?"

"Corn bread, too."

Soon, the aroma of simmering, spicy chili filled the cottage.

Tessa fell into a chair at the kitchen table, a table older than she was.

Nonna handed her a large serving of chili in a white bowl, the one with a tiny chip on the edge.

"Smells good. Thank you."

"You're welcome." Her grandmother lifted the checkered napkin off the cornbread. She always covered bread with a cloth napkin, as if she were tucking it into bed.

Tessa crumbled cornbread into her chili and stirred. She blew on a small bite.

Like the chocolate milkshake the other day, it was the taste of childhood—a time when problems could be solved by kisses and comfort food.

"When did life get so complicated, Nonna?"

"It's always been complicated, darling." Nonna gave her a gentle smile. "You know that."

Tessa rubbed her face with both hands, smearing the heavy eyeliner she'd worn for Halloween. Black smudges appeared on her palms like a dark omen.

Nonna wiped away the smudges with a dishtowel dipped in water. "Tell me what's tormenting you," she said, her eyes dark with concern.

"I have a decision to make."

"Can I help?" The wrinkles in Nonna's face deepened.

"I wish you could. But no, not this time." Tessa couldn't remember ever feeling so alone.

She continued eating as Nonna ladled chili into a container. "I promised Marco leftovers." She wrapped up the rest of the cornbread and placed it in a bag with the chili.

Tessa had a vision of Marco at age three, dipping cornbread into his great-grandmother's chili. The flashes of his childhood were haunting her. She washed her bowl, dried it, and put it in the cupboard.

"Thanks for feeding me," she said.

"I love feeding you, my bambolina." Nonna cradled Tessa's chin and kissed the tip of her nose.

They walked to the door hand in hand. "Whatever it is you have to decide, remember you must look forward, not back."

Tessa furrowed her brow. "I'm not sure what that means."

"Envision the future, darling, *your* future. And no matter what you see, be true to your values."

Sometimes her grandmother's advice was hard to decipher, bits of wisdom buried inside of clichés and predictions.

Tessa gave her a tired smile. "My values? I don't even know what they are at this point."

"Of course you do, darling." Nonna gripped her shoulders with surprising strength. "Just remember, it is only when we face the most difficult challenges that our true character is revealed."

∿

The botanical garden was Crystal's idea—quiet paths, benches, peaceful shades of green. It was neutral ground, a place where neither had been before and wouldn't bump into anybody they knew.

Tessa inhaled the scent of flowers, trees, wood. It was the first of November, the midst of autumn, but the air was warm and still, as if summer were trying to hold on a little longer.

Both women shed their jackets and sat on a bench in the sun.

"Want some goldfish?" Crystal asked.

"Sure." Tessa held open her palm and watched the little yellow crackers spill into her hand. She ate one. "Marco used to love these. I'd forgotten how good they are."

Crystal popped them into her mouth one after another, like popcorn at the movies. "Yeah. I knew I was pregnant the minute I started craving them. Happens every time."

Tessa finished her handful and brushed the crumbs from her hands. "Well, here we are."

"Here we are." Crystal rested her hands on her stomach. "Thank you for seeing me again."

"You're welcome," Tessa said. In the two days since she'd seen Nonna, her perspective, as well as her values, guided her decision.

"I want you to know I've done a great deal of thinking since the other day."

"Okay." Crystal pulled her long hair over one shoulder and

twirled it with both hands. "This is crazy, but I feel like I'm about to be sentenced."

Tessa laughed. "Relax. There's no great revelation coming. And I am not going to tell you what to do. I'm going to give you my honest opinion and a few thoughts. That's all. And then it's up to you to make your choice."

"I understand." Crystal swallowed and took a tremulous breath.

Tessa brushed her bangs out of her eyes. What had seemed an impossibility at first had become clear. "You already know that Marco is my priority. He is my world, and that's why what I'm about to tell you is really quite simple."

She shifted and tucked one leg under the other, facing Crystal directly.

"First off, regarding your concern that Victor still has feelings for me, I sincerely doubt it. In fact, I'd bet a lot of money on it. We've put each other through hell for years. We married too young, had different aspirations, and fought all the time. That said, I do believe he respects me, and that makes him resent me. He seeks my approval and then gets angry because he wanted it."

"Wow," Crystal said, her pupils dark. "I get that."

"I think if he ever does compare you to me," Tessa said, twisting the diamond stud in her earlobe, "it will only be because you've made him far happier than I ever could."

Crystals eyes turned misty, and her lips curved with the trace of a smile. "I appreciate you saying that."

"It's the truth."

"Maybe. But it's also true Victor would never have asked me to marry him if it weren't for the baby."

Tessa pressed her lips together and said nothing. It wasn't her place to confirm or deny it.

"To be honest," Crystal said, "I wasn't ready to get married either. I mean, I'm not saying I wouldn't have wanted to marry him, you know, down the line, but—but it all happened too fast."

She leaned her head on the back of the bench and looked up at the sky. "I just have to make up my mind and move forward, stop obsessing over every what-if scenario."

Tessa shifted. "There's more for you to consider in making your decision. Some things I need to tell you that might, well, that might help you decide one way or the other."

Crystal turned the ring on her left hand. "I'm listening."

"About two months ago, Victor came by my house to tell me about the two of you getting married." Tessa paused, remembering the beautiful Sunday morning when her life, which was just getting back on track, had been thrown into chaos. "He insinuated he might pursue custody of Marco. Did you know about that?"

Crystal went back to twirling her ponytail. "He—he mentioned it."

"Well," Tessa said, choosing her words carefully, "as far as I know he hasn't made a move in that direction. But if he does, if he takes me to court, I'll fight him to my last breath." Her chest expanded. The statement sounded threatening, but it was no threat. It was just a fact. And Crystal deserved full disclosure. Being married to a man in a custody battle would bring on all kinds of stress and misery. "And he knows it."

"Okay," Crystal said, her voice as small as a baby bird's chirp. "I'm glad you told me." She toyed with the strap on her satchel.

"Good." Tessa smiled. The conversation was going well. She was in control, and her message was clear and rational. "Now, I'd like to ask a few questions. And I hope you'll be as honest with me as I've been with you."

Crystal lowered her chin and crossed her arms. "I will be."

Tessa believed her. "Are you moving to San Diego?"

She rubbed the back of her neck. "We've talked about it. My parents, they, um, they want us to."

"Makes sense. They probably want their grandchildren nearby."

"It's more than that." Crystal gazed into the tree overhead. "With them it's never simple, always a hidden agenda."

"I understand."

A sad smile appeared on Crystal's face. "I knew you would. But to answer your question, I don't know yet. There are compelling reasons for us to live there."

"I see," Tessa said, her chest tightening.

"And if Victor and I don't stay together, I'll have no choice. I can't do this on my own." Her face paled. "I don't want to live with my parents, but I have to do what's best for Henry and the baby."

Tessa imagined Victor driving up and down California every other week, trying to be a father to a teenager in one location and a baby in another. What a disaster that would be. Marco would hardly know his half-brother, and his relationship with Henry would wither.

Crystal picked up Tessa's hand. She placed it on her round belly and covered it with both of hers. "I want this baby to know Marco."

As if he'd heard his mother speak, the baby moved under Tessa's touch. The feeling of another woman's baby stirring inside his mother's womb went straight to her heart. She and Crystal were bonded. They were two mothers who loved their children more than anything and two women who knew how hard life could be.

"I'm going to make you a promise," Tessa said, resisting the urge to take Crystal into her arms. "No matter what happens, our boys will know they are brothers."

36

A dull pain on the back of Tessa's head woke her from a deep sleep in the middle of the night. She went downstairs to check on Marco. As usual, he was sprawled across his bed with the down comforter falling off to one side. She straighten it out and covered his shoulders.

"Mom?" Marco rolled over.

"Sorry, I didn't mean to wake you."

"What's wrong?"

Tessa placed a hand on his cool cheek. "Nothing, sweetheart. I just, well, I thought I heard something." She sat beside him on the bed and stroked his hair. He didn't mind her touch when he was half asleep.

Marco rolled over again, mumbling something about going back to sleep.

When his breathing grew soft and rhythmic, Tessa stretched out on top of the comforter and wrapped an arm around him. If only she could hold him like that forever.

~

The winery sat on a hillside with views of the valley all around. In the distance, a lake glistened under the sun.

"This is a beautiful spot," Owen said. "Very peaceful."

They sipped a 2005 Cabernet from a balcony overlooking a vineyard that stretched out as far as they could see.

Tessa leaned against the railing. A hummingbird hovered nearby, then darted away. "I think so, too. It's one of my favorite wineries, and this is an award-winning Cabernet."

"I knew that." He winked.

"Now you're teasing," she said, enjoying the humorous side of him. She wished she could let down her guard and fall into the unknown. "Let's go sit."

They moved to a wooden love seat with thick white cushions and a small cashmere blanket on the arm.

"I have a question for you," Tessa said. "Kind of personal."

"That's intriguing." Owen put his glass on the table in front of them. "What would you like to know?"

"Tell me about the beautiful blonde."

"Who?"

"The woman you brought to the art show."

His laugh was wide and generous. "First of all, she brought me, not the other way around. And it was a setup, a very regrettable one to say the least. The only thing that made the night memorable was running into you."

Tessa covered her smile. "Come on. Be serious."

"I couldn't be more serious." Owen draped an arm over the back of the couch. "I should've known better than to go on a first date that required a tuxedo. First dates ought to be simple and low stress. You know, like coffee in a garden."

Tessa's mind drifted back to the day they'd had espressos beside a trellis of roses. "Coffee is a safe first date. Find out if you have anything in common."

"Like fountain pens," he said.

"Yes, fountain pens."

Owen poured more wine into her glass. She sipped, tasting blackcurrant and a hint of licorice. The sun had dipped, beginning its descent. The winery closed at dusk, and dusk was fast-approaching.

"This might sound odd," Tessa said. "But I get the feeling you know more about me than I do about you."

"I probably do. Between my google search and your grandmother, I know quite a bit."

"Hardly seems fair," Tessa said, attempting to keep the conversation light while her heart pounded and her palms felt sticky. Her mind drifted, and it struck her as ironic that she and Crystal had parallel dilemmas—Tessa unsure about starting a relationship and Crystal unsure about ending one.

"Hey, where'd you go?" Owen brushed the back of his hand over her cheek.

"Sorry," Tessa said. "My mind wandered for a moment."

Owen moved closer to her. His eyes were dark with concern, and she wondered how he had come to care for her so deeply.

"Did my grandmother tell you about my life?"

"Your grandmother told me about *her* life."

"She did?"

"Yes, and I've got to say, it had quite an impact on me."

Tessa wasn't surprised. Nonna understood others with rare clarity and empathy. She must have tapped into Owen, reaching something buried deep inside.

"In what way?" Tessa asked.

"In a way that changed how I view my life—that moving forward doesn't mean forgetting the past."

Tessa inhaled. "Sometimes a simple truth is the most life-affirming."

Owen's gaze shifted. "That sounds like something Rosa would say."

"I get my best material from her."

They shared a moment of levity before Owen grew somber

again. "I want to tell you something about myself, something I rarely talk about. Would that be okay?"

"Of course it would." Tessa put a hand to her chest.

Owen ran a hand through his hair. He stared at the sky for several seconds and puffed his lips, as if he weren't sure where to start.

"I was married for a while, but I've been alone for a long time."

Tessa pulled the blanket onto her lap. It didn't surprise her that he'd been married, but she sensed a dark turn.

"We met in medical school. She went into family practice, and I continued into orthopedics. We were good together, both of us focused and structured. Everything was going according to plan. A few years later, and right on schedule, our son was born."

Owen paused. He crossed and then uncrossed his legs. The corners of his mouth flickered upward, but only for a moment.

"The happiest moment I'd ever known lasted barely a day. My son was born with a complicated heart defect."

Tessa pressed her knees together to keep them from trembling.

"For the next eight years, it was one emergency after another. Surgeries, weeks in the hospital, round the clock care." Owen let out a puff of air. "It was awful."

Tessa said nothing—no words in the world could measure up to such devastating grief. She laid her hand on top of his and squeezed gently.

"We had bouts of hopefulness, periods when he was stable and we could pretend to be a normal family. I even took him to baseball games, which he loved. Those times were like rare sunny days in a storm that never ended." Owen coughed, his fist in front of his mouth. "He died two days after his eighth birthday."

Tessa had been holding her breath. She released it, and a tear rolled down her cheek. Owen brushed it away, and his sorrowful smile tore into her.

"I couldn't get past the fact that both of us were doctors, and we couldn't do anything to save our son. It destroyed us. Eventually, we went our separate ways. A loss like that either cements two people together or rips them apart. I can't imagine any middle ground."

Tessa couldn't either. She wiped away another tear.

Owen rested his elbows on his knees and turned his head toward Tessa. "Rosa was the first person to put into words the way I've felt for the last twelve years."

Tessa touched her earring. Of course she had—Nonna knew the pain of losing a child, too.

"I don't remember exactly what she said," he continued. "But I'll never forget how she made me feel. It sounds cliché, but she understood me and the unbearable pain of having to live when my son had to die." His voice cracked.

A soft whimper escaped Tessa's throat. The cruelty of life astounded and infuriated her. Owen couldn't save his son. Nonna couldn't save her daughter. And Tessa, no matter how hard she prayed and bargained with God, could not save her mother.

She rested her hand on Owen's arm. He looked away, cleared his throat and swallowed.

"And now," he said, turning toward her again, "after all this time, I think I'm ready to move forward. I never thought I'd say this, but I want to start living again."

Tessa nodded, unable to speak.

Owen caressed her cheek, his gaze dark and searching as if he could see into her soul. She closed her eyes as he lowered his mouth onto hers, sharing the taste of wine and tears. She'd never known a kiss so consuming, a kiss that shattered her heart and healed it in the same moment.

37

*T*hey drove in silence along a rural road, the landscape zipping by in a blur of green and brown. Tessa leaned her head against the soft leather and sank into the warmth of the seat heater beneath her.

She glanced to the side, wondering what Owen was thinking. The tension he'd held in his jaw and forehead had faded, as if relieved of a burden.

"What was his name?" she asked.

A smile flickered. "Joseph. We named him after my grandfather."

"It's a beautiful name," Tessa said. The story he'd shared about his son explained much about him. It answered some of her questions, but not all. "Where's your ex-wife, if I may ask."

"You may, and to tell you the truth I'm not sure. Somewhere in Africa, I think. She turned her heartbreak into a mission to save the lives of children in third world countries."

"That's amazing," Tessa said, feeling small by comparison.

She thought of Crystal's concern that she wouldn't measure up to Tessa. How could Tessa, a simple sommelier and shop owner, measure up to a woman saving lives?

"I hear from her on occasion, a card at Christmas sometimes. But—but that's all." Owen added that last bit of information as if to wrap up the subject.

Tessa glanced outside and watched the sky turn black, giving the stars a velvet backdrop upon which to shine. "I have some big decisions to make," she said.

His jaw twitched. "I'm aware of that, and I know your situation is complicated, even a little crazy. I saw it that day when you were struggling with Henry. You have a lot of moving parts there."

Moving parts—exactly. "Sometimes I feel like I'll never get a handle on things. Everyone in my life is going in different directions, and I can't get them under control."

"That is one thing we definitely have in common. Both of us like to be in control."

"It's not just that I like to be." Tessa paused before revealing her tremendous weakness that, at times, was her greatest strength. "I—I need to be."

Owen nodded. He glanced in his rearview mirror, and the headlights from the car behind them illuminated his serious face.

"The first time you came to my office with Rosa, I could see that. Although, if I recall, you were no match for your grandmother."

Tessa recalled the appointment and how much she'd disliked him. "And no match for you either."

A soft laugh, then he said, "You're a formidable opponent. But when it comes to medical decisions, I do assert myself. However, when it comes to food and wine, I promise to defer."

His promise spoke of future dates, ongoing encounters.

"Speaking of food and wine," he said, "let's get some dinner."

And there it was, the first future date.

They discovered a roadside barbecue joint off the beaten path. The parking lot was full of motorcycles. Tessa opened her door, and the aroma of burning apple wood greeted her. Smoke rose off of an enormous Santa Maria grill under a spotlight where slabs of ribs sizzled.

Owen came around and took her hand. "This okay?"

"It smells like heaven."

Bikers drinking beer and families with boisterous children occupied most of the tables. Music blared, dishes clattered, laughter and loud voices bounced off the wood paneled walls.

The hostess seated them next to a family of five. The mother rocked her baby while the father coaxed a toddler into eating tiny bites of chicken. The older child, maybe six, was watching a cartoon on a cell phone and gnawing on an ear of corn. Butter dripped down his chin.

"Cute family," Owen said, his gaze on the little boy eating corn. "That one reminds me of—of Henry."

She nodded, wondering if he'd really meant Joseph. Tessa imagined every little boy Owen saw probably reminded him of the son he lost.

They ordered ribs, baked beans, coleslaw, and beer—a Bavarian dark lager that paired well with barbecue sauce.

When the food arrived, Tessa filled her plate. "You know, ribs are not good first date food. Much too messy."

"This isn't really our first date." Owen tipped back his beer. "I'm just hoping it's the first date we get to finish. Where's Rosa tonight?"

"Home as far as I know. My aunt is visiting. And Marco's with his dad, so unless you get an emergency call, I think we're good." Tessa sipped her beer. It was sweet with a hint of toasted caramel. "Oh, that's excellent."

"Are you a beer expert, too?" Owen asked, finishing one rib and starting another.

"Not really, but I'm an encyclopedia on the science of pairing flavors and compounds. That's how I knew this particular beer would be good with the tangy sauce on the ribs."

"Really? That's quite fascinating."

Tessa appreciated his keen interest. "The mouth craves balance. Do you know what creates the most perfect pairings?"

Owen shook his head. "Tell me."

"It's the elegant connection between flavor and taste, the balance between something creamy, like ice cream, combined with something acidic, like soda."

"Like a float?"

"Exactly." She grinned at him. "Next time you drink a root beer float, hold it in your mouth and notice how the vanilla complements the sassafras. Those flavors are good on their own. But together," she raised her hands like a preacher delivering a sermon, "together they are extraordinary."

Owen rested his elbows on the table. "That's actually very beautiful."

"It is." Tessa suspected they were thinking the same thing. The concept of perfect pairings went beyond the culinary.

The server delivered a basket of hot buttermilk biscuits.

Owen broke one in half, and steam rose from the middle. He placed a pat of butter on it and bit into it. "Bread and butter, another perfect combination?"

"Absolutely," Tessa said.

"Does Marco eat ribs?"

"He's going on fourteen—he eats everything and lots of it."

"Maybe we could take him here sometime." Owen glanced at the family. "And Rosa, too."

Tessa's face heated up. He was speeding along while she was idling in neutral. Owen reached for Tessa's hand, but she withdrew it.

"Did I do something wrong?"

"It's just a little soon to be thinking about, you know, family dinners with my son and grandmother."

"You're right. Forget I said it." Owen ate another rib and licked barbecue sauce off his thumb.

Tessa felt bad—she'd made them both uncomfortable with her *it's too soon* comment. "Owen, I'm sorry I—"

He held up both hands. "Don't worry about it."

They continued eating, but the mood had changed. Tessa wished she'd been gentler with her response.

Owen scratched his brow. "Here's the thing," he said suddenly, as if the thought had just occurred to him. " It feels as if you're pulling away, but at the same time, I sense that you don't want to."

Tessa regarded his evaluation of her mental state. In truth, he was spot on. "I'm a single mother of a teenage boy." She said it as if it were an excuse for sending mixed messages.

"I know that."

"What you don't know—" Tessa paused and asked herself if she should go there. It wasn't about keeping it a secret; it was about stripping off a layer of protection, showing her vulnerability and allowing Owen access to a deeper part of her. She took the leap without any idea of how she wanted him to react. "There's a good chance I'm heading into a custody dispute with my ex-husband."

Owen's eyebrows formed a deep V. "I'm sorry to hear it."

"Yes, well, thank you." She swallowed some beer.

"We can talk about it if you want to."

Tessa tucked her hair behind her ears. Her fingers found her earrings, plain pearl studs. "There's not much to talk about. Victor threw the idea at me two months ago and then did nothing about it. I've been hanging in limbo ever since."

"Why don't you ask him what he intends to do?"

It was a straightforward question, and it made no sense that she hadn't asked it. "I'm afraid if I push, it'll force his hand. Doing nothing allows for the possibility that the whole mess might blow over." Tessa was ashamed of her admission. She'd never been one to bury her head in the sand, but that was exactly what she'd been doing.

"And to make matters worse," she continued, "I've gotten myself embroiled in the middle of Crystal's turmoil."

Owen rubbed the stubble on his chin. "Crystal's the fiancé, Henry's mother, right?"

Tessa nodded.

"She has turmoil, too?"

"She certainly does." Tessa felt the weight of so much angst coming from so many directions. "But, well, it's not something I should talk about."

She found a rough spot on the table's edge and ran a finger back and forth over it. Her cheeks burned. She'd successfully turned the conversation away from the two of them and made it about something entirely different.

Owen started to say something, but then he stopped.

"What?" Tessa sensed criticism.

"You're very good deflecting. It's like…"

Tessa waited for him to finish the thought, but he didn't. "It's like what?"

Owen drank the last of his beer and shook his head. "Never mind."

The server came by to clear their plates. "Would you like to see the dessert menu?"

"No, thank you," Owen said, taking out his wallet. "Just the check, please."

Tessa watched the server walk away. Owen had put an end to the meal.

"I might have wanted dessert," she said.

"Did you?"

"I would've looked at the menu."

"If you'd like to see the dessert menu, I'll be happy to go get you one."

Tessa regretted her childish retort. "No, it's okay. I don't really want to see it. I'm just being difficult."

"Why?" Owen asked, turning his palms up.

Tessa didn't know why—or did she? "I shouldn't have brought up my problems with my ex-husband. They have nothing to do with—with us."

"On the contrary, I think your problems with him have everything to do with us."

"Excuse me?"

"You don't want to depend on anybody, especially men, because you can't be sure they won't hurt you like he did."

Tessa choked on a derisive laugh. "Are you trying to analyze me?"

"Of course not. Fear is a normal reaction—it's how we stay safe."

She rearranged a few pieces of silverware left on the table. "As my grandmother would say, that's just common sense."

Owen chuckled. "Common sense isn't obvious to everyone."

"So now I've missed the obvious?"

"Maybe." Owen rested his chin on his folded hands. "There's no shame in being afraid, Tessa. Why do you think I've been alone for all these years?"

Tessa's chest rose and fell. He had dug around inside her, found her most vulnerable spot, and poked it with a stick.

If only she'd never let it get this far. She'd allowed attraction to become affection which led to caring and longing, dragging her down the slippery slope toward vulnerability.

Tessa gazed into his greenish-gray eyes, afraid to speak and release the tears pooling around the edges of her lashes.

"Here's my truth, Tessa. I never thought I'd find somebody again, and then you came along and shook everything up." He gave her a sad, wistful smile. "My life has been on hold for twelve years. Thanks to you, I've decided that's long enough. I don't want to be alone anymore."

Dizziness made her see double for a moment. Her life had been on hold for over seven years, but with good reason. Marco, Nonna, and a business that demanded constant attention.

"That sounds a little like an ultimatum," she said.

"I don't mean it to, but I want to move forward, Tessa. I want a relationship. I want to fall in love and get married and be part of a family. I was hoping you might want that, too."

Tessa blinked, and the tears she'd held at bay fell. She brushed them off her cheeks and pictured her son. Owen's fantasy was just that, a dream that would not come true. At least not with her. At least not now. "I'm sorry." She didn't even hear herself speak.

Owen inhaled, and his eyes glistened. "I'm sorry, too," he said.

Inside her chest, something cracked.

38

They rode in silence to the spot where Tessa had left her car. Classical music played softly. She glanced at Owen every few seconds, but his attention remained on the road ahead, as if she weren't even there. It felt as if he'd already forgotten about her.

Owen parked his car behind hers and shut off the motor. Tessa didn't move. This was her last chance to change her mind, but her throat closed around the words.

"I suppose I should thank you," Owen said.

"Thank me? I'd hate me if I were you," Tessa said, relieved they at least were talking. She'd half expected him to drop her off with the car still running.

"God, no. This might sound melodramatic, but you've changed my life." Owen lifted her hand and kissed it. "I only wish I could've done the same for you."

"At the risk of using a cliché," Tessa said. "It's not you, it's me."

Owen laughed. "You know what? I believe you." He got out of the car and walked around to her door. A gentleman to the bitter end.

Tessa buttoned her coat and got out. The air was cold and heavy, as if rain were on the way. Owen walked with her to her car door. Tessa planned her departure—she'd say goodbye, get in, and drive off, avoiding any awkwardness or embarrassing tears.

But Owen directed the scene. He wrapped her in his arms, and held her tightly. Tessa's body stiffened.

"Relax," he said. "I'll let you go in a second."

Tessa looked up at him, her pulse thumping. Under the street-light, she saw his sad eyes and regretful smile. Owen put his hands on her face and stroked her cheeks with his thumbs. "Goodbye, Tessa."

His lips touched hers with tenderness, longing, and the unmistakable sadness of letting go.

～

The following morning, after a sleepless night, Tessa put on a cheerful act for Marco's sake. She dropped him off at school and then went to see her grandmother, hoping for some common sense advice that would support her decision.

They sat on the couch, and Tessa poured out the story.

After listening without comment, Nonna said, "I must admit, I'm disappointed. But I also think you're more upset about the outcome than you care to admit."

Tessa couldn't grasp why ending a relationship that had never even started was causing such pain. "I know, but I didn't have a choice."

"Of course you had a choice, darling."

Did she? Tessa had so many reasons to push Owen away, good reasons. Although she recognized that reasons were only one step away from excuses.

"Obviously, you're afraid to let a man get close to you again." Nonna brushed Tessa's bangs out of her eyes. "First your father left you, then your husband. It's understandable. But you're denying yourself a chance at love out of fear."

Fear, the same word Owen had used. Why did everyone think she was fearful? "I'm not afraid, Nonna. I'm practical."

"I'm practical, too, my dear. And practicality means stating facts." She set her jaw and gave Tessa a stern look. "The next four years will fly by, and before you know it, Marco will be off to college. And eventually, I'll be gone. I'm sorry to be so blunt, but you need to face reality."

"Are you kidding? I've been in the midst of a brutal reality check for months now. Even my nutty therapist at the wellness retreat knew that."

"But you're still paralyzed. I'm begging you, regardless of what's happened with Owen or what will happen with Marco, let yourself live." Nonna pressed a hand to Tessa's chest. "Your heart's still beating, my love. It's not too late."

"That's a rather trite statement coming from you," Tessa said with a quiet laugh.

"Trite but true, my dear. Listen, we can talk more about it later. You have to get to the shop, and I have to get dressed." Nonna patted Tessa's cheek. "But we're making progress, I can tell."

Tessa had no idea what kind of progress she thought they were making.

"Whatever you say, Nonna. Love you." She kissed her grandmother and left for work.

It was the first Monday in November, one of Tessa's favorite days of the year—the day her shop transitioned from Halloween to Thanksgiving.

Clearwater was an explosion of holiday preparations. Halloween morphed into Thanksgiving when the groundskeepers replaced ghosts and witches with turkeys and pilgrims.

At Betsey's Blooms, the windows and doors overflowed with buckets of orange, yellow, and ivory flowers, cinnamon scented candles, and baskets full of pinecones, mini pumpkins, fall foliage, and multi-colored gourds.

A new month, a new holiday, a new perspective, but Tessa hardly noticed. She was too busy facing reality. Owen was never far from her thoughts, lingering around the edges of her mind.

She had awakened in him a desire to carry on with life, yet she wouldn't allow herself to join him on that journey. No doubt, there'd be many other women happy to take her place.

On Tuesday afternoon, after two hours of non-stop customers, Patty presented Tessa with a new idea.

"Hey," she said, stepping over Buttercup sprawled across the floor, "what would you think about hiring another part-timer?"

Tessa stopped reading an email from a vintner in Montana. "You want me to hire somebody new?"

"Maybe just for the holidays. Liza's baking business is really taking off, and I don't want us to be caught short-handed."

"I don't know." Tessa rocked on her feet. "I'm so used to it being just you and Liza. On the other hand, it's not a bad idea."

"You want to think about it?" Patty asked.

"Actually, no, I don't need to," she said firmly. "Let's do it."

"Yeah? Really?"

Tessa felt good about it already. "You have anybody in mind?"

"Actually, yes. What do you think about Rebecca? She's always looking to earn some extra money."

"Rebecca? I'm not sure about that. She's so—so effervescent." Tessa imagined having to withstand a bear-hug every time they crossed paths.

"Yeah, she has a big personality, but I can work with that. You know how smart she is, and everybody loves her."

"And," said Tessa, "she's very tall."

Patty pointed at her boss. "She's even taller than Liza."

"You know what? I'm going to leave it up to you." Tessa held her palms out, as if handing something off.

"Really? Wow, great." Patty stood up straighter. "I'll talk to her and let you know what she says."

"Sounds good." Tessa said, forcing confidence into her voice. Patty practically skipped away.

Tessa ignored the twinge of anxiety. She was proud of Patty —and pleased with herself. But her moment of satisfaction was usurped by a text from Elaine:

Coming by shop around six. I have new news.

New news these days was never good. Tessa responded with a simple:

I'll be here.

She spent the rest of the day with a churning stomach, watching the clock.

Shortly after Patty left for the night, the bells on the door-knob jingled.

"Helloooo?" Elaine Cooper waltzed in. She shrugged off her raincoat, uncovering a turquoise pantsuit.

Tessa tied a ribbon around a gigantic gourmet basket she'd just wrapped in clear cellophane. "Hi, there." She took Elaine's wet coat from her and hung it on the rack.

"Can you believe that rain?" Her lawyer looked at a display of new items and picked up a jar of savory tomato jam. She handed it to Tessa with a coy smile. "This looks delicious. I'd love a taste."

Tessa opened it, and the lid released a satisfying pop. She stuck a plastic spoon into the jam and set the jar on the sample platter.

"So," Tessa said, her anxiety reaching new heights. "What's the news?"

Elaine spread jam on a cracker and tasted. "Mmm, delicious."

Tessa pulled the samples out of reach. "News?"

"Oh, right." The lawyer sat on a stool. "I have a question for you."

Tessa's eyes narrowed. "Okay."

"Do you know Crystal's last name?"

"I don't think so," Tessa said. "Why?"

"Because it's Deckland." Elaine reached for a glass from the rack above her head. "Wine?"

Tessa grabbed the closest open bottle. "Crystal Deckland—should that mean something?"

"Only if you live in Southern California."

"Which I don't." Tessa didn't bother to hide her sarcasm.

"No, you don't. So, I assume you've never heard of Deckland Development either."

Tessa shook her head. "It sounds like some kind of real estate thing."

"It's real estate all right, big real estate. And the major shareholder is none other than Don Deckland, Crystal's father, who happens to be a millionaire many times over." Elaine's eyes grew wide. "And I'll bet that's why Victor went to see his lawyer."

The cogs in Tessa's brain turned over as things started making sense. The new bicycle on the porch, the fancy swing set in the yard—gifts from Henry's grandparents. "You think Crystal wants him to sign a prenuptial agreement?"

"Either she does or her daddy does." Elaine licked her pinky finger. "And if I were her lawyer, I'd tell her she'd be crazy not to have one. If you only knew how many problems could be avoided with prenups. Divorces are much easier when they're all planned out ahead of time. Of course quick and easy divorces don't generate those nice fat fees, so there is that."

"My God, Elaine, sometimes I can't believe the things that come out of your mouth."

The lawyer ate another cracker slathered in tomato jam. "I hear that all the time, but I'm just telling you the truth."

The truth—Tessa was getting a lot of truth thrown at her

lately. She locked the door and hung the closed sign in the window, thinking hard. Crystal coming from money might mean something, but it might not. "Do you think Victor is marrying Crystal for her money?"

"He's your ex-husband, you tell me. But if she has that kind of money, he sure as hell doesn't need yours."

Tessa scratched her head. "I really don't think they'd be getting married if not for the baby. And as much as I can't stand him sometimes, I have a hard time believing he'd be so opportunistic."

"Oh please, of course he's opportunistic, all men are. But I suspect Crystal might not be rich yet. Old man Deckland has three ex-wives and seven children, most of whom hate him but love his money."

"How do you know all this?" Tessa asked, appalled yet impressed.

"Easy-peasy. I went to law school with the lawyer who represented the third wife in their divorce. When the time comes, there'll be a ton of money to fight over. And fight they will. Every kid and grandkid will want a piece of that pie." She stood and started her pacing ritual, wine in hand, then stopped and stared straight ahead.

It took a full minute for her to snap out of the trance and start talking again.

"Just so you know everything's public record, so I'm not telling you anything you couldn't find out yourself. Although, you'd never know where to look, but that's neither here nor there." Elaine paced a few steps then stopped again. "We still don't know if Victor plans to file for custody of Marco, do we?"

"No." Tessa poured herself a half-glass of wine. "I tried to get information out of Crystal when I saw her last week."

"What?" Elaine's eyes popped. "You saw the fiancé?"

Tessa shrank from her lawyer's horrified glare. "Yes, twice."

"You're cavorting with the enemy? You can't do that!"

"It wasn't a big deal," Tessa said defensively. "We actually met to talk about the children. No matter how this all shakes out, her son and my son will be brothers."

"Until your custody issue is put to bed, it's a huge deal."

"I think you're overreacting."

"Oh, honey, Elaine Cooper, Esquire does not overreact." She pointed at her head. "When it comes to custody fights I could fill an ocean with what I've seen. If I know anything, and I know plenty, you never, ever let the opposition get the upper hand. For all you know, she has some *Yours, Mine, and Ours* fantasy."

"I don't know what that means." Tessa was exhausted from trying to keep up with Elaine. It was like running a marathon.

"You're kidding," Elaine said, a huge smile lighting up her face. "*Yours, Mine, and Ours* is an old movie. I can't believe you never saw it—Henry Fonda and Lucille Ball—it's hilarious. Anyway, she has kids, he has kids, they get married and have a kid together. Boom!" She clapped once, making a loud smack. "One big happy family."

Tessa gulped. It all started clicking into place.

His son, her son, their son—*one big happy family.*

39

essa did everything she could to avoid falling into a simmering cauldron of anxiety—she meditated, drank herbal tea, and ate sardines, oysters, sauerkraut.

Elaine, who realized she'd sent her client over the edge with the *big-happy-family* idea, called every day throughout the week to reiterate that family court judges don't even consider changes in custody without good reason.

Tessa accepted the reassurance, but the idea of going to court and dragging Marco into a fight made her physically sick. And now with the possibility that Victor would be backed by his future father-in-law's fortune, the tables had turned. She no longer had the upper hand.

Despite her distress, she put on a brave face in front of her son and tried to act as if nothing were wrong. But night after night she lay awake, unable to quell her fears. At any moment, her world could come crashing down around her, and she was a sitting duck waiting for it to happen.

~

Rebecca blew into the shop like a hurricane for her first day of work at *Mariano's Cheese and Wine*.

"Tessa!" She practically lifted Tessa off the floor. "Oh my God, I'm so excited. I've wanted to work here forever! Thank you, thank you, I'll be the best employee you've ever had, after Patty and Liza of course. And I can do anything you want, really, anything."

"You can start by letting go of me." Tessa grunted.

"Right. Sorry, I just get a little over excited, you know?"

"Yes, I know. Now don't go crazy, but I have something for you." She reached under the counter and pulled out a bright white *Mariano's Cheese and Wine* apron with Rebecca's name embroidered in the upper corner.

The tall girl with frizzy red braids burst into tears, clutching her new apron against her chest. "This means so much to me, you have no idea, so—so much."

Tessa couldn't help being cheered by Rebecca's Academy-Awards-level acceptance speech. "Put it on and dry those tears. Your work day begins in one minute."

"Okay," Rebecca said, sniffling. She put the loop over her head and tied the strings behind the back. "What can I do?"

"Go to the storeroom and find Patty. She's your new boss."

Rebecca spun around, braids flying, and dashed through the swinging door.

As soon as her new employee vanished, Tessa's flat mood returned. She worked the rest of the day holed up in the cellar, leaving the shop to Patty and Rebecca.

At six, her cell buzzed with a text from Natalie:

Marco with Vic tonight?

She responded:

Yep. You want to have dinner?

Natalie replied:

Sure. I'll pick up Chinese and bring it to your house.

. . .

Natalie arrived at seven with a plastic bag full of Styrofoam containers. "I got all your favorites," she said, unloading the bag onto the island.

Buttercup sat at attention right beside her leg.

"She's drooling on my foot," Natalie said, nudging Buttercup with her knee.

"Sorry." Tessa tugged the dog away. "That's a ton of food."

"I know, but I'm starving. A dancer's gotta eat. Besides, now you'll have leftovers for Marco." Natalie loaded her plate with chow-mein, spicy beef, chicken and mushrooms, and fried rice.

"Thanks, Nat, this is sweet of you."

"You're welcome. Here, have some Kung Pao shrimp."

Tessa took a few bites, but she had hardly any appetite.

"What's wrong?" Natalie asked. "I've been so busy at the studio, I don't think we've talked all week. Did something happen? Is Nonna okay?"

"Nonna's doing great, actually. But it's been a hard week." Tessa stirred her food with her chopsticks. "I saw Owen on Sunday."

"You did?" her friend asked. "What happened?"

"Basically, I ended it, whatever *it* was." Tessa ate a shrimp and chewed slowly.

"I'm sorry. That must've been hard."

"It was." Tessa didn't want to get into the details, so she moved on. "And then the next day I found out from Elaine that Crystal's father is a real estate tycoon."

"Geez, no wonder you're stressed."

"Yup." Tessa released a loud sigh. "Maybe I should do a weekend refresher at the wellness center in Big Sur. As much as I hated it, I did feel better afterwards."

"I don't think so," Natalie said, wiping her mouth with a paper napkin. "I think you just need to find out once and for all what Victor intends to do. Maybe it won't be as bad as you've imagined."

Tessa stopped mid-bite. "Losing custody of my son is pretty bad."

"But you have no idea if that'll happen. Come on, Tessa. Do what you do best. Take control, be strong—make him make a decision."

Tessa put down her chopsticks. "Maybe I do need to force his hand."

"Exactly. It's time for him to show his cards." Natalie broke open a fortune cookie and smoothed the tiny slip of paper.

"What's it say?" Tessa asked.

"*Success is doing what you love and making a living by doing it.*" Natalie perked up. "Wow, that works for me. Okay, your turn."

Tessa opened hers and read it aloud. "*With strength you meet challenges, and with challenges you build strength.*" Tessa's eyes widened and met Natalie's.

"You see?" her friend said. "Be strong. Meet the challenge. Grow stronger. The fortune cookie is always right, just like Nonna."

40

*A*fter Natalie left, Tessa cleaned up the kitchen. Buttercup sat beside the back door waiting patiently for her to finish. When the dishwasher went on, the dog let out a low bark.

"I'm coming." Tessa slipped on her jacket, clipped the leash to Buttercup's collar, and went out into the damp, dark night.

Somewhere in the distance, an owl hooted. Smoke from a nearby chimney drifted over, and Tessa breathed in the smell of burning cherry wood. A shooting star launched across the black sky, leaving behind a trail of flickering light.

When Buttercup stopped to sniff a bush, Tessa stuffed her hands into her pockets, deflated. What had happened to her? Where was the survival instinct that had steered her through every crisis and propelled her success, the strength she was born with? For two months, she'd felt as if she were chasing something that couldn't be caught. It exhausted her. She was so tired of chasing, of not knowing, of imagining every worst case scenario. It had to stop. The time had come to confront her fear, ask Victor the ultimate question, and then, if need be, take decisive action to keep her son with her.

Tessa tugged on the leash. "Come on, Buttercup, we gotta go home."

She jogged back with the dog loping along beside her. As they came around the side of the house, Tessa saw Victor's car pull into the driveway. "This is it," she said to herself.

Marco opened the passenger door and got out of the car. "Hi, Mom."

"Hi, sweetie."

It would be so easy to wrap an arm around him, walk inside, and close the door, leaving the conversation for another time. Instead, she poked her head into Victor's car.

"Would you mind coming inside for a minute?"

"Now?" Victor balked. "It's after nine."

"I know, but I need to talk to you." Tessa kept her voice calm but firm.

"Fine." Victor got out of the car and followed her, his annoyance evident in the way he clomped up the steps.

Tessa had imagined the conversation many times, but now that she was about to make it happen outside of her head, her nerves were on alert. She closed the door, removed her jacket, and unhooked Buttercup's leash.

"Can I go take a shower?" Marco asked.

Tessa nodded. "Sure, honey, go ahead."

Victor gave his son an awkward kiss on his head. "G'night, buddy. I'll see you, um, in a few days."

"Okay, g'night." Marco disappeared, as if grateful he wasn't part of the conversation, taking Buttercup with him.

Victor turned and rested a hand on the banister. "So, what's up?"

Tessa peered down the hall to make sure Marco's door was shut tight. "Would you like to sit on the couch?"

"Not really. I'd like to talk about whatever it is you want to talk about and get home."

"Fine." Tessa inhaled and raised her chest. "Two months ago

you stood in this very spot and suggested Marco should live with you. And for *two months*, I've been waiting for you to make a move. But you've done nothing." She maintained a quiet, calm voice.

Victor shuffled his feet. "I know."

"So tell me—are you going to file for custody or not?"

He tilted his head, cracking his neck. "I—I'm not sure."

Tessa closed her eyes and pinched the bridge of her nose, simmering with frustration. "After all this time, you're still not sure? I don't get it. Did you toss the idea out there just to see how I'd react? To throw a wrench into my life because your life is in chaos? For God's sake, Victor, since we divorced you've gone through umpteen girlfriends, moved at least four times, and had I don't even know how many jobs."

She paused, trying to keep her voice in check, but impatience and exasperation won out. "I've done everything, *everything* in my power to keep Marco's life stable and to make sure he never had a moment of insecurity!"

"I know that." Victor bowed his head like a scolded child. "But there are certain things that—that changed."

"Not on my end." Tessa swept her hair out of her eyes. "You're the one who changes, the one who moves on, the one who has a life outside of—"

"Mom?"

Tessa spun around, her hand on her throat. How long had he been standing there?

"Honey," she said with tight smile. "I thought you were going to take a shower."

Marco pinched his lower lip between his fingers, his gaze fixed on his mother as if her words were sinking in.

Tessa was furious with herself. It was foolish and impulsive to confront Victor tonight. Why hadn't she waited until Marco was at school? Now that he'd overheard her rant, all she could do was downplay the situation. "Your dad and I are just talking."

"That's right, buddy," said Victor. "No big deal."

Their son swiped his sleeve across his eyes. "It is a big deal. I know what you're fighting about, and it's all my fault."

"Nothing is your fault," Tessa said.

"But it is my fault, right Dad?"

Victor ran the back of his hand over his lips. "No, well, I don't know. Maybe."

Tessa glowered at her ex-husband. "Not maybe; not at all. Marco, you didn't do anything."

"Yes I did!" His eyes filled with tears. "I know you always tell me things aren't my fault. But this time, it really is."

Tessa ached to hug him, but she knew he'd resist. "You're wrong, honey. Please, just let us work this out."

Marco turned to his father. "I'm gonna tell her, Dad."

"Tell me what?" Tessa asked, growing agitated.

Victor shook his head. "You don't have to, son."

Tessa stopped breathing. What secret existed between the two of them that she wasn't privy to? She pushed a hand against a sharp pain on the side of her head. "What are you talking about."

Marco's face reddened. "It was my idea." He blurted the words. "I asked Dad if I could live with him."

Tessa froze. Her throat tightened, and her mouth went dry. It had been Marco's idea, not Victor's? It didn't make sense. But if her son didn't want to live with her anymore, well, that changed everything.

"I'm sorry, Mom." Marco's skinny shoulders folded inward. "I'm sorry, but the thing is I only asked him because—"

"Don't be sorry," Tessa said, faking equanimity. Her worst fear had materialized. The question had been answered without ever being asked. Given the choice, Marco would choose Victor. She summoned every ounce of strength within her. "I get it."

"You don't get it." Marco lifted his head and stepped back, his cheeks streaked with tears. "And neither does Dad."

Victor looked lost. "What do you mean? What don't I get?"

Tessa's palms were wet with perspiration. She had tried so hard to piece together bits of information and random hints, but everything she'd thought made sense no longer did.

Marco twisted the bottom of his shirt into a knot. "I didn't mean to cause all this trouble. And now I—I don't know what to do!"

Tessa didn't know what to do either. Fight to keep her son, even if he wanted to live with his father, or give up and let him go.

No matter which way she went, she'd already lost.

41

Tessa closed her eyes and willed herself to do what she did best.

"Listen to me," she said, her voice surprisingly steady. "You're almost fourteen, so it's—it's up to you. If you want to live with your dad, I won't prevent you from doing so. I get it, and it's okay. You're the love of my life, and nothing—*nothing* will ever change that." She forced down the sob in her throat.

"I know." Marco dragged his sleeve under his nose. "That's why I did it. I mean, it's how come I could." Marco rubbed his face with both hands, leaving red marks on his cheeks. "I don't know how to explain it, and no matter what I do now I can't be sure it's right."

The epitome of an impossible choice—how does a child choose one parent over the other without overwhelming guilt?

"Sometimes we can't know if a choice is right until we make it." Tessa knew this from experience. She'd made countless choices on a leap of faith.

Marco sucked in his trembling lower lip, refusing to look at either one of them. "But I'm scared to hurt your feelings."

Tessa smiled sadly. "I told you, sweetie, I understand. If you—"

"Not yours. Dad's."

"Mine?" Victor cocked his head.

Marco wrapped his arms around his stomach.

Tessa fought back tears. Their little family of three had held such promise at first—proud father, adoring mother, beautiful baby—the perfect picture. But once the unraveling began, it refused to stop. Even so, through every fight and crisis, Tessa had protected her son. But the cocoon she'd wrapped around him was no match for the realities of life.

Victor's voice pulled her out of her trance. "Marco," he said. "Whatever it is, my feelings won't be hurt. I promise."

Marco raised his gaze and looked at Tessa. She wished she could absorb his pain and make it her own.

He looked at his father for several seconds before speaking. "I don't really want to live with you. I mean I don't *not* want to live with you, but I only asked if I could because—because I wondered what you'd say. I wondered if you'd want me." He blinked and released a river of tears. "And you're not like Mom. I—I don't know if you can love me no matter what."

Tessa's legs almost buckled underneath her. She felt no triumph in being the better parent, only despair that her son had lost faith in his father's love.

～

Seeing Marco and Victor both come apart was one of the lowest moments of her life.

Victor had been blindsided by their son's confession even more than Tessa. But he did his best to hold it together and said the right things, reassuring Marco that he loved him and wanted him—no matter what.

Marco leaned heavily against his father chest as if he

couldn't stand without the support. He was part boy, part man—a child navigating his way toward adulthood.

In that moment, Tessa's love for him felt more profound than ever. There was nothing she wouldn't do for him. And now she had to do whatever it took to help her son and his father through the darkest moment, to help renew the trust and mend the hurt. Marco needed his father as much as Tessa had needed hers. In the days and months ahead, she'd do everything in her power to save Marco's heart, to prevent the wounds that cut so deep they were impossible to heal, protect him from the scars she bore.

Tessa waited a few minutes before coaxing Marco into bed. She rubbed his back just like she had when he was a little boy, matching her breathing with his.

Once he fell asleep, she tucked the quilt under his chin and went to find Victor.

Her ex-husband sat in the kitchen at the island with a bottle of whiskey.

He picked up the bottle. "Care to join me?"

"Sure." Tessa got herself a glass, and Victor filled it with amber liquid. She took a small sip and felt warmth spread from her throat down into her chest. "That felt good, but it tasted awful."

Victor smirked. "Still don't like whiskey, do you?"

"I don't."

They laughed together—a sad, bitter laugh.

"It's late," she said. "Crystal must be worried."

"I called her, told her what happened."

"What did she say?"

"Truth?" Victor's gaze flickered upward then returned to the glass in his hand. "She said she hopes to be as wonderful a mother as you are some day."

Tessa appreciated the sentiment. "Crystal's a very good mom."

"She is." That was all he said.

Tessa ruminated a moment. Victor had no idea how much time she and his fiancé had spent together. It was up to Crystal to tell him, if she chose to. She sat on the stool beside her son's father. "You need to know, this wasn't what I expected or wanted. I had no idea Marco felt the way he did."

"Me neither, but at least it's settled now. He wants to stay here." Victor downed the whiskey in his glass and poured himself another one. "God, Tessa, I'm so sorry."

"I am, too. We both could have done better."

"Not true. You've done everything right, sacrificed way more, always put Marco first. I didn't do that." He held his whiskey in both hands, looking like a down-and-out guy at a bar drowning his sorrows.

Tessa wouldn't contradict him. She had put Marco ahead of everything and had no regrets. The resentment and hostility she'd felt toward her ex-husband gave way to pity and compassion.

"Listen," Tessa said, "we can make changes to the custody arrangement. I think it'd be good for Marco to spend more time with you. Of course, that depends on where you live."

"Oh, right, about that—we're not moving to San Diego. We made the final decision the other day."

"That's good news," she said. "I'm relieved."

"Yeah, just one more thing you were right about. Living in two places would've been impossible."

If they were staying put, that meant Crystal had made her decision about Victor, too.

"When do you think you'll get married?"

"I don't know. Maybe around Christmas, maybe in spring. Whatever she wants."

"Sounds nice." Tessa sipped her whiskey.

"I do love her, you know. And for some crazy reason, she's nuts about me."

Tessa laughed. "Well, even I can see you have a few redeeming qualities."

Victor lifted his head. "Look at us having a civil conversation. Who knew we could actually be nice to each other?"

Tessa emptied her glass. "It's about time."

Over seven years divorced, and finally they had come together. And there was still time to repair the damage, strengthen the relationships, and do better going forward.

They had exactly four years, nine months, and two weeks (give or take) until Marco left for college.

42

$\mathcal{M}$arco and Tessa stayed home together on Monday. Tuesday, she went into work for a few hours while he spent the day with Nonna.

By Wednesday, Marco was ready to go back to school.

"You want fried eggs?" she asked, her head in the refrigerator. "With hot sauce?"

"No, I'll have a cheesy scramble."

"Okay." Tessa cracked two eggs into a pan and scrambled them with cheddar, not saying a word about his choice to go back to his old way of eating eggs.

Victor picked Marco up for dinner on Wednesday. Instead of pulling into the driveway and delivering the usual beep-beep, he knocked on the front door.

Tessa invited him in. "You look better," she said. "Rested and all clean-cut."

He rubbed his whiskerless face. "Yeah, I shaved, got a haircut. And this morning, believe it or not, I saw my therapist."

"You did?" Tessa didn't even try to hide her shock.

"Yep. I need to, you know, figure things out and make sure I don't—don't screw up again. I might ask Marco if he'll do a few sessions with me. What do you think?"

"I think it's a good idea," she said, thankful for the dramatic change in him. It gave her hope that they'd all come out on the other side of the crisis.

Marco's footsteps padded down the hall.

"Hey, Dad."

Victor held his arms open wide. "Hey, buddy."

Marco hesitated, then ventured forward. He fell against his father and wrapped his arms around his waist. Victor closed his eyes and rested his cheek on top of Marco's head. They stayed that way for a very long time.

~

As the days passed, Tessa's routine returned to normal. Marco went to soccer practice after school. Nonna was back to all her activities—walking, baking at church, and delivering meals-on-wheels. And Tessa immersed herself in all things work related.

She attended a grand re-opening of Pierre Fabron's wine cellar. Vintners and wine sellers from Santa Ynez to Mendocino were there, all vying for a few minutes with the great sommelier, Tessa Mariano.

She met with Angela Reid, who needed wine for another reception at her San Francisco mansion, a fundraiser for the Symphony with over three-hundred guests.

She accepted an invitation to speak at one of the most prestigious wine academies in the country.

All in all, and on the surface, she was back to her old self. The tension in her shoulders dissipated, and her headaches were fewer and milder. She started meditating again and even let Natalie and Cece drag her to yoga.

~

The Monday before Thanksgiving, as Tessa was placing an order from a winery in Washington state, Crystal called and asked her to join them for the holiday. "And of course, bring your grandmother. My parents are coming, too."

"That's very sweet of you, but we—we have a whole thing planned."

Despite the calm, Tessa wasn't quite ready for a big family affair.

"Okay, well, if anything changes, let me know. I—I'd love to see you." Crystal cleared her throat. "You helped me a lot, Tessa, you helped both of us. I want you to know how much I appreciate it."

"I don't think I did much, but you're welcome." Tessa thought for a moment, wondering if it were possible to be friends with her ex-husband's new wife. She'd have to see. "Have a good Thanksgiving, Crystal."

She ended the call, hoping she hadn't been standoffish.

Patty popped up from behind the counter. "What was that about?"

Tessa jumped. "Jesus, you scared me."

"Sorry. Was that Crystal on the phone?"

"It was. She invited me to Thanksgiving. It's Victor's year to have Marco, so I guess they thought we could, you know, all be together. But I'm not up for it."

"Too much too soon, huh?"

Tessa nodded. "Exactly."

"You should come with us to Cece and Brad's." Patty looked at her with wide, sympathetic eyes. "They'd love it if you did."

"Aww, thanks for asking." Tessa put on a cheery smile. "But Nonna and I are—we're all set." *All set to be all alone.*

The bells on the door jingled, and Rebecca blew in holding a pink box from Nutmegs. "Breakfast!"

"Rebecca, you can't yell like that," Patty said. "We might have had customers."

"But it's not even nine. Are we open?"

"Not yet." Tessa took the box from her. "What did you bring?"

"Sticky buns!" She shouted again. "Oh my God, crazy story. I was working the six am shift, and somebody—well, me—dropped a tray and smashed a tray of sticky buns. They're perfectly fine, but we can't sell them because they're kinda smooshed. So I bought them for like way discounted, like well, actually, I got them for free. Where's Liza? Is she here? I hope she's here."

"I'm here," Liza said, coming through the swinging door. "And I smell sticky buns."

Tessa opened the box and inhaled. She removed one of the lopsided pastries and ate the entire thing herself. The problems that had been plaguing her for months—custody of Marco, Nonna's recovery, her headaches and stress—had been resolved.

She should be happy, but she wasn't.

Thanksgiving morning, Tessa awoke to a silent house. She rolled over and dangled her arm, searching for Buttercup's soft head. She didn't find it. That could only mean one thing.

Tessa ran downstairs to the kitchen.

"Oh, no, what did you get into?"

Buttercup raised her giant head, crumbs all over her snout and up to her eyes. Tessa could tell she was thrilled with her discovery, a package of gourmet stuffing cubes and seasoning.

The dog let out a sneeze, and crumbs flew.

"You might as well finish it. But that's all you get for breakfast."

As Tessa put on the kettle for coffee, her thoughts went straight to Marco—he was already at his father's house for the holiday weekend. She wondered if she might have been too quick in turning down Crystal's invitation to join them. But as Patty had said, it was too much too soon.

She went upstairs and threw on her walking clothes. When she returned to the kitchen, Buttercup had her nose submerged in her water, lapping at it as if she'd been lost in the desert.

"I knew you'd be thirsty." Tessa made a quick coffee and poured it into a travel mug. "Walk?"

Buttercup looked up, water cascading from her jowls, and barked.

They strolled down the path toward the road as a cool breeze kicked up leaves and shook the branches overhead. Mrs. Nelson, the nosy neighbor, stood in front of her house, leaning over to pick up the morning paper.

Tessa trotted past her like a horse with blinders, but then Buttercup made a sudden stop to sniff a gigantic tree trunk. She had no choice but to wave.

"Good morning, Mrs. Nelson."

"Tessa, hello, happy Thanksgiving." Her neighbor, bundled in a thick green bathrobe, her hair askew, scurried across the street. "What are your plans today? Big family gathering?"

"Oh, sure," she lied, "how about you?"

"We're heading to Marin. My daughter and her husband are having both sides of the family, so it'll be a big crowd—in-laws, cousins, and all the grandkids."

"How nice," Tessa said, meaning it. Some people were truly blessed with big happy families.

"By the way," the woman said, sidestepping Buttercup's curious sniffing. "Did you hear the stupid stop sign is coming down tomorrow?"

"Really?" Tessa brightened. "That's great."

"I know! I can't tell you how many times that trouble-maker Glen Duffy pulled me over. And after all I did for him. You know, he was my son's best friend for years. But then of course they had that falling out in high school over that—that girl, what was her name?" Mrs. Nelson tapped on her head as if trying to jolt her memory. "Anyway, doesn't matter. The good news is, after tomorrow no more sign. I'll tell you, I never thought I'd— oh, oh dear, your dog…"

Buttercup's entire head was inside the woman's robe.

"I'm so sorry." Tessa tried not to laugh. She yanked on the leash. "I'd better go, Mrs. Nelson. Have a nice Thanksgiving."

"You, too, dear." She scurried across the street, the green robe flying behind her like a cape.

43

*N*onna shook a finger at Buttercup. "You're a very bad girl eating all our stuffing cubes."

The dog panted and wagged her tail.

"It was my fault for leaving it on the counter." Tessa uncorked a bottle of Grenache. "I sometimes forget how far she can reach when she stands on her hind legs."

"Maybe she could be better trained." Nonna opened the oven and basted the turkey. "I guess we can live without stuffing seeing as how it's just the two of us."

Tessa peered over her grandmother's shoulder and watched the rich, savory juices flow over the perfectly browned skin. It was a lot of turkey for two people.

She had set the dining room table with antique china, crystal, and sterling silver. A flower arrangement of yellow roses, sunflowers, eucalyptus, and gold candles sat in the center.

Nonna placed the wine bottle on the marble coaster. "The table's beautiful, darling."

"Yeah. Pretty dreary with only two places though."

"I know." Nonna rubbed her back. "But at least we get Marco

for Christmas. Now, how about we enjoy a glass of wine together?"

"Good idea," Tessa said, appreciating her grandmother's attempt to distract her. She was about to pour the wine when her cell chimed with a call from Natalie.

"Happy Thanksgiving," Tessa said.

"Happy Thanksgiving. What are you doing?" her friend asked.

"Just getting ready to eat. What about you?"

"We had an afternoon supper, and my mom's already gone to bed. It's so quiet here. Can I come over?"

"Yes, of course! We'd love it. Get here as soon as you can." Tessa ended the call and said to her grandmother. "Guess what? We're having company."

"Wonderful, I'll set another place at the table."

Tessa, her mood much improved, went to work carving the turkey, mashing potatoes, and steaming green beans.

By the time Natalie arrived, dinner was on the table.

"Everything looks amazing," she said, presenting Tessa with a pumpkin pie decorated with a wreath of sugary crust maple leaves. "One of the dance moms made this for me."

"It's gorgeous, and it smells divine." Tessa set the pie beside the flowers. She dimmed the lights in the dining room, lit the candles, and filled the wine glasses.

The three women took their seats around the table.

"A toast," Nonna said, raising her glass, "to two beautiful, successful, wonderful women. May you both find love before it's too late."

Tessa choked. "What kind of toast was that?"

"A sincere and heartfelt one. I merely toasted to your futures, I didn't mean to offend anyone. Natalie, dear, did I offend you?"

"Not at all, you're just being honest. And you're right. We both deserve love in our lives." Natalie pointed her fork at Tessa.

"But you're way ahead of me. By the time you were my age, you had Marco."

"Yes, I did. The only bright spot in my otherwise disastrous marriage." Tessa pictured Marco with Victor, Crystal, and Henry. She imagined the four of them posing for a Christmas card photo in matching outfits. "Why don't we move on to another subject?"

"Good idea." Natalie filled her plate. "Like stuffing, why didn't you make any? It's my favorite."

"You'll have to talk to Buttercup about that," Nonna said, reaching for the gravy boat. She ladled a spoonful over her mashed potatoes and tasted it. "Oh dear, the gravy's cold."

"Here," Tessa said, "hand it to me, I'll go heat it up."

"I'll do it, dear. You just stay put and tell Natalie what your dog did this morning." Nonna pushed herself out of her chair. She took two steps, stumbled, and fell against the table. "Oh!"

Tessa jumped to her feet. "Nonna! What happened?"

"I—I don't know. It's my hip."

"The new one?"

Her face scrunched up. "The other one!"

44

*T*essa refused to let Nonna go home, despite the fact that her hip felt better after a couple of pain relievers. She tucked her grandmother into bed in the guest room and spent the next eight hours worrying and not sleeping.

On Friday, a huge shopping day at Mariano's, Tessa darted back and forth between the shop and her house.

"This is silly, darling, you don't need to be coming home every hour. I'm not in pain as long as I don't move around too much."

"Tell you what," Tessa said, setting Nonna's turkey sandwich on the coffee table. "I'll stay at work, but only if you answer my texts and calls. And promise me you won't get up unless you absolutely have to."

"I promise."

Tessa put her hands on her hips. "Are you sure you're comfortable on the couch? It's kind of soft."

"I'm comfortable enough. Now go." Nonna waved her away. "Just don't forget, I made an appointment with Dr. Barnes on Monday."

How could Tessa forget that?

~

In the parking lot of the medical building, Tessa opened the passenger door and helped Nonna out of the car. As concerned as she was about her grandmother, it was the prospect of seeing Owen again that had her on pins and needles.

"You look very cute today," Nonna said, rolling the walker in front of her.

"I'm just dressed for work." In leopard print ankle boots with cropped jeans and a white silk sweater, she clearly was not just *dressed for work*. "I'm meeting with a client this afternoon."

"Oh, dear. What if we're not back in time?"

"Don't worry about it." Tessa said of the pretend appointment. "I can always rearrange. Besides, I'll probably have to take you for an MRI."

"I hope not. That was miserable."

Tessa hated the idea of her grandmother going through any more discomfort, but she'd already convinced herself that Nonna would be getting another new hip.

There were three people in the waiting room when they entered.

"Here," Tessa said, "you sit down, and I'll check in."

"Thank you, darling." Nonna pushed the walker with halting steps.

Tessa held her arm as she sank into the chair with a little groan.

"Are you okay?" Tessa winced, feeling a sympathy twinge in her own hip. "Did that hurt?"

"I'm fine, darling. Just go sign in."

While the receptionist wrapped up a call, Tessa stood by, tapping a foot and twisting an earring. In a matter of minutes, she'd be seeing Owen. Her heart thumped wildly.

The receptionist hung up the phone. "Hello, Ms. Mariano. I see you've brought your grandmother in again. I'm sorry she's experiencing pain."

"Thank you." Tessa glanced back at Nonna who was thumbing through a magazine. "How long is the wait?"

"Well, you know we squeezed your appointment in, so it could be while. But Dr. Finley's very efficient, so I'd say—"

"Who?"

"Who what?"

"Who's Dr. Finley?"

"A colleague of Dr. Barnes. He's still on vacation."

"Oh." A mix of relief and disappointment stirred in Tessa's stomach. She didn't know what she'd expected or hoped for, but what did it matter? They were there for Nonna's hip. "Okay."

Tessa returned to her grandmother and sat beside her. "We might be waiting a while since they worked us in. Did you know you were seeing Dr. Finley?"

"Who?"

"Dr. Finley. Dr. Barnes is on vacation."

"He's what?" Nonna shouted so loudly she attracted the attention of everyone in the waiting room.

"Calm down," Tessa said, surprised by her grandmother's reaction. "He's on vacation, but I'm sure this other doctor will be just as—"

"I don't want to see this other doctor." Nonna jumped out of her seat. "I want to see Dr. Barnes."

She marched to the window and yelled at the receptionist.

Tessa was mortified to hear Nonna reprimanding the shocked woman. Not to mention stunned by her sudden agility.

"You should have told me when I called that Dr. Barnes was on vacation," Nonna said.

"I did tell you, Mrs. Mariano."

"You did not tell me! Just cancel my appointment." She turned to Tessa. "Let's go home."

Tessa grabbed the walker and followed her grandmother out the door and into the hall. "Nonna. Stop. What on earth did you do?"

Her grandmother turned, chagrined. "I'm sorry."

"Are you kidding me?" Tessa refused to believe her grandmother would deceive her. "You were faking it?"

"I—I, uh, well, I…" Nonna bowed her head. "Yes."

Tessa poked the elevator call button, taking her anger out on the plastic. "What were you thinking? You can't make a doctor's appointment for a fake problem."

"Well, actually, you can."

"Oh my God, do you have any idea the trouble you caused? I was worried to death about you, not to mention how much aggravation I had trying to—"

The doors opened on a packed elevator. Tessa folded the walker, slamming the sides together, and maneuvered in with Nonna. She continued berating her in a hushed tone.

"Did you even think about how your little ploy might affect me? As if I haven't been stressed enough?"

"I know, and I am sorry." Nonna leaned toward her ear. "But I only wanted to bring you and Dr. Barnes together again."

Tessa rubbed her brow. Her grandmother's scheme, while well-intentioned, had backfired. But she couldn't stay angry with the woman who always wanted the best for her.

"It was terrible what you did, but I know it came from a good place." She lowered her voice. "I know you want me to—to have someone in my life."

"Not just someone, dear. I want you to be with *Owen*."

Tessa sighed. "It's too late, Nonna." It pained her to say it, but a man like Owen would get snapped up faster than a Silver Oak Cabernet at fifty percent off, not that she'd ever seen one of those. "I can assure you, he's probably fallen for some other woman by now."

The doors separated, and people filed out.

"And I can assure you, he hasn't." The voice was low and masculine.

Tessa's stomach dropped to her feet. She turned and looked at the man standing behind her.

45

*T*essa wished she could sink into the floor and disappear. Owen had heard everything.

"Dr. Barnes," Nonna said, tugging on Tessa's arm to get her to move. "I had an appointment with you. And we drove all this way, only to find out another doctor was going to see me."

He stepped out of the elevator. "Dr. Finley's an excellent orthopedist. She's the one I'd recommend for a second opinion, or..." he glanced between the two of them, "or if you want someone's who's not me."

"Don't be ridiculous," Nonna said. "I have no intention of changing doctors."

"Okay," Owen said. "Well, why did you need an appointment, Rosa? Are you having a problem?"

"No. I'm fine. In fact, I'm so fine I'm going to take a little walk. My granddaughter can explain everything, and hopefully she won't mess it up." Nonna marched off, her steps brisk and light.

Tessa gripped the handles on the walker her grandmother had left behind. "Well, this is certainly awkward."

"I suppose it is." Owen took off his baseball cap and raked a hand through his hair. "Is Rosa really fine?"

"She is," Tessa said, leaning against the wall for support. "I guess you heard our conversation in the elevator."

"Some of it. Your grandmother is one determined lady."

"That she is." Tessa smiled and took a deep breath. Being near him again set every nerve in her body on alert. "So, um, how have you been?"

"Okay." Owen rocked on his heels. "What about you?"

"Same."

"Shall we sit?" he asked.

Tessa nodded, pleased he suggested it.

They walked down the corridor to a small atrium, and Owen motioned toward a bench surrounded by potted plants. Tessa parked the walker and sat on one end. Owen seated himself on the other.

Tessa's knees bounced. "How funny we ended up in the same elevator at the same time. I mean, what are the chances of that?"

"Unlikely, I'd guess."

"Especially with you on vacation—if you actually are on vacation, not that that's any of my business." It was part question, part apology.

Owen rubbed the scruff on his cheek. "I was out last week and just took an extra day to catch up on paperwork. If I hadn't been upstairs consulting with a colleague, we never would've bumped into each other."

They definitely wouldn't have. And although Tessa was hardly one to engage in the romantic notion of something *meant to be,* maybe this time something was.

"I can't believe my grandmother went to so much trouble to get us in the same room." Tessa's laughter was louder than she'd intended. "I mean, she faked a problem with her hip all weekend to get me here."

"Pretty clever." One side of Owen's mouth turned up. "I'm just glad she's okay."

Tessa sensed his apprehension, the distance between them like cold air. She recalled their last kiss, their final goodbye, the night he'd bared his soul only to be rejected. His wariness was understandable, and it was up to her to break through it. No doubt, this moment was her last chance.

"So, you overheard what I said in the elevator about you, you know, falling for…"

"I did," he said, sparing her the embarrassment of having to finish the sentence.

"Some things have changed since we—since we last saw each other."

"I see," he said in a quiet voice. "How so?"

"Well, for starters, the custody issue is settled."

A crease appeared in his forehead. "I hope it went your way."

"It—it did." She elaborated, but only a little, sharing a few details from Marco's emotional outburst.

Concern darkened Owen's handsome face. "That must have been painful for him. For all of you, actually."

"It was." Tessa pulled a thread on her white sweater, unsure about how much to reveal. "I—I feel like I owe you a little more explanation about the last time we—we were together."

"You don't owe me anything, Tessa. In hindsight, I'm pretty sure I pushed too hard and said too much."

"You didn't say too much." She hesitated. Vulnerability made her feel weak, but she plowed forward anyway. "The truth is, I didn't say enough."

He tilted his head. "What didn't you say?"

Tessa sensed him softening, a willingness to hear her out. As he let down his guard, she did, too. "I didn't say that you were right about my being afraid. I was; I still am. And to be honest, fear is an emotion I'm not comfortable with."

She paused for his reaction, but all he did was look at her as if waiting for more.

"And, um, you were right that I have trust issues when it comes to men. I've known it for a long time, but I wouldn't admit it."

Owen inched closer, and the tension in his jaw seemed to relax. "Well, I have something to admit as well. I got a little ahead of myself, rushed things. I'm sorry I did that. But the thing is, when I decide something, it's decided. And I move on it."

Tessa understood. She was the same way, strong and resolute in most situations. She scooted toward him. "I can't say I made a mistake, because a month ago I was in a different place. But that's changed, and I've changed. And something is telling me to put my trust in you, because in my heart I truly believe you'd never hurt me." She swiped away a tear. "I only hope I'm not too late."

The corners of Owen's mouth turned upwards. "You're not."

"Are you sure?" she asked, her stomach fluttering.

"Yes." He closed the gap between them and kissed her with a tenderness that stole her breath and made her tremble. "Absolutely yes."

EPILOGUE

*O*NE *year later, Christmas Eve*

Tessa and Owen snuggled together on the couch. The house was quiet except for the crackling logs in the fireplace and Buttercup's soft snores.

The Christmas tree, adorned with twinkling white lights, blue and silver balls and ornaments, smelled like an entire forest of pine trees.

Tessa kissed Owen's cheek. "I have to go get ready. Our company's coming soon."

The company was her unconventional family—Marco, Nonna, and Owen's father, Abe; Victor and Crystal, Henry and the baby.

The friendship between Tessa and her ex-husband's new wife had flourished. She'd even felt protective of Crystal at first, concerned that Victor be a better husband this time around. From what Tessa could tell, he was up to the task. Age, mistakes, and life experience had a way of changing people for the better.

"I don't want to move," Owen said, wrapping her in his arms. "I could stay like this forever."

"Maybe you could, but I need to go get dressed. And, unlike you, I need makeup."

"I think you look perfect."

"Of course you do. You love me."

Owen nuzzled her neck, sending a shiver up her spine. "More than you know."

"Oh, believe me, I do know." She tried to stand, but he pulled her back.

"Wait," he said. "Close your eyes."

"You're going to make me late."

"This'll only take a minute, now close your eyes," he said again. "Please."

"Okay, but hurry up." She closed them. "If I don't get started soon I won't be—"

He picked up her left hand, and Tessa's mouth snapped shut. She felt the ring glide onto her fourth finger.

"You can look now." There was a note of anticipation in his voice.

Tessa held her breath. She opened her eyes and gasped. The diamond sparkled and flashed as if tiny fireworks were exploding inside it. "Oh my God. Oh my God!"

"Tessa Mariano, you've turned my life upside down and inside out. You've brought me the kind of happiness I didn't even know existed. And now that I know it, I can't imagine living without it."

Her vision clouded. "This is—I mean I—I…" Tessa paused, still in disbelief. "Are you sure?"

Owen laughed. "Of course I am. As sure as I've ever been." His greenish-gray eyes were full of love and hope and the promise of forever. "Do you like the ring?"

"Are you kidding? I love it." And she did—the ring and all it represented.

"So, what do you say?" He pressed a lingering kiss on the back of her hand. "Will you marry me?"

"Yes," she said, looking from *her fiancé* to the ring and back to him again. "Absolutely yes."

～

Nonna was beside herself. She wouldn't stop hugging Owen or gushing over Tessa's gorgeous engagement ring.

Victor gave Owen a hearty handshake and toasted the happy couple with an expensive bottle of whiskey he'd brought as a gift.

Abe, walking with only a cane now, beamed. He declared he knew the moment he'd first set eyes on Tessa that she'd be the woman to win his son's heart.

Crystal behaved like an excited little sister, clapping her hands and insisting on giving Tessa a wedding shower.

And Marco, who had just turned fifteen and grown five inches in the past twelve months, threw his arms around his mother and told her nobody deserved happiness more than she did.

As they gathered around the table, Tessa cherished the scene. The people who filled her house were a gift beyond measure.

She glanced at the diamond on her finger, and the corners of her mouth turned upward.

"You really like it?" Owen whispered into her ear.

"I really do," she whispered back.

After dinner, soft Christmas music playing in the background, Victor and Marco cleared the table, Nonna loaded the dishwasher, Crystal fed the baby, and Abe snoozed on the couch with Buttercup's head in his lap.

Tessa was slicing Nonna's homemade pies when she noticed Henry and Owen sitting on the floor by the Christmas tree.

She licked a bit of apple syrup off her thumb and wandered over to eavesdrop, catching Henry in mid-sentence.

"... thinking about things, you know, in my head."

"Hmm," Owen said. "I get that. I like to think about things, too."

Henry looked up. "Like what?"

"Well, I think about being a doctor and how to take care of people."

"Like when you fixed my chin?" Henry pointed to the spot.

"Exactly." Owen ruffled the back of Henry's hair. "What about you? What do you like to think about?"

Henry pulled his knees up to his chest. "I don't know. Just stuff."

Tessa was drawn into the sweet conversation. He must be thinking about Santa Claus and presents and treats—what else would a child be thinking about on Christmas Eve?

Henry poked a silver ornament, making it shimmer in the firelight. "Are you gonna be Marco's dad now?"

Tessa nearly tripped over the ottoman.

"No, Marco's dad will still be his dad," Owen said, seemingly unfazed. "When I marry Marco's mom, I'll be his stepfather."

Oh dear. Tessa clenched her teeth. Explaining the ins and outs of blended families to a six-year-old was probably not in Owen's wheelhouse. This could go wrong in any number of ways.

"You mean Marco gets two moms and two dads now?"

Tessa heard bewilderment in Henry's voice. He'd gone from being an only child to a middle brother sandwiched between a teenager and a baby.

She bumped her leg against Owen's back. He looked over his

shoulder, and she gave him the *you-want-me-handle-it?* look. But Owen put out his hand as if to say, *don't worry I got this.*

As difficult as it was, she stepped back.

"It's not really fair," Henry said, rubbing his eyes with the backs of his hands.

"I suppose it's not. And it's confusing, too." Owen sounded confident, as if the topic were one he addressed every day. "Maybe I can help. You got any questions?"

"Yeah, but I don't know what they are."

Tessa began to think the kid was a genius.

"Right. It's because you want to understand things better," Owen said. "Probably a lot of things."

Henry blinked and his shoulders rose as he took a few breaths, as if absorbing the concept. "I just don't get who belongs to *me.*"

Tessa caught her breath. Such an extraordinary statement from a child—and a complex, heartbreaking question.

"Well, if you want," Owen said, "we can belong to each other. Family is all kinds of people, you know, like moms and dads and brothers. But it also can be people we love. And there are a lot of people here who love you."

Henry's head turned. "Do you?" he asked.

Owen looked at Henry with an intensity that caught Tessa by surprise. She covered her mouth, containing the wave of emotion that struck hard.

Every little boy must remind him of the son he lost.

"Yes, Henry," Owen said. "Yes, I do."

The little boy climbed into Owen's lap and rested his head on his shoulder.

Tessa's heart swelled with gratitude and contentment. Somehow, they'd all become a family—a wonderful, crazy, far-from-perfect family cobbled together from broken parts.

She closed her eyes and planted the moment in her mind.

Marco came over and stood by her side. He was so tall now

she had to look up at him. Tessa wrapped an arm around her son's waist, marveling at the changes in him.

Only three years, eight months, and a couple of weeks until he left for college.

The time would pass quickly. But when the day came for Marco to leave home, she knew for certain she would not be alone.

AFTERWORD

I hope you enjoyed Tessa's story and your visit to Clearwater!

Recommendations and reviews are the best ways to share your love of reading and to let an author know you enjoyed her work. Please take a moment to post a review of *The Lonely Sommelier* on Amazon. Thanks so much!

Find out what's up next and keep in touch by subscribing to my newsletter at juliemayersonbrown.com

Easy links for e-readers:
    Post review on Amazon
    Julie's Newsletter
    Julie's Reader Group on FB
    Julie's Website

ABOUT THE AUTHOR

Julie M. Brown is an author, playwright, and essayist. A California girl, she lives in Los Angeles on the Palos Verdes, California surrounded by trails, horses, random critters, and wild peacocks. Wife, mom, and dog-lover, Julie enjoys mentoring young writers and interacting with readers and bookclubs. When not writing, rescuing dogs, or trying out new recipes, Julie can be found in a quiet corner of her local library working on her next book.

~

View my website
juliemayersonbrown.com

While you're there, be sure to subscribe to my newsletter ~ it's a great way to get in touch and find out about my new books and projects.

Let's connect on social media, too!